THE TALLULAH BANKHEAD
MURDER CASE

THE
TALLULAH BANKHEAD
MURDER CASE

GEORGE BAXT

G.K.HALL &CO.
Boston, Massachusetts
1989

Published in Large Print by arrangement with
St. Martin's Press, Inc.

British Commonwealth rights courtesy of
St. Martin's Press, Inc.

G.K. Hall Large Print Book Series.

Set in 18 pt Plantin.

Library of Congress Cataloging in Publication Data

Baxt, George.
    The Tallulah Bankhead murder case / George Baxt.
        p.   cm.—(G.K. Hall large print book series)
    ISBN 0-8161-4707-8 (lg. print)
    1. Bankhead, Tallulah, 1902–1968—Fiction.   2. Large type books.
I. Title.
[PS3552.A8478T35   1989]
813'.54—dc19   88-35547

---

for Jean Muir

THE TALLULAH BANKHEAD MURDER CASE

ONE

NOT EVERYONE was privileged to dance to their death, but Nance Liston was one of the fortunate few. At forty there wasn't a telltale line on her face or an extraneous ounce of fat on her long, lithe body. There should have been lines and there should have been fat because for the past six months, from December of 1951 to April of 1952, Nance had been drinking and eating as though she'd been privy to the news of an imminent famine. There was now a famine of sorts in her life, but it had nothing to do with food or drink. It was a matter of unemployment.

Of course many of you recognize her name. Nance Liston. The sexy, sensuous, magnificent siren of the Rhine in the musical comedy sensation of ten years ago, *Bunker!* A musical about a Nazi courtesan daringly produced at the height of the war seemed doomed to disaster as a monument of poor taste until Nance made her entrance in the middle of the first act, writhing on a rock

1

overlooking the Rhine and mesmerizing the audience with some of Barry Wren's most outrageously innovative choreography. Success followed success, and then wisely recognizing that encroaching age made one less seductively appealing to audiences despite the gorgeous body and the classically beautiful face, she embarked on a career as a choreographer. In rapid succession there was a hit musical, two big film hits, and a series of television spectaculars.

And then six months ago, silence.

Six months ago Barry Wren had been subpoenaed to appear before the House Un-American Activities Committee. Nance didn't go to Washington to attend the hearing, but others did and told her how he sat on the stand, staring at those who accused him of communist affiliations, and then at his lawyer. Barry, Nance was told, looked as though he was suffering from the aftereffects of swallowing a tainted clam. Barry Wren, her friend, her mentor, the magnificent dancer who partnered her in her first pas de deux with the old Baronovitch Ballet Company.

"The little weasel was sweating like a pig," Nance was told. "You could see the beads of perspiration on his bald head, twinkling like fairy lights. We thought he'd take the Fifth.

He didn't. Yes, he told them, I was a communist, but I was very young, I was in my teens, it was at college. His inquisitor wasn't interested in a schoolboy communist. They wanted big stuff. Big names. Headliners. Who did you associate with in films and television and the theater who you knew to be communists? And the names came vomiting out. We'd heard most of the names before from previous testimonies of those who'd chosen to inform rather than risk the blacklist. And then he named you, Nance. It was absolutely unbelievable."

Nance was slowly descending the stairs into the Times Square IRT subway station. She hadn't been in the subway in years. She used taxicabs or chauffeured limousines or she walked usually preferring walking if she had the time. She seemed impervious to the noise, the smell, the occasional admiring look, a whispered innuendo. It was spring, it was April, and it was surprisingly warm even for that time of the year. But Nance was as cool as a virgin's rebuff. She wore a flared skirt, a blue blouse with a Peter Pan collar, no stockings, and a pair of blue flats she'd bought at Capezio just a few days earlier in a sudden but briefly experienced burst of enthusiasm that the dark cloud would lift and there'd be

3

a call from a close friend in the business brave enough to defy the blacklist and offer her an assignment.

There had been a call from a friend, but it wasn't an offer of a job. It was Tallulah Bankhead inviting her to a drink at Sardi's. They had been seated at the first table to the left of the entrance, the one reserved for the royalty of show business. "It's awful, dahling, absolutely awful. I mean you don't know what I go through booking guests for my radio program." Tallulah was applying a match to a Craven A; she went through four packs a day of the English cigarettes. "Waiter!" she barked, and when she had the man's attention she said with a seductive smile, "Can't you hurry those drinks, dahling, we're late for an A.A. meeting." To Nance she said, "We're radio, we're not visual, if there was a way to work you into the show, so help me God, dahling, I'd do it. I mean I've forced them to use Eddie Robinson, Judy Holliday, and Gypsy Rose Lee." She thought for a moment as she directed a smoke ring to the ceiling. "True, they're graylisted rather than blacklisted, but what in God's name would Gypsy be doing in a communist cell? I mean even my fertile imagination can't conjure up the image of

Miss Lee addressing someone as comrade and then suggesting a plan for a raid on the Pentagon. What about your agent, dahling? Is he trying? Or has he given up on you?"

"Not George," said Nance. "George doesn't give up." The drinks arrived and Nance sipped her martini. "There's a community theater in New Jersey that would like me to do a production of *Oklahoma!*"

She hadn't noticed Tallulah's shudder. Community theater, Tallulah was thinking, the elephant's graveyard of show business. Tallulah forced a smile and said, "Wouldn't that be wonderful, dahling. I mean once you get the job machine rolling, one thing leads to another and the next thing you know you're in demand in Delaware, Ohio and"— she added for no reason in particular— "Fairbanks, Alaska." Tallulah didn't notice Nance's shoulders shaking, but she heard the sob. "Oh, dahling"—Tallulah put her hand on Nance's—"do you need money? Let me help you. Please, Nance. When I get home tonight after rehearsal, I'll call everyone I know who might help. I'll badger them, I'll threaten . . . what's so funny?"

Nance was laughing almost uncontrollably. "I have to think of something funny to beat the blues. I suddenly remembered what you said to John Garfield after that roll in the hay with him."

"Was it that funny, dahling? Really? I don't remember. I never remember what I say. That night with Julie was weeks ago. I can't remember what I said ten minutes ago. Oh control yourself and stop laughing and tell me what I said to the great movie star . . . Waiter! Another round! And step on it, we're not here to establish residence!" John Garfield, another blacklisted actor, another victim. "Oh, do control yourself, Nance!" The smile was back on Tallulah's face. "What did I say to him?"

Nance wiped her eyes with a napkin and said, "You said . . ." now giving a fair imitation of the celebrated smoke-and-whisky-bruised Bankhead voice, " 'If that was sex, dahling, you should be arrested for loitering.' "

The Bankhead laugh had boomed through the restaurant.

Now the sound of an approaching train boomed into the station. People on the platform were used to just about anything occurring in their notorious subways, but they'd rarely been privy to a sight as lovely and as touching as that of Nance Liston dancing.

Only she could hear the music trapped in her brain. The choreography was fresh and innovative. She had just created it, special for today, special for her farewell performance. Some of the people waiting for the train to arrive seemed embarrassed; a few dug their noses into their newspapers; the blasé ones leaned against the pillars with arms folded and on blasé faces a variety of expressions ranging from smirks to amusement. And then Nance broke into a series of pirouettes. She was sixteen years old again, auditioning for the ballet. From a corner of her eye she could see old Vanya Baronovitch, a look of pleasure on his face. She could see some of the other aspirants, some supportive, some envious, a few hostile. She saw the balding young dancer who had been the only one to offer words of encouragement, the one to whom she would always be grateful. And as she spun into a final pirouette, the people on the platform heard her shout, "Thank you, Barry Wren!" as she leapt in front of the incoming train.

Tallulah Bankhead was not alone in the living room of her suite in the Hotel Elysee on East Fifty-fourth Street between Madison and Park when she heard the news of Nance

7

Liston's suicide. Sitting across from her on a divan was her best friend, the English actress Estelle Winwood. At the bar pouring drinks, a cigarette hanging somewhat precariously from her mouth, was another good friend, Patsy Kelly, who'd known success as a film comedienne. Tallulah was exhausted as she stood at the window looking down into the street, the inevitable Craven A held between index and middle fingers and the ash dropping onto the windowsill. She had sobbed and railed and cursed and thrown a vase at the wall and then calmly phoned others to make sure that Nance Liston would be given the beautiful funeral a woman of her stature so richly deserved. Patsy served the drinks and then settled herself on the divan next to Estelle Winwood.

"Tragedy begets tragedy," Tallulah said darkly.

"What's that from?" asked Patsy, whose voice was a combination of screeching tires and a chorus of irascible parrots.

"It's from me," said Tallulah as she moved away from the window and began slowly pacing the room. "It's the dark ages, the Inquisition, the reign of terror, Torquemada has been reincarnated in Washington, D.C. Mady Christians dead. J. Edward Bromberg dead. And my dahling Canada Lee, oh what a joy it was to work with him in *Lifeboat*, my dahling Canada dead. How he had suffered. No work anywhere. Broke." She sighed heavily. "Now Nance." She was raging again. "And tomorrow? Who'll die tomorrow? Who'll suffer that fatal stroke, the heart attack, another suicide and then another . . . oh my God, it's too awful to contemplate!"

Estelle said impatiently, "Must you be so morbid, Tallulah?"

"Yeah, Tallulah," chimed in Patsy, "it's bad for your ulcer."

"You insensitive bitches!" shouted Tallulah as she circled the two women seated on the divan, a war party attacking the wagon train. She addressed the ceiling. "That's what I get for associating with two women born out of idle curiosity!"

Patsy was on her feet and spoiling for an argument. "I resent that! I'll have you know I'm descended from one of the first families to land in New York!"

"Oh now really, Patsy," said Estelle, assuming one of her favorite positions when skeptical, her right wrist propping up her chin, the lids half-masking her eyes, her thin lips drawn in a tight line, and one leg crossed over the other, swinging back and forth like a pendulum out of control.

"Estelle dahling," said Tallulah, "Patsy's family came over on the Hoboken ferry."

The phone rang. Tallulah growled into it and heard the pleasantly familiar voice of Lewis Drefuss. Lewis coordinated the talent for her highly successful radio show, an anachronism in these days of live television. "The Big Show" ruled radio every Sunday night on the NBC network from six until seven-thirty P.M. Its astonishing success was attributed to Tallulah's still remarkable hold on a large coast-to-coast audience, this plus the cleverly assembled variety of major stars she presented as her guests.

"Lewis dahling," she said as she watched Patsy pouring herself another large scotch, "I'm really not in the mood to discuss next week's guests. You just don't know what Nance Liston's suicide has done to me. I mean really, dahling, I'm completely unraveled. Patsy for crying out loud, why don't you just drink from the bottle!"

Lewis was sympathetic. He was young, handsome, ambitious, and as Tallulah had told him the previous season, if he developed a strong sense of ruthlessness to add to his other assets, he could rule the world. Lewis wasn't all that ambitious. "Actually, Tallulah," Lewis said in a voice that made her wonder what he might be like in the sack, "I want to talk to you about someone who's in the same situation as Nance was." Tallulah said nothing. She waited to hear the name. "Abner Walsh."

"Abner?" Tallulah was truly astonished. She knew the celebrated folksinger socially and had always considered him a sweet, kindly soul who would surely prefer the top of old Smokey to a communist meeting. "I can't believe it. They must be mistaken! I mean I know he sings all those protest songs, but they're so dahling, dahling. Oh Christ, I can't believe it, I just can't!" She thought for a moment. "Who turned him down?" Lewis mentioned a network executive whom Tallulah had once described as being asocial, apolitical, and a pain in the ass. Red signals flashed in her brain. The anger mounted. "Book him."

"Just like that?" Lewis wished he was standing next to her so he could throw his arms around her and give her a big kiss.

"Book him. I've had enough of this crap, dahling."

"Lady, I love you."

Tallulah's face lit up. "Do you really,

11

dahling? Why don't we have dinner this week?" They made a date, Tallulah hung up, and Patsy suddenly emitted a mournful howl. "What the hell's the matter with you? Have I run out of scotch?"

"You hire everybody for that goddamn show of yours but me! You know I can't get arrested in Hollywood anymore, they tell my agent my type of comedy's dated. For chrissakes, that's a pail of bilge and you know it!"

"Calm down, Patsy!" shouted Tallulah.

"I can't calm down. Lately I've been thinking—"

"Don't think, Patsy. It could cause brain damage."

"I thought you were my friend!"

"I *am* your friend," said Tallulah as she lit a fresh Craven A.

"You have a hell of a way of showing it! How long can I go on borrowing money from you! Tallulah, if I don't find work soon—"

Estelle interrupted. "Now Patsy, I don't want to hear any suicide talk from you!"

"I would never commit suicide," screeched Patsy. "It's un-American!"

In the Oak Bar of the Plaza Hotel, across the

street from Central Park, Dorothy Parker smiled at detective Jacob Singer while waiting for the waiter to serve their drinks. "I don't know why they sing songs about April in Paris," said Mrs. Parker, "when they should be singing about April in New York. Collared any interesting felons lately, Jacob?"

They hadn't seen each other in almost twenty years. It was back in 1926 that Mrs. Parker had been of such invaluable assistance to Singer in the celebrated case in which she and Alexander Woollcott had helped to break up a dangerous murder ring operating in New York and Los Angeles.

"Nobody as interesting as Lacey Van Weber."

Lacey Van Weber. Mrs. Parker sipped her Jack Rose as she tried to recall Van Weber's face. "Isn't it funny," said Mrs. Parker to Jacob Singer, who was munching a peanut.

"What's funny?"

"I can't remember Lacey's face. I was in love with the man and I can't remember his face."

"You're lucky. There's a lot of faces I wish I could forget. You're looking great, Mrs. Parker. What brings you back from Hollywood?"

"I'm in exile."

"You broke up with your husband?"

"What husband? Oh you mean Alan. *That* husband. No such luck. Haven't you been reading the papers lately? I'm washed up. I can't get work at the studios anymore. I'm blacklisted. I'm a dangerous subversive. As a matter of fact, maybe you'd better sit at the table across from us. You might get fingered, guilt by association."

"You know, I'm really flattered. After all these years you haven't forgotten me. I mean, when did you get here?"

"Day before yesterday."

He sounded and looked pleased. "And right away you invited me to have a drink."

"Unlike George Washington, who was a fraud, I cannot tell a lie. There were several others I contacted first"—she smiled a very small smile—"but the several others weren't in to me. I've left lots of phone messages, but just like in Hollywood, even the nobodies don't return my calls." She sipped her Jack Rose. "Except Tallulah."

"Tallulah Bankhead?" Singer was impressed.

"I don't mean Tallulah Horowitz. Why are you wolfing those peanuts? Haven't you eaten today?"

14

"I'm nervous," he replied candidly.

"Do I make you nervous?" He said nothing, but his cheeks had reddened. "Is it because you're an officer of the law, and a bastardized offshoot of the law accuses me of being a subversive? Why, Jacob, just about the only subversive thing I've ever done in my life was write a movie for Ginger Rogers."

"That's not why I'm nervous."

"I'd suggest another drink, but you haven't finished the one in front of you."

Jacob Singer shifted in his seat. "Mrs. Parker, after all these years I have to tell you the truth. Ever since we worked together on that case back in 'twenty-six and you fell for that shit Van Weber—"

"Now Jacob, he wasn't all that much of a shit. I mean he was a killer, Jacob, but he had lovely manners."

"I was jealous of him."

"But why, for heaven's sake? Surely you've killed a few people in your time."

"I was jealous you were in love with him."

Mrs. Parker's mouth formed an O and then with twinkling eyes she said, "You're such a dear old-fashioned boy, Jacob Singer. Why didn't you come right out with it and say you wanted to go to bed with me?"

"I couldn't. You were a somebody. I was a nobody."

"Well, now that I'm a somebody who's threatened with being a nobody, Jacob Singer, you just speak your piece."

"Mrs. Parker, now you're Mrs. Alan Campbell."

"Don't tell me, tell him." She stirred her drink with her index finger, licked the finger, and then spoke quietly. "My husband, my dear old friend, is a very attractive man. He is my collaborator on film scripts, most of which he writes, because I hate writing anything, let alone film scripts. He is dear, attentive, and like me, he drinks too much, and also like me, is a very good drinker; he's never obstreperous or obnoxious. But unlike me, Mr. Singer, my husband is a homosexual. Oh, don't look so shocked. Everybody knows it. Even Alan knows it." Her glass was empty. "I need another drink. And very soon, I'm going to need another husband. And that's not why I asked you to have a drink with me today." Singer signaled the waiter for refills and returned his attention to Mrs. Parker. "I need to work, Mr. Singer. I've never been very good with money. I need to get my name cleared. The only prospect I have in New York is to collaborate on

16

a play for Broadway, and you know how chancy that is. After all these years, you *must* have friends in high places. Mr. Singer, can you help me?"

In a small room on the seventeenth floor of the very same hotel, the brilliant actor Michael Darnoff was speaking to his son Gabriel, the author of a play now trying out in New Haven.

"Don't you dare do that, Gabriel," said Michael Darnoff sternly. "Don't you dare fire an actor out of your play just to give me a job."

"I should have insisted you played it in the first place, Pop. I swear this guy's a bum, he's no good. He's fucking up the whole second act."

Michael Darnoff stared around the room, fighting back the tears.

"Pop? Pop?" shouted the young playwright in New Haven.

"I'm here, I'm here. I'm tired. I can't think anymore. A whole lifetime of work and respect down the drain because a son of a bitch fingers me to HUAC."

"He'll burn in hell, Pop. Lester Miroff will burn in hell."

"You're right. He just signed a deal with

17

CBS-TV to host a new weekly program. Can you imagine that son of a bitch singing love songs again? You'd think he'd be hoarse from all the singing he's been doing in Washington."

"Come to New Haven, Pop. See the show. See for yourself what I mean. My producer's all for it! He wants you to replace this schmuck!"

"Damn it, Gabriel. It's just one scene, just one scene!"

"It's a terrific scene!"

"I'm a star! I'm a star! My Cyrano was legendary! Actors can't do Iago or Lear without being compared to me!"

"You'll be a big star again! I'm writing my next play for you! It's for you and someone like Bankhead . . ."

"Oh, my God. Me on the same stage with Bankhead? She'll chew me up. It'll never work. Oh, what in the hell are we talking for? Don't you realize what a threat it would be if I did your play now? Isn't it enough you're my son and the innuendos are already flying?"

"Let 'em fly!" shouted his son. "Screw 'em! Screw 'em all! Screw McCarthy and his fag stooges! Screw Vincent Hartnett and his threats to finger everybody. These are cretins! These are brainless cretins!"

"You're right, my boy," said Michael Darnoff, as he poured himself a tall vodka, "but think if they had brains, then they'd really be dangerous." Michael heard his son's laughter in New Haven as he took a swig of the vodka.

"Pop, it's good you still have your sense of humor."

"Without it I'd be Lee J. Cobb."

"Come to New Haven."

"Maybe. I'll think about it."

"Don't think so much! Just come!" His voice broke. "Pop, I love you so much. I can't stand to see this happening to you!"

"I got news for you! Neither can I!"

In the Oak Bar, Jacob Singer was trying to reassure the worried Mrs. Parker. "I know a couple of biggies in Washington. Let me feel them out. It'll take time. I have to be subtle about it."

"Oh, be very subtle, Mr. Singer, I mean what the world needs now is subtlety. There's so little of it. Shall we have another drink and be carefree?"

"I'd be delighted, Mrs. Parker. And then perhaps you'll join me for dinner."

19

"That would be charming. Signal the waiter. I'm parched."

They heard the screams from outside in the street and then they heard the thud of something heavy hitting the pavement. Singer was fast on his feet and rushed to a window. The body was lying flat on its back, in a pond of blood. He heard a gasp from behind him. It was Mrs. Parker.

"My God," she said softly. "It's Michael Darnoff. I haven't seen him in ages."

TWO

THERE WAS a look on Tallulah's face that could wilt flowers. The two middle-aged men in the room watched as she stalked about the office with the slinky, sinuous movements of a caged panther, the inevitable Craven A poised between her lips, her voice breaking the sound barrier. "You're damn right I'm a household name. I'm bigger than Brillo! I'm the star of this show and I have a right to demand appearances by people I respect and feel comfortable with! Damn it, I want Abner Walsh on the show next Sunday!"

The two men were advertising agency ex-ecutives, and therefore very dull and pedan-

20

tic. Osgood Platt had red hair, and Vernon Crane, dyed brown hair. It was said of Vernon Crane he used more hair dye than a television anchorman. The difference in hair color was the only way you could tell them apart, at any rate the only way Tallulah could tell them apart. Describing them to Estelle and Patsy, Tallulah said they were both so parched and wooden, if you struck a match near them they'd go up in flames.

The two men made eye contact and then the red-haired Osgood Platt cleared his throat. "Miss Bankhead . . ."

"And another thing," roared Tallulah, a match for a cleared throat or a soft-spoken voice, "I intend to do a sketch with John Garfield which Goodman Ace is going to write for us. And don't you dare tell me Julie Garfield is unacceptable!"

"Miss Bankhead, will you kindly listen!" It was the dyed brown hair who had banged his fist on the desk and dared challenge her.

Tallulah stopped in her tracks and stared at the dyed brown hair who had unfortunately positioned himself under one of those framed god-awful prints of a little wide-eyed girl clutching a little wide-eyed doll, which were a big hit at Woolworth's. Tallulah drew her paisley shawl tightly around her shoul-

21

ders in protest against the air-conditioning. "I'm listening, Mr. Craig . . ."

"Crane," he corrected her.

"Oh really, dahling? When did you change it?"

"Miss Bankhead, you are in serious danger of losing several of your sponsors." Platt the redhead was nodding in agreement. It suddenly struck Tallulah he resembled Edgar Bergen's other dummy, Mortimer Snerd. "Do you understand what I mean?"

"Frankly I don't. I thought in my time period I was beating all the competition including television."

"You are," said Crane, "but they are thinking of withdrawing to bring home to you the importance, the seriousness of defeating the threat of the red menace in America."

Tallulah sat in a chair opposite them. "What the hell do you mean by *that?*"

"It's not just the fact that you insist on booking suspected subversives—"

"What nonsense!"

"But it's your own past record."

Tallulah paled, and she stubbed out her cigarette. "What the hell do you mean by that!"

Platt the redhead adjusted his pince-nez

("Pince-nez, dahlings, pince-nez, can you believe it! I presume he writes his memos with a quill!") and referred to a document on his desk.

Platt cleared his throat, cocked his head, and looked like Uriah Heep. "Miss Bankhead," he said, speaking the name in a tone sepulchral and forbidding, "you've heard of Vincent Hartnett?"

Of course she knew the name. Vincent Hartnett, the scourge of the blacklist. John Garfield had told her, "If he says you're red, you're dead. If he says you're red, you're listed in *Red Channels* and *Aware*, the official, deadly blacklist periodicals, and you're finished. And Tallu, you won't believe the old friends who are squealing on each other to save their own necks or just to get rid of the competition."

Tallulah stared at Platt coldly. "Mr. Plate . . ."

"Platt."

"Whatever. . . . I know a cockroach when I see one. Apparently the only difference between the vermin and Mr. Hartnett is that he's just a bit too big to be stepped on."

"He has provided us with a dossier of your past and present associations."

Tallulah leaned forward, her hands

23

clenched tightly together to keep them from trembling. "What the hell are you insinuating?"

"I am not insinuating," said Platt with a voice of solid steel. "I have before me in black and white the true, irrefutable facts." He referred to the dossier. "You appeared in a play called *The Little Foxes?*"

"Of course I did. It was my greatest triumph on Broadway!"

"It was written by a Miss Lillian Hellman?"

"It was."

"She's been subpoenaed by the committee. You appeared in the play *The Skin of Our Teeth?*"

"Are you trying to tell me Thornton Wilder the playwright is also accused?"

"No, they can't get anything on him." He sounded like a child who'd just had his all-day sucker stolen. "But they will be questioning the director of the play, Elia Kazan. Also one of your co-stars, Fredric March."

Tallulah was astonished. "Freddie March suspected of being a communist? They must be mad! The only threat he poses is to little girls' behinds! He adores pinching them." Then came the afterthought. "Big girls' too."

Platt ignored her verbal footnotes and con-

24

tinued in an ugly monotone. "You appeared in the play *Clash by Night* by Clifford Odets and co-starring Lee J. Cobb?" Tallulah just stared at him, her face no longer masking her contempt and revulsion. "Both men are in serious trouble."

Slowly Tallulah arose and leaned her hands on the desk. The paisley shawl fell to the floor as she addressed both men, coating every word with her own special brand of deadly venom. "How dare you! How dare you two little obscene toads threaten me with this stinking blackmail as repulsive as revolting as the ugly dye in your hair, Mr. Place—"

"*Platt!*"

"Don't interrupt me, you rodent!" The other man closed his eyes and pressed his lips together. He'd heard tell of the Bankhead temper but never dreamt it could be this horrifyingly ferocious. Tallulah snatched the dossier, tore it to pieces in her uncontrollable rage, and flung the tatters, she hoped equally distributed, in their faces. "How dare you! How dare *they!* Whatever they say about me, just you assholes remember this. I'm Tallulah Bankhead, a legend in my own slime! My daddy, God rest his soul, was Speaker of the House of Representatives! My uncle and my grandfather, God rest their souls, were senators from Alabama!" She spat the next words. "All three were registered Democrats! And if they were alive today, they'd be spinning in their graves! Very well, gentlemen." She retrieved the shawl from the floor and with two magnificent theatrical gestures, draped it back around her shoulders. Now looking like Joan of Arc armed for battle, she resumed speaking. "I shall live up to the letter of my contract. If you attempt to brand me a communist or cancel the program before the end of the season, I shall sue you for fifty million dollars and, dahlings, remember this, not you, not Hartnett, not any member of the fucking House Un-American Committee is as powerful as I am with the press and the public. I'll see you all in purgatory before I permit you to try and make me bend before you. If there is a whisper, an insinuation, an innuendo about me as a suspected subversive, I shall destroy you."

"Now really, Miss Bankhead," demurred the redhead, "we have no intention of cancelling the program. We have every intention of living up to the terms of your contract."

"You damn well better. It's ironclad."

"Indeed it is, but, Miss Bankhead, we will not permit John Garfield or your folksinger

Abner Walsh or even Charlie Chaplin or Larry Parks or Sterling Hayden or the rest of them there pinkos. If you try to put them on the program, the engineers will be instructed to pull the plug and substitute organ music!"

"What organ? Certainly not yours, Mr. Plant, or yours, Mr. Crunch. Gentlemen, this is my last season with you. I will not renew should you want me to renew. And this is going to be one red-hot chapter in my forthcoming autobiography, which is being written by my press agent Richard Maney. Let me tell you, I may be a firebrand but Maney's a volcano!" With which words she swept out of the office, slamming the door behind her but politely remembering to say goodbye to the office staff, who were gathered outside the door. They knew better than to applaud the performance she had just given, but they would each dine out on it for months to come.

Gregory and Anya Hagle, both in their mid-fifties, had been writing collaborators since their student days at New York's City College. It had truly been love at first slight, since Anya insulted him in the cafeteria when he usurped a chair she had been occupying.

Later at a protest rally (they both forgot what they were protesting, since rallies got them out into the fresh air and provided exercise) she apologized and accepted his invitation to see Rudolph Valentino's *The Sheik*. A few weeks after graduation, they were married, setting up housekeeping in the one-room apartment they rented in one of Brooklyn's meaner districts. Gregory waited on tables, and Anya sold notions in a local five-and-dime. At night they started to write plays together. After three years of this blissful life, they had a play produced on Broadway. It wasn't a success, but their combined talent was recognized.

Talking pictures were on the horizon, and soon the Hagles were recruited to go to Hollywood to write pictures for such theater stalwarts as Ruth Chatterton, Claudette Colbert, Fredric March, Edward G. Robinson, and so forth. Within a few years, they were solidly established in Hollywood, lost forever to Broadway, and leading a crusade to unionize scriptwriters, most of whom were sadly underpaid. After years of bitterness and struggle, the union was established and grudgingly accepted, and the Hollywood moguls swore revenge against those who had fought to create the union.

And so, in 1952, Gregory and Anya Hagle were subpoenaed to appear before the House Un-American Activities Committee, did appear, refused to testify on the grounds of self-incrimination, and now were unemployable. Childless, rootless, they left Hollywood and settled in a small but charming cottage in Bucks County, Pennsylvania, near such old friends as playwrights Moss Hart, Joseph Schrank, George S. Kaufman, and others, who urged them to write a play. They wrote the play, but the magic was missing. A producer friend offered charitably to give it a summer tryout at the popular Bucks County Playhouse, but both the Hagles were too wise not to realize there was no future to the play beyond the tryout.

They sought work as script bootleggers, the way Dalton Trumbo and Ring Lardner Jr. and Ian McClelland Hunter and others were doing with varying degrees of success, but what offers (one) they received were degrading and humiliating. Then Anya learned she had cancer. She didn't despair, nor did Gregory. Although it had been unspoken for months, both were very tired of living. They went to New York to dine with Dorothy Parker, who herself was tottering bravely on the brink of disaster and looking for a play collaborator. At least Dorothy had some income from her earlier short stories; the Hagles were flat broke.

"We could all use some kind of a break," Dorothy said in her soft voice, which they could barely hear above the din in Barney's Steak House. "The trouble with us is we don't have cookie-cutter talents. We're unable to worship at the feet of that great Greek god, Mediocreties. God, at a time like this I wish I were vastly untalented so I could make a living. Don't look so sad, my darlings. Somehow the wheel has got to start revolving again in our favor. I know! Let's order champagne! That's what we need, the babbling bubbly to buck us up."

"We can't afford champagne," said Gregory.

Anya said, "We can't afford borscht."

"Hush!" cautioned Mrs. Parker as she stole a quick glance under the table, "Mustn't say borscht! It's subversive!"

In their battered Chevrolet, driving back to Bucks County later that night, Anya snuggled next to Gregory. "It was sweet of Dottie to order the champagne. Did you notice how worn her gloves were at the fingers?"

"I noticed only how worn her eyes were."

"Darling, have we anything on for tomorrow?" She was staring up at the skies which were aglitter with stars, shining brilliantly as stars could shine brilliantly only in the clearer firmament of the suburbs.

"Nothing special."

"And the day after?"

"Likewise."

"And after and after and after."

They had reached the old road along the Delaware River.

"I guess we just ain't got nothing much to look forward to, Miss Scarlett," he said in one of his better imitations of Butterfly McQueen.

"So why don't you take your hands off the wheel and put your arms around me and pepper me with some hot kisses."

He was looking straight ahead through the windshield. He didn't see the tears in her eyes, but he knew they were there. He didn't speak because he knew if he did, the words would choke in his throat. He relinquished the wheel; he drew his wife tightly to him and pressed his lips against hers.

It took three days of dragging the river to find the Hagles clutching each other tightly in death in their battered Chevrolet.

"I'm reading George Santayana," Dorothy

Parker said to Tallulah Bankhead in Tallulah's suite at the Elysee.

"I thought you were a Nietzsche girl," said Tallulah as she worried a fingernail with an emery board.

"I find Santayana more comforting. Nietzsche come, Nietzsche go." She studied Tallulah in profile. "You're still very beautiful, Tallulah."

"Oh really, dahling? Marcus Blechman says he has to spend a day in bed after a session of airbrushing my photographs. I don't feel very beautiful these days, dahling. It's all too depressing. This epidemic of suicides. Nance Liston, Michael Darnoff, now the Hagles. Who's next?"

"I suppose it's time for me to make another stab at suicide . . . oops . . . no pun intended."

"Oh, Dottie, please don't. You're such a bungler at suicide. You have no discipline."

"What will you do if your show is canceled? They can cancel, can't they?"

"Yes, the bloody bastards, they can," admitted Tallulah ruefully. "Some act-of-God clause in my contract that can have various interpretations, all in their favor. And then there's the morality clause, and Christ could they do me in with *that* one!" They burst into laughter. "So Tallulah's being a good girl, or as good a girl as Tallulah can ever be or else she'll be at the mercy of one of those." She pointed to a pile of scripts on a desk.

"Well, aren't you the lucky one getting all those plays submitted to you?"

"Lucky!" cried Tallulah with a snort. "One of them is one of those dreary boulevard comedies in which both the setting and the heroine are laid in Paris. Then there's one set in San Francisco at the turn of the century where they want me to play a Chinese mail-order bride!"

"Special delivery?" inquired Mrs. Parker, "or returned for insufficient postage?"

"Returned for insufficient interest, dahling. Get this. My entrance line sticks in the brain like a plunged dagger." She was on her feet, shuffling about the room, hands clasped, head lowered to one side, a picture of obsequiousness. " 'Oh honorable Hung Low . . . or something like that . . . I am Moo Goo Gai Pan, fifth daughter of third cousin of eighth aunt in the honorable house of Anna May Wong.' " She sighed. "And in this day and age too." She reached for the pile of scripts, took one from the top, and turned to the title page. "Oh God, yes, there's *this* one. An adaptation from the Hungarian of Melchior Lazlas."

"Who's Melchior Lazlas?"

"I think it's a state of mind." She flung the script aside. "My character's named Fritzi Mitzi, believe it or not, and I'm a duchess masquerading as a B girl in a nightclub and the Grand Duke Hymie—or is it Irving?—out slumming with his valet, played by Edward Everett Horton, comes in, takes one look at me, and goes berserk."

"Why?"

"I thought we were friends."

Patsy Kelly came bursting into the room and in a tear-stained voice screeched, "I just read for some rotten play about Hollywood and you know what the sons of bitches said to me, 'You're not the type, Miss Kelly, we need someone funnier.' Funnier! Oh my God, me, Patsy Kelly, a Hollywood fixture for twenty years, and these two schmucks in swaddling clothes tell me I'm not the type. How are you, Dottie?" She grabbed the scotch Tallulah had poured for her. "Can somebody tell me what I need?"

"A blood transfusion," suggested Tallulah.

Patsy took a swig of her drink, wiped her mouth with the sleeve of her dress, stared at

34

the two women, and asked, "Well, what are you two so glum about?"

Tallulah gravely intoned her favorite lines from Psalm 7, Verse 1. "Oh Lord My God in thee do I take refuge, save me from all my pursuers and deliver me."

"Nice title there," said Mrs. Parker. " 'All my pursuers.' "

"Dottie," said Tallulah in a voice that demanded attention. "I'm going to fight them. Next Sunday I'm going to do one of your monologues."

"It's not the gift, it's the thought that counts," commented Mrs. Parker. "No, Tallulah, no no no. I know you adore treading where angels fear, and you're an angel for offering to be my angel, but don't tilt at windmills. At any rate, don't tilt at this set of windmills."

"But I can't stand this feeling of helplessness!" exploded Tallulah. "I can't use you, I can't use Julie Garfield, I can't help Abner Walsh . . ."

"Well, if you're so goddamned anxious to help somebody," screeched Patsy, "help loyal faithful trustworthy dead broke me!"

"What I love about you, Patsy dahling, is that when you have absolutely nothing to say, you go right ahead and say it."

It was as though Abner Walsh couldn't remember ever not living in Greenwich Village. He had migrated there from a small midwestern town, discovering it by instinct and knowing he was at home the minute he set foot on Christopher Street. Now thirty-five years later he was in a bigger, much more expensively furnished apartment in the more exclusive area of the Village on West Tenth Street off Fifth Avenue. He sat on the floor of his living room with his legs crisscrossed, strumming a guitar and staring at Lewis Drefuss, who was standing by the fireplace staring into a glass of wine as though uncovering hidden secrets there. Abner shook Lewis from his reverie. "Bankhead can't do anything?"

"She tried. Believe me, how she tried. Now she's under fire herself."

"You're kidding."

"Oh, she knows it's a setup just to keep her in line. But it could be harmful. They could pull the show out from under her. Just this morning she tried to sneak in a monologue by Dorothy Parker. It was as though an earthquake shook Rockefeller Center."

Abner set the guitar aside and stretched out his legs. "One miserable schmuck like

36

Lester Miroff names names and careers are shattered. Lives are shattered. Oh shit"—he rubbed his eyes—"I'm so tired. I'm so damn tired. I don't have anybody to talk to anymore."

"I'm talking to you."

"You're a good boy, but you be careful. Forget you know me."

"Don't be ridiculous!"

"You listen to me, kid. Better safe than sorry, if you'll forgive a cliché. Your bosses find out you've been pushing me the way Tallulah's been trying to use old friends in trouble, and you'll be feeling the axe. Believe me, kid, there's no profit in being a martyr. Even Nanette's walked out on me." He sighed and shook his head from side to side. "To think I left a wonderful woman for Nanette Walsh. Oh well, she was a great lay while she lasted. But she sculpts better."

"Abner, have you thought of going out on tour? You know, like colleges and universities?"

"Are you nuts?" With an effort, Abner was getting to his feet. "You read what happened when Paul Draper and Larry Adler tried a tour? Picket lines, threats, cancellation on top of cancellation. Not me, kid, I've still got footprints on my back from where people have been walking all over me. As of now, kid, Abner Walsh is officially retired."

"Come on, Abner!"

"The hell with it. I've had it. I'm fed up. I need to get laid. I wish I had the guts to murder Lester Miroff. Oh yes I do. I really wish I had the guts. Can you imagine that? Talk about fate's fickle finger. Me, the big star, the big box-office draw, blacklisted, unemployable. But Lester. The stool pigeon, the informer, the little fucker whose talent you could fit in a nutshell and still have room for a sofa, he gets a new TV show! Jesus, is there no justice anymore in this world?"

At the chic "21" Club on West Fifty-second Street, Detective Jacob Singer was flirting blatantly with Tallulah Bankhead. Tallulah was cooing and gurgling like a girl guide in heat, and Mrs. Parker sipped her Jack Rose while dwelling on a memory of meeting the elegant Lacey Van Weber back in 1926 in this very same room.

"Dahling," Tallulah asked Mrs. Parker, "are we boring you?"

"No more than usual."

"Oh do be kind, Dottie. Detective Singer

is such a marvelous salve for my bruised life."

"You two just keep on flirting with each other. I'm just the comic relief." Singer smiled. Mrs. Parker commented on two midgets at the next table whom she assumed were sharing some small talk. "Actually, watching you two batting your eyelashes at each other and trading sweet nothings that are sweet but nothing, reminds me of that afternoon in Venice some twenty or more years ago . . . don't you remember, Tallulah, you were well along in years even then." Tallulah's eyelids fell to half-mast as Mrs. Parker turned to the detective. "There was a bunch of us at a table at Harry's Bar. We were just sitting around, killing time and reputations, swapping shaggy Doge stories. Tallulah was flirting with Ernest Hemingway, and she soon got bored with that, which wasn't hard to do, and then she zeroed in on Scott Fitzgerald, but he was already on his way to his favorite spot under the table, so Tallulah chose to favor a film director with the most enchanting name."

"*What* film director with *what* enchanting name? You don't mean Ernst Lubitsch, for chrissakes. There was nothing enchanting about him unless you found the odor of stale cigar smoke intoxicating."

"No, dear, the man's name was Harry D'Abbadie D'Arrast." She smiled and asked Jacob Singer, "Isn't the name heaven?"

"It's a mouthful," commented Singer.

"The name was heaven," said Tallulah while lighting a Craven A, "he wasn't. Married some film star of the silents, didn't he?"

"Yes. Eleanor Boardman. I saw them recently. She's still gorgeous."

"Probably because she's not blacklisted."

"Oh dear, Jacob," said Mrs. Parker. "Tallulah's going to get morose on us. Just when I was having such a good time wallowing in tired memories and the embarrassing behavior of my dinner companions, and goddamn it I forgot the point I was trying to make. Oh yes. Venice. Tallulah. Flirtation. The fourth man she flirted with, a correspondent for some news syndicate. He asked her to go to bed with him and she slapped his face."

"That's right!" bellowed Tallulah. "I remember! I told him I never fuck when I flirt. Ooom Wah Hah Hah Hah Hah . . ." The raucous laughter petered out. She had recognized someone across the room making a hurried departure.

Jacob Singer commented on the strange expression on Tallulah's face. "You see someone you hate?"

"No, I saw someone I adore."

"Who?" asked Mrs. Parker, her curiosity piqued. There were so few people that Tallulah adored. She called everybody "dahling" because she could rarely remember anyone's name.

"Abner Walsh."

"Abner?" Mrs. Parker stared at Tallulah with disbelief. "Abner didn't say hello to us? Well, maybe he didn't see us."

"He saw us," said Tallulah. "And there was a perfectly dreadful expression on his face."

THREE

MARTHA WALSH, Abner's first wife, was surprised when he phoned and asked if he might visit her. When he had left her for the elegant Nanette, a successful sculptor whose work was coveted by museums and collectors, she didn't fight the divorce or make impossible financial demands despite the advice of friends and her lawyer. She was still very much in love with him, and it would be

41

alien to Martha to hurt anyone she loved. Even now, sitting across from him at the kitchen table in her basement flat on West Fiftieth Street in the heart of Hell's Kitchen, she ached to feel his arms around her once again, to press her lips eagerly to his, to make love and then phone for a pizza. He hadn't wanted a drink so she brewed tea. She had baked that morning, but he was only toying with the almond cake. He looked old, drawn, drained, wretched, but not in Martha's eyes.

"If you don't like the cake, I can get you something else. A sandwich? I've got onion rolls."

"Nothing, Martha. I've got no appetite these days." He couldn't mask his despair. "I didn't intend to visit all this operatic tragedy on you, Martha. But I don't know how to cope any longer. There's no way for me to fight the blacklist."

"Why can't Harvey do something?" Harvey Eilers was Abner's lawyer, who specialized in theatrical luminaries. As his star had ascended, he was as adept at dropping friends as he was at dropping names. Once when he broke his leg, Abner assumed he'd dropped a very heavy name on it. "I thought the law was supposed to protect people, not condemn them."

"Harvey suggests I go to Europe, to England. A lot of others have fled there. Lionel Stander's in Italy with a gang of others. Some are in Mexico. How do you think 'Blue Tail Fly' would sound in Italian?"

She tried to smile, but the effort was as weak as the tea in her cup. "Abner, are you broke?"

"Oh no no. I'm okay. Don't you worry about the payments."

"I wasn't thinking about myself."

"I forget. You rarely did." He looked across the table at her and he could still see the bright, fresh-faced girl who had captivated him over thirty years ago.

"How could those people do it? How could friends betray friends? I wonder if some day I'd be desperate enough to dishonor myself."

"Oh Christ, Martha, who knows what people can do when they've been pushed against the wall? Eddie Dmytryk went to jail with the Hollywood Ten and what does he do when he gets out? He recants, beats his chest, crying *mea culpa* so he can maybe go back to work again." He rested his hands on the table. "I can't do it. I just can't do it. If I

43

did, I wouldn't just hate myself in the morning, I'd hate myself forever."

"What does your wife say?"

"She said goodbye."

"I'm sorry." A pause. "Are you?"

Abner laughed. "You still know where to plunge the knife."

"I'd like to plunge it into Lester Miroff and Barry Wren and—"

"Martha. If you outlive me, and you probably will, I want you to make me a promise. Cremate me and throw my ashes in Lester Miroff's face."

Lewis Drefuss phoned Tallulah to break their dinner date. He apologized, explaining an overload of work. Tallulah was surprisingly understanding about the rejection. After returning the phone to the cradle, she stared at Estelle and Patsy, who were at the card table playing gin rummy. She sat back in her chair and thought about her assets. Windows, her home in Bedford Village, a short drive from the city, was worth a great deal of money. She had solid investments, and her father had left her and her sister Eugenia a surprisingly healthy amount of money. The autobiography was due in September, and her publisher predicted landslide sales. Magazines were already bidding for the serialization rights. Aloud she said, "I suppose I could always take out a tour of *Private Lives*."

"Why?" asked Estelle as she laid her ten cards on the table. "Forgive me, oh Lord, for I have ginned."

"Shit," said Patsy eloquently as she began counting her penalties. "My mother used to beat up on my father for doing that. Hell, she was always beating up on the old man."

"Really?" said Estelle, her beautiful eyes wide with astonishment. "Why didn't he leave her?"

"He couldn't borrow the carfare."

The phone rang. Tallulah answered it. It was her agent relaying a proposition. As she listened, Tallulah's grip tightened on the phone. Blood began boiling in her veins. And then words erupted from her mouth like hot lava pouring down from a volcano, spilling over the phone, across the room, inundating Estelle and Patsy, devastating everything in its path. In his office, her agent had dropped his phone and rushed to open a window. "Me do a show with Barry Wren? Why, that son of a bitch would betray his country for the right price! Don't you keep reminding me he's been cleared! He'll never get Tallulah's seal of approval! Of course I'd

love to do a musical, but not with that con-
taminated barrel of offal." She paused to
light a cigarette and then said into the phone,
"How's your mother?" A minute later she
was pacing the room, hands clasped behind
her back, muttering dark thoughts.

"Now, Tallulah, you mustn't be too harsh
on your agent. He works very hard for you
and he's sincere." Estelle snapped each card
as she dealt a fresh hand.

"His sincerity is about as heartfelt as that
of a French maître d'." She picked up the
script of her next radio show from the desk
and began flipping pages. Then she threw
the script on the floor and stomped on it.

"Tallulah!" screeched Patsy. "The neighbors!"

"Screw my neighbors. There are two
things in this world I can easily do without,
cancer and neighbors! Oh my God, why am
I so uneasy? Why do I feel as though heavy
heavy hangs over my head?" The phone interrupted her. "Goddamn it, how I hate that
phone!" She attacked the instrument and
snarled into it, "What?" She listened to
Dorothy Parker's soft, sad voice. "Oh, no.
Oh my God, no. How? Where?" She listened. "Well," she said through a dry laugh,
"if you have to go, it's a lovely way to go.

46

Let me know when they decide on the ser-vices." Estelle and Patsy were waiting. Tallulah hung up and covered her face with her hands. "Julie Garfield's dead."

"Hell, oh hell," said Patsy. "He's so young."

"Julie who?" asked Estelle.

"John Garfield, damn it!" shouted Tallulah.

"Oh my heavens," twittered Estelle as she adjusted her scarlet wig. "He was so sexy."

Tallulah roared with laughter. "Well, dahlings, he died fucking! He had a heart attack in his girlfriend's bed!"

The television networks early that evening paid brief, heartwarming tributes to the late John Garfield, tactfully omitting the truth surrounding his sudden death. Choreogra-pher Barry Wren watched one of the tributes in his living room, and then suddenly dropped the glass of wine from which he'd been sipping and bolted for the bathroom, where he stood over the sink with the dry heaves. Lester Miroff was in a sleazy bar on West Forty-third Street off Seventh Avenue having a bourbon with a beer chaser; for the first time in months, he had the decency to feel some remorse.

47

In another part of the city, an expensive apartment on upper Fifth Avenue, the celebrated young film and theater director Theodore Valudni was shutting the door behind him and placing his overnight case on the floor. He could hear the television set in the living room. "Honey," he called out, "I'm home." There was no response.

He entered the living room. His wife Beth was watching a kaleidoscope of scenes from John Garfield movies. Her eyes were red, though tearless. She had acted with Garfield in their early days on Broadway with the Group Theater. Ted Valudni had been an actor then too, not a very good one. But with the help of his friends in the Group, he'd found his true vocation as a gifted director. In the past ten years, he'd notched up an enviable string of film and theater triumphs. "What's that about Julie?" His voice was dry and parched.

"He's dead." It was Beth who certainly spoke, but the voice belonged to someone else. It was hollow and lifeless. Ted said nothing. "He had a heart attack." She arose from her seat and turned the set off. She picked up her glass of scotch and soda and then looked at her husband. "And so what happened in Washington? Did you take the Fifth?"

"Now look, Beth, we've been through this over and over again and I'm fed up discussing it!"

"Who did you name?"

"I don't want to talk about it."

"What would you like to talk about?"

"I want to talk about packing and heading for the Coast, that's what I want to talk about. I've decided to take Zanuck's offer . . ."

"Who did you betray?" He recognized this voice. "How many people will be crossing to the other side of the street when they see me coming? Who can I no longer phone and invite over for lunch? Did you name me? We met at the same fund-raiser. We acted in three plays together. We've been sharing the same bed for a long time." Her voice rose a few octaves. "How many lives did you destroy, my beloved husband? How many?"

He repeated the names of the men and women he had betrayed to save his own professional skin. She threw the drink in his face and then went to the bedroom to pack a bag. He sank into a chair without drying his face. Then he wondered if Broadway was ready for a revival of *King Lear*.

Abner Walsh cried as he watched the eulogy to John Garfield on his television set. The vial of sleeping pills was uncapped in his hand, and one by one he popped a pill into his mouth, helping it along with a sip of vodka. He was still popping pills when the eulogy was over and a cutesy weather girl was promising lovely weather for tomorrow. He kept downing pills and vodka until the vial was empty. He took all the pills because he wasn't sure how many were necessary to complete the job of dying satisfactorily. He had never tried to commit suicide before, except that one time he had recorded a romantic ballad, "You'd Better Go Now." The record was a flop and sent him back to folk songs with alacrity. He staggered to the record cabinet and through a bleary vision rummaged and found the recording. He had enough strength to put the record on the turntable and while he listened, he felt his life slipping away, without regret.

"You'd better go now . . . because I like you much too much . . ."

Abner sank to the floor with his head against the speaker. He whispered softly, "Okay . . . I'm going."

Abner had died early enough in the day to provide headlines for the afternoon newspapers. Gabriel Darnoff bought one at Times Square and thought: Another valiant is gone. My father's friend, my father's comrade, they fought together with the Abraham Lincoln Brigade during the Spanish Civil War. They always marched to the tattoo of the same drummer. They lived the same way, more or less, and they died the same way, more or less. Gabriel leaned against the news kiosk while crumpling the paper. My father defenestrated and Abner took pills. Both methods were highly effective. Maybe I should write my next play about them. They deserve a worthier epitaph than the ones they've received. Newspaper print is cold and heartless. No number of words can give the reader the true measure of these wonderful men. They weren't subversives. They were causists. They believed in something and fought for it and for this they were condemned. Men such as they fought in the Revolutionary War and it was men such as they who wrote the Constitution of the United States. My God, thought Gabriel as he started walking slowly to the theater where his play would have its first preview that night after a disappointing run in New Haven, if Nathan Hale or Patrick Henry or Thomas Jefferson were alive today, they'd be subpoenaed by HUAC! My, what another good idea for a play.

"What did you say, young man?" asked a feisty little old lady prepared to hit Gabriel with her umbrella.

"Are you talking to me?" asked Gabriel, waiting for the traffic light to change.

"Well, you were talking to me! I didn't hear what you said! Do you need help crossing the street? I hate boy scouts."

"What I said? Oh . . . yes . . . I said the world is rapidly running out of heroes."

"You some kind of a nut case?" The light changed and Gabriel fled.

In Studio 8H of the NBC Studios in Rockefeller Center, from which "The Big Show" was broadcast, a pall hung over the rehearsal. The news of Abner Walsh's death had brought a fresh spate of vituperation from Tallulah aimed at anyone silly enough to step into her line of verbal fire. The orchestra conductor, Meredith Wilson, doodled at the piano a melody Abner had composed many years ago and Tallulah's guest stars wisely repaired to their dressing rooms. Tallulah spotted Lewis Drefuss talking on the phone, crossed to him, and put her arm around his shoulders. He finished talking and hung up.

"I'm so sorry, dahling. You tried so hard to save Abner."

"We both did."

"My God, Lewis. The world's gone mad. Absolutely mad. Oh for the good old days when people making speeches from soap boxes were a popular vaudeville joke!" She was hunting in her handbag for her cigarettes and when she had one between her lips, Lewis struck a match and lit it. "I'm a fighter, Lewis, but now I'm beginning to think I'm getting too old for it." She savagely blew a smoke ring that barely missed hitting a stagehand. "Maybe I should retire quietly to Windows and spend the rest of my life taking nips from a bottle of gin while listening to my arteries harden. Well, aren't you going to talk me out of it?"

"What?"

"Oh, Lewis, you poor dahling. You haven't been listening." She put her arm through his. "Let's get some coffee and talk about the people we hate. Who's that woman over there who keeps smiling at me? Even with my glasses on I don't recognize her."

"That's Beth Valudni. She's doing the tea party sketch with you."

"*That's* Beth Valudni? Why dahling, she looks as though she's just been in a train crash. Beth! Dahling! Forgive me! It's been so many years, I didn't recognize you!" They fell into each other's arms. Then to Lewis, Tallulah said, "Beth was my understudy in a piece of crap I did with that profile I was married to. For God's sake, Beth, what are you doing working?"

"I've left Ted. I need to work."

"Congratulations! Come have some coffee with us and we can verbally destroy the villain. Is it true he named *you* too?"

"He named me and God knows what I'm doing here. I was stunned when I was told I had the job."

Lewis explained, "They couldn't find any incriminating documentation on you."

"That must have ruined their day, dahlings." She asked Beth as they reached the elevator, "Did you know Ted was going to name names?"

"Well, Tallulah, I knew he had an offer from Hollywood that was contingent on his clearing himself. He's going there in a few weeks."

The elevator arrived. Although it was

crowded, Tallulah took the two by the arm and pressed in. "Sorry, dahlings," she said over her shoulder to the discomfited ones, "but my girlfriend's pregnant and we're late for my abortionist." Beth blushed. She had seen an abortionist three days after leaving Valudni.

They found a vacant table in Cromwell's drugstore on the lobby floor that not only provided refreshments but was a clearing-house for radio and television actors trading tips and gossip. The young waiter was having trouble taking their simple orders of coffee and sandwiches, and Tallulah, impatient with his ineptness, asked, "Young man, are you an actor?"

"Why, yes!" he said brightly, glowing in his one and probably only moment in the sun.

"Oh, good! Because you're certainly not a waiter." With sagged shoulders he went away. "Something's got to be done about this."

"The waiter?" asked Beth.

"Hell, no, let's leave him to heaven. These betrayals. The destruction of the innocent. Have you heard even *I've* been threatened? The next thing you know they'll be after

Lunts, and then God help them. Well, any ideas?"

Lewis crumbled a breadstick and the table fell silent.

Martha Walsh wandered about the apartment trying to come to a decision. She had swallowed her pride and phoned her successor, Nanette Walsh, to offer her condolences and to tell her Abner wished to be cremated. Nanette said she knew that and he was to be cremated in the morning.

She told Nanette of Abner's visit a few days ago and of his strange request about the disposal of his ashes. There was silence from Nanette for a few seconds, followed by a hoarse laugh, and she said, "I'll have them delivered to you."

And so Abner had been cremated and the tin of ashes now sat on the mantelpiece next to a photo taken many years ago of Abner, Martha, and their son, Leo, a small boy with a jagged scar on his left cheek. Martha touched the photograph gently, then touched the tin of ashes and, with resolve, referred to her book of phone numbers and dialed Lester Miroff.

"Hello?" said Miroff while watching his friend, Oliver Sholom, stare dumbly out the window. Sholom had not been as fortunate as Miroff and so many others who had been cooperative witnesses. He'd blabbed all over the place, but still couldn't get a job as a director. He couldn't even get a job directing traffic.

"It's Martha Walsh, Lester."

"Martha Walsh?" He couldn't believe his ears. He had named Abner, everyone knew she was forever loyal to Abner, and here she was on the phone speaking to a man who had betrayed the only great love of her life. Now he needed a scriptwriter but there was none at hand. He had to improvise on his own. "Er . . . hello, Martha."

"I have something for you, Lester. Abner wanted you to have it."

"Me?"

"Will you be home for a while?"

"Why, sure, sure I will. Actually, Oliver Sholom's here. Visiting." Sholom turned from the window when he heard his name.

"I'll be right over," said Martha and hung up. Taking the tin of ashes, she left the basement apartment and walked purposefully the three short blocks to Lester Miroff's building. When she reached his door, she pried the lid from the tin of ashes, and when Lester opened the door wide, a carefully manufactured smile on his face, Martha said, "Compliments of Abner Walsh." She flung the ashes in his face. "Those are his ashes! I wish they were yours!"

"Oh my God!" cried Oliver Sholom. "Oh my God! Such bad taste!"

Lester Miroff neither said anything nor did anything. He was shocked with horror.

When Martha returned to her basement apartment, she sat at the kitchen table penning a brief note. When she was finished, she put it in an envelope and sealed it. She took a five-dollar bill from her purse and went out into the street. She recognized the teenage boy playing stoop ball and called his name. "Nick!" Nick frequently ran errands for her and was generously rewarded. "Can you use five dollars, Nick?"

Nick crossed to her and she explained the errand. Half an hour later he was in Studio 8H asking for Tallulah Bankhead. Lewis Drefuss suggested he wipe his nose. The boy smiled and inhaled. Lewis took him to Tallulah's dressing room. "There's a young man here to see you, Tallulah."

"Not too young I hope. I'm not the girl I used to be."

"He has a note for you."

"Yeah," piped up Nick, "she gimme a

58

fiver to make sure it's delivered to you poisonally. You rilly Talluler Banghead?"

"Bankhead. Yes, dahling. Is this the first you've ever seen me?"

"Yeah!"

"How I envy you." She took the note, patted him on the head, offered him a martini which he refused, and then ushered him out the door. "Sweet child, probably contemplating a life of crime." She tore open the envelope and extracted the note. She scanned it swiftly and then emitted a cry of dismay. "It's from Martha Walsh! Thanking me for what I tried to do for Abner . . . and oh my God . . . she says she's gone to join him!" Lewis ran out of the dressing room. "Where are you going? Phone the police! Someone! Phone the police! But where does she live? There's no return address! Somebody help me!"

A neighbor had smelled the gas while in the basement to dispose of her garbage. She banged on Martha's door, shouting, "Mrs. Walsh! Mrs. Walsh!" but there was no response. She ran upstairs and alerted the building superintendent. With his oldest son, the man rushed to the basement and together they broke the door down. Martha was on the floor of the kitchen, towels stuffed around window edges and under the doors. They turned off the gas and the son phoned for an ambulance. The neighbor patted Martha's wrist and the janitor applied a damp dish towel to her forehead. But it was too late.

Later Lewis Drefuss told a distraught Tallulah, "By the time I got there, the ambulance had gone. But someone told me she was dead. Gas."

Tallulah stubbed out her cigarette and then said in a husky voice, "If there's a God, someone will pay for this."

"Miss Bankhead! Miss Valudni! We're ready to rehearse your sketch!" they heard the floor manager call.

Tallulah said to Lewis, "Find out if she had any money. If she didn't, then I'll pay for the funeral. She and Abner were always so kind to me. They put up with so much. And I've got a bloody sketch to rehearse."

Oliver Sholom waited a decent ten minutes before leaving Lester Miroff in his apartment and hurrying back to his own shabby walk-up apartment on Tenth Avenue. A job, he was thinking, a job. I've got to find a job. Somebody out there has got to offer me a job. I've had some good successes on Broadway. I've directed big stars. Mary Boland. Jane Cowl. Lenore Ulric. Real big stars. I've got to find a job. Ashes. Abner's ashes. Well, he was lucky she wasn't carrying a gun. She might have murdered him. *Murder*. Oh my God, can it be that all this mess is coming to that? *Murder*.

Lester Miroff had bathed and now sat wearing a bathrobe staring out the window. It had taken the ashes of an old friend flung in his face to finally bring home to him the enormity of his betrayals. He would have to live with this for the rest of his life. Soon he'd be singing on his own TV show, but was it worth it? Was it really worth it? Who was still speaking to him these days? His agent, his mother and father who couldn't understand why he was still a bachelor at the age of forty, the neighborhood tradespeople and . . . who . . . oh yes . . . Oliver Sholom, poor bastard, begging me to get him the job directing my program. Oh, what the hell, maybe it's worth a shot trying to get it for him. Oh my God, oh my God, what have I done to myself?

The phone rang and he stared at it. Maybe it was wired to explode. He was feeling paranoid. It rang again. Answer it, you dummy;

it didn't explode when Martha phoned you. Martha. Abner. Ashes. He reached for the phone. "Hello?"

"Lester Miroff." The voice sounded faint, muffled.

"Yes, could you speak up, please. I can barely hear you."

"Martha Walsh is dead." Still faint, still muffled, but Lester heard. His mouth went dry and his skin was pale and clammy. "Lester, you'll never sing again."

Click.

FOUR

"So TELL me what to do!" shouted Lester into the phone.

"You're getting hysterical, Lester," said his agent, a formidable middle-aged woman named Leona Clystir who loathed her clients en masse.

"Hysterical! I've just had a death threat!"

"Lester, it's just a crank. Face it, dear." She had the phone cradled between her shoulder and chin while applying polish to a fingernail. "You'll be getting a lot of flack from these pests. Crank call, crank letters, I mean for some kookieboos, it's a hobby."

"I'm going to call the police!"

"Lester, save the effort. The best they'll offer to do is tap your phone and believe me, it's not worth the invasion of privacy. Don't sit around the house either. Go to a movie. Go to a Turkish bath. Go to a supermarket and shove geriatrics."

Lester went to a Turkish bath. It was located in the West Twenties off Broadway. It was a homosexual hotbed and named, amusingly enough, the Everhard. He taxied down from his apartment, too nervous and edgy to notice he was being followed.

It was too early in the day for much action, and Lester was grateful for the comparative peace and quiet. During rush hour the place sounded like the invasion of a chicken coop by fox and vixen. A towel comfortably wrapped around his potbelly, Lester settled down on a ledge in the dimly lit steam room. When his eyes became accustomed, he realized he had the place to himself. It was almost an intrusion when the door opened and through the steamy mist Lester saw a man enter. The man was fully clothed. Fully clothed, in a steam bath? Well, maybe that's how he gets his kicks. Lester closed his eyes and leaned back; he could almost hear his pores opening and exuding body poisons, or at least that's what they were supposed to do in a steam room. He sneezed and then yawned and then wondered what the other man was doing and if perhaps he was attractive. He opened his eyes and saw what the other man was doing. He was pointing a small gun at Lester, and before Lester could realize he was doomed, the man pulled the trigger. Lester heard a little *ffffuttt*, and that was the last thing he heard. The bullet hit him right between the eyes and killed him instantly. The man left the steam room cautiously; he made his way out of the building without being seen; and then he went to a Jewish delicatessen on Broadway and ordered a hot pastrami and corned beef combo, as lean as possible, please, and a celery tonic. Yes, a slice of half sour pickle would be nice too, but no cole slaw, thank you. Fascinating, the man thought as he waited for his order, absolutely fascinating. Killing is so easy. It's such a cinch to commit the perfect crime. Lester Miroff. That's one down, and just a few more to go. He smiled. Murder is like eating peanuts. Once you start, it's hard to stop.

A young man with a father fixation entered the steam room of the Everhard baths. When his eyes became accustomed to the dimly lit mist, he saw Lester Miroff sitting with his head back against the wall. The young man with a highly practiced and professional eye whispered to himself, "Bingo!" and zeroed in on his potential daddy. He sat next to Lester and seductively rearranged his towel. He stared carefully out of the corner of an eye to see if Lester was responding. Lester, albeit in a steam room, appeared cool and aloof to the young man. The young man was neither a quitter nor a dropout. He edged along the seat a little closer to Lester. Weird, he thought, sitting there with his head back and his mouth open. The young man moved his hand so that it now gently touched Lester's thigh.

He decided it was time to stop wasting time and with the cheery voice of a seasoned campaigner, plunged right in. "Hi there! Do you come here often?" Lester's head fell forward and drops of blood fell on the young man's hand. His shriek might have gone down in gay steam-bath history for the magnitude of its pitch, but there was nobody around to record it for posterity. The young man fled to the hall, found an attendant, and babbled there was a stiff in the steam room, stiff hardly being the word he should have used on these premises. The attendant finally cottoned there was a dead man on the premises, said "Shit," and hurried to the steam room.

At least one person in Tallulah's audience was spellbound. Detective Jacob Singer was as mesmerized as a cobra held in thrall by a Hindu's pipe. Dorothy Parker was more amused watching Singer watching Tallulah than she was by Tallulah's account of a recent Hollywood rejection that would pain her until death.

"Can you imagine what that son of a bitch Jack Warner did to me? To me, mind you! That he dares ask me to do a screen test in the first place was insult enough!"

"Didn't you do a test of Scarlett O'Hara for David Selznick, dear?" asked Mrs. Parker while fingering the small strand of pearls around her neck.

"But dahling, that wasn't just a test, it was a production! They took three days. And Selznick was a gentleman. He knows how to treat a star!"

"For what disease?"

Tallulah's look was withering, but Jacob Singer urged her to get on with her story. "Where was I, dahling?" she said, now favoring Singer with a smile that scorched and held some promise.

"That son of a bitch Jack Warner," prompted the detective.

"Oh, do you dislike him too?"

"Oh, get on with it, Tallulah." Mrs. Parker went to the bar and poured herself another drink.

"So they convince me to fly to Hollywood to test for Amanda Wingate in *The Glass Menagerie*. I mean it's bad enough I'm years too young to play a mother of two grown children—"

Interjected Mrs. Parker, "And it's bad enough they didn't offer it to Laurette Taylor, who created the part . . ."

"Dahling, Laurette was dead by then."

"Oh, I hadn't noticed."

Tallulah returned her attention to Singer. "So I make the test and everyone is thrilled, including, I must admit, myself. My agents are ready to negotiate. And what happens? What happens?"

"What happened, Tallulah?"

"Oh, shut up, Dottie! What happened was *this*. Jack Warner says I don't want Bankhead, she's a drunk! We have enough trouble with Errol Flynn, we don't need another rumpot on the lot." Her voice choked.

"Me! Tallulah! I've never been drunk on stage or in front of a camera in the entire lifetime of my career! I'm a disciplined actress and I do my job. I've never been sick. I've never missed a performance. And who do they sign for the part? Are you ready for *this*, dahlings?" She paused dramatically and then spat out the name. "Gertrude Lawrence, for chrissakes! A bloody soubrette with the voice of a sodomized cockatoo! Well, I'm happy to add the movie was a disaster and it serves the bastards right. I might add, and I don't mind telling you, I wanted to murder Jack Warner. It would have been the perfect crime!"

"There's no such thing," said Jacob Singer complacently.

"Oh, isn't there?" challenged Tallulah.

"Oh, some people get away with murder occasionally because there's insufficient evidence to make a collar. Vagrants and people like that get killed. It's hard to trace who might have done it. But celebrities, that lot, no way."

"You're wrong, Mr. Detective!" Tallulah swayed slightly, and Mrs. Parker worried she might soon topple over. "Ever hear of a movie actress named Thelma Todd? She was murdered in nineteen thirty-five and the murderer's never been found."

"Miss Bankhead," said Singer, "the files on Thelma Todd no longer exist in the Los Angeles police department, but they knew who murdered her and to expose the killer was to expose a political mess that would have rattled the city and the studios."

Tallulah was not about to be defeated. "You ever heard of the tobacco heir Smith Reynolds?"

"Sure. Libby Holman the singer, she was his wife at the time, they brought her to trial."

"And the trial was discontinued and all charges against Libby were dismissed. I can tell you who murdered Smith Reynolds."

"Oh, stop teasing us," said Mrs. Parker edgily, "who is it?"

"Blanche Yurka.'

"Tallulah, you're mad! She was a divine Gertrude to John Barrymore's Hamlet."

"So what? She was a brilliant Madame Defarge in Ronnie Colman's *Tale of Two Cities,* she was also one hell of a shot with a handgun. Ha-ha-ha-ha-ha! If you could see the expression on your faces! Got you on that one, haven't I, Mr. Detective Jacob

69

Singer with those adorable brown eyes, and you look so edible when you flutter them."

"Tallulah, you're drunk. You're making this up!"

"Like hell I am and like hell I am. I got the story from someone who got it from Blanche when she was drinking heavily. Blanche was Libby Holman's lover then." Singer was beginning to feel giddy. "She was in the house as Libby's guest. Libby was pregnant with Smith's child, though there's those who suggest the father might have been Smith's best friend."

Tallulah turned to Singer. "Well, Jacob, why aren't you off to East Seventy-second Street to arrest Miss Yurka?"

"Well, second of all, I'd have to pick up a warrant."

"What's first of all?"

"Proof. Tallulah's story is hearsay."

"It's the fucking gospel according to Saint Bankhead!" shouted Tallulah. "Oh, let's go eat. I refuse to suffer fools any longer."

"Now why don't we order room service?" suggested Mrs. Parker. "It's so snug and comfy here, and there's more room to spread your insults and innuendo."

Tallulah laughed and then said, "I do adore you, Dottie. You have such a one-smack mind." Singer asked if he could use the phone.

Mrs. Parker took charge. "What do you feel like eating?"

"Order me some vichyssoise and a bottle of champagne."

"That's not a fit dinner for anyone. I hear they do a nice chicken here. Wouldn't you like a nice chicken?"

Tallulah was lighting a Craven A and folded one leg over the other. "Sure, bring the young man in." They could hear Singer speaking to the desk sergeant at his precinct.

"What part of the chicken would you prefer, dear?"

Tallulah couldn't resist. "The left wing."

Mrs. Parker exhaled, conceding defeat. Singer had finished with the phone. "You ladies know Lester Miroff?"

"My dear Jacob," said Mrs. Parker, "to speak that name here is to wave a red flag at a bull. Who's he betrayed now?"

"Himself. He's dead. Murdered." He told them where Lester was murdered and how.

"The bastard," said Mrs. Parker, "a man who suffered the impoverishment of courage."

The news did much to sober Tallulah. She

71

was on her feet with her arms folded around herself to ward off a sudden chill.

"What's wrong, Tallulah?" asked Singer.

"Someone just walked over my grave. The killer got away I assume."

"Without a trace."

Tallulah smiled. "Well, not too bad a candidate for the perfect crime, Mr. Singer."

Singer shrugged. "Too soon to tell, Tallulah. Ladies, it's been nice, but I've got to go to work."

"What? Without dinner?"

"I often go without eating, Tallulah."

"Ridiculous, but oh well. You had a hat, didn't you? I'll get it." She went to the bedroom and Singer watched her leave with hungry eyes.

Mrs. Parker said, "Why Jacob, you're smitten."

He blushed. "Yeah, I kind of go for her."

"She's a dangerous woman."

"That's why I go for her. What do you suppose it would take to get her into the sack?"

"Courage."

"Just ask me!" shouted Tallulah from the bedroom. "You dear sweet old-fashioned boy!"

She entered twirling his hat on her index

72

finger. "Now seriously, about Lester Miroff. Oh, do sit down the two of you; you don't have to go rushing off, Jacob, Lester isn't going anywhere. There's a lot to be considered here. The murder of that man could lead to serious consequences for a lot of people."

"Such as?" asked Singer as he took his hat and sat.

"All the people he named before the House Un-American Committee! He fingered at least a dozen."

"More," said Mrs. Parker.

"The greedy sod. I mean he helped destroy Abner Walsh and Michael Darnoff and that writing team the Hagles."

"They're all dead," reminded Mrs. Parker.

"But there are plenty still living."

"On the other hand, Tallulah," said Jacob Singer, "it might just have been your everyday run-of-the-mill sex crime. The steam room he was killed in is part of a notorious fag hangout."

"Oh really, dahling, the boys don't go cruising packing gats or rods or whatever. At least not the ones I know and I know a great many and they only shoot off their mouths." She turned to Mrs. Parker. "What do *you* think, Dottie?"

"Well, thank God my husband's in L.A."

"Are you sure, dahling?"

"Yes, darling, I spoke to him a couple of hours ago. I'll tell you what I really think! If one of the blacklisted murdered the little bedbug, I'll help raise money for his defense if they ever catch him."

"I think they'll have a hard time catching him," said Tallulah. "That chill I had, I'll tell you why. It occurred to me, and much too quickly I might add because I'm not all that quick a thinker. It occurred to me that Lester Miroff was the first. There'll be more. All the others who cooperated with the committee. I think they could be marked for murder."

"Tallulah, how morbid." Mrs. Parker sipped her drink and then said, "How wonderful."

"Ladies," said Singer, "I'd appreciate your help. Offhand, which of these people do you think might be in line to draw the black ace?"

"Have you got all night?" asked Tallulah. "Oops."

For the next fifteen minutes, Jacob Singer was busy writing names in the notebook he always carried with him. He had a cast list of stars, supporting players, bit players, and walk-ons. He had directors and writers, composers and choreographers, singers and charlatans; the size of the list was mind-boggling, a list, Mrs. Parker insisted, that would someday cause historians to break down in despair.

"Now there's another thing to consider," said Singer when he was finished writing. The women waited. "These blacklisted people who are dead. Some of them had families? They have children?"

Said Tallulah, "You mean avenging angels swarming about bleating threats of revenge?"

"Don't take it so lightly, Tallulah," admonished Singer. "I've turned up some very strange murder suspects in my time. I mean there was this here private secretary who bumped off a whole board of directors who had destroyed her boss."

"He must have paid her handsome bonuses," said Mrs. Parker.

"These dead ones have children or lovers or sweethearts or somebody connected with them who gets it in their head to revenge their deaths. Isn't that likely?"

"Well, let me think," said Mrs. Parker, back at the bar for a refill. "There's Gabriel Darnoff, he's the actor's son. But he's got a play opening in a few days, when he'll probably be thinking of murdering the critics." Singer was scribbling rapidly. "The Hagles had no children. Julie Garfield had kids . . ."

"Oh, dahling, they're just babies," said Tallulah, "and as for his wife, if Robbie was ever going to kill for him, she would have done it years ago when he was just getting started in Hollywood. But today . . ." Tallulah shrugged.

"What about Abner Walsh?" asked Singer.

"There was Martha, his wife," said Mrs. Parker, "but now she's dead too, a suicide."

"There's a son," said Tallulah.

"There is?" Mrs. Parker was honestly amazed at the news.

"Well there was," said Tallulah. "I don't know, he might be dead for all I know. Something about some awful tragedy some years back, a plane crash or maybe it was a train crash. I'm really not sure, dahlings. I do remember Abner mentioning the boy once, and then, come to think of it, he clammed up as though it was privileged information not meant for sharing. Oh, the hell with it. I'm starving. Come on, Dottie, let's go eat at Tony's and make Mabel Mercer miserable."

"I will go nowhere if you're planning to make a spectacle of yourself. And I adore

Mabel's singing and will not tolerate your badgering her. Wait, Jacob, and we'll go down with you."

"And, dahlings, it just might be the only time the three of us will go down together!"

FIVE

"WHERE'S THAT sandwich and coffee I ordered an hour ago!" Jacob Singer bellowed from his office to no one in particular.

"It's on the windowsill!" someone yelled back, and it was. Jacob rolled his chair over to the food and carried it back to his desk. When he unwrapped the sandwich, the Swiss cheese was soggy and the ham was wilted. The coffee was cold. He committed the mess to the wastepaper basket behind him and then returned to studying the list of names he'd taken from Tallulah and Mrs. Parker. He had a man investigating Abner Walsh's first wife, Martha, and the whereabouts of the son, name unknown. He had another man tracing Lester Miroff's movements that day. He had located Miroff's agent, Leona Clystir, who told him about the threat Lester had received on the phone. She could tell him little else about Lester or his movements

77

and said it was she who suggested he go to a movie or a steam bath to calm his shattered nerves.

Leona had never met Lester's family but knew where to reach his parents. The officer who went to their apartment to break the sad news to them reported there was no crying or sobbing or tearing of hair, but a gentle inquiry as to the whereabouts of his insurance policy. Leona said she didn't know any of Lester's friends because since his command performance in Washington, he didn't have any friends, but oh yes, there was this director Oliver Sholom, who Lester still saw because he'd also ratted and the two of them were a case of misery loving company. Jacob duly jotted down Sholom's name.

In response to the question did she know either Abner Walsh or his first wife, Martha, Leona Clystir was a jackpot of Walsh history. She kept transferring the phone from one ear to the other while talking to Singer, trying to watch a client performing on a variety show on the television screen (the reception was dreadful and so was the client) and fixing a salad for her dinner. "I knew Abner and Martha when they were first married. There was a child. A boy, I think. I was booking club acts then for some goniff in the Brill Building and I used Abner as often as possible. Then we lost touch, but later, when he was a big success, Martha and the boy were in some dreadful accident. I think it was a plane, or maybe it was a train."

"About how long ago would you say that was?"

"Oh, hell," said Leona as she screwed up her face and looked out the kitchen window, hoping she'd find the answer on the billboard on the roof of the building across the street. "It must have been at least twenty years or thereabouts. You know, I think the boy was killed." She thought for a moment, "Yes, that's what happened. The boy was killed and Abner dumped Martha for that sculptor thing he's married to now. I mean she's his widow, or something. Nanette. A maneater, I've been told. When Abner met her she was known as 'No No Nanette.' Listen, Mr. . . . what's your name again, dear?" Singer told her. "Of course, Detective Singer. Have Lester's parents been told or do I have to do the dirty work?" He told her they were told and were making the funeral arrangements once the autopsy was performed. "Oh, poor Lester," she wailed. "A TV series up in smoke," and with it, she diplomatically refrained from remarking, her ten percent commission. "I'd arrange a memorial service, but who'd come?"

While chewing on a chocolate bar he found on somebody else's desk, Singer began phoning the people he wanted to talk to starting the next morning. He left messages for Gabriel Darnoff, Barry Wren, Ted Valudni and his estranged wife Beth, Oliver Sholom, and so on and so forth. He wasn't looking forward to the tedium of the investigation, nor was he relishing the prospect of the inevitable false leads and blind alleys and reluctant cooperations. He was hoping somebody would suddenly leave town. That was always a healthy sign that the person knew too much or with any luck was the guilty party.

There was a tapping on his window. Singer yelled "Come in!" and the young man who had discovered Lester Miroff's body entered. He had a look of exasperation on his face.

"Are you Jacob Singer?"

"That's what it says on the door."

"I'm Clive Osgood Thrum the Third."

Singer looked up. He wondered what the first two Clive Osgood Thrums looked like. This one was no beauty-prize winner. Singer indicated the only other chair in the cubicle. "Have a seat, Mister Thrum the Third."

"Now can you please tell me what I'm doing here? I told that cop down at the Everhard everything I knew, which wasn't much."

"Sit down. This won't take long."

"Well, I hope not. I've got a late date at the East Five Five and I have no intention of keeping him waiting."

Singer referred to a memo on his desk. "Mister Thrum, it says here you've had seven arrests over the past six years for soliciting in public toilets, attempted extortion . . . and *rape?*"

"I can assure you it wasn't worth the bother. How was I supposed to know he was a rabbi?" Thrum the Third finally sat. "I hope it says on that sheet I beat the rap on all seven counts."

"You must have a very smart lawyer."

"My sister."

"Tell me what happened in the steam room."

"So I go in, there's nobody there but the stiff, except he don't look dead when I get in. Anyway, the place is so dimly lit and full of steam I could have made a pass at and laid my father without either of us recognizing each other."

81

"You're positive there's nobody else in the steam room when you're there?"

He smiled. "Honor bright. There's very little action there so early in the afternoon— it's too soon for the ribbon clerks and too late for the night shift because by noon they're on their way home to their wives or whatever."

"So what were you doing there?"

"Looking for a leftover or a stray. You know, potluck."

"Who'd you see when you checked into the place?"

"The guy who rents the lockers and the roomettes, period. There wasn't a soul on the premises. I looked in the pool and the game room and the refreshment . . . ha . . . bar, and oh yes, there was the guy who does the coffee and goodies, but he's been there for years—the only thing he'd kill is your appetite."

"When you were entering the place, did you perhaps notice anyone leaving?"

"You mean like coming out the door?"

"That would help."

"Listen, that place is located in the heart of the shmotter district . . . ."

"The what district?"

Thrum the Third rolled his eyes with exasperation and explained, "Shmotter . . . rags . . . garment center, get it? I mean the crush of humanity there from nine to six is unbelievable. Face it, I'm a lousy witness."

And that's how it was with the steam-bath personnel when Singer got around to them. But someone had entered the place and plugged Lester Miroff between the eyes. How, Singer wondered, did the murderer know where to locate Miroff? Easy. He'd tailed Miroff from the singer's apartment. He'd phoned him from a nearby booth, gambled Miroff would panic and very soon come flying out the door looking for someplace to hide. And the gamble had paid off. If it hadn't, well, thought Singer, he'd be having dinner right now with Tallulah and Mrs. Parker.

Tony's Restaurant on West-Fifty-second Street between Fifth Avenue and the Avenue of the Americas was a reformed speakeasy located in the street-level basement of a brownstone. After prohibition, Tony, the owner, had converted to a restaurant club where the food was sometimes good and the black singer Mabel Mercer sang nightly, except Mondays, before a legion of loyal fans. It was a celebrity hangout, although Tony's daughter, who was recently married to the film director John Huston, was never seen there with her husband. The tiny stage on which Miss Mercer reigned with her pianist had been constructed against what had once been the windows overlooking the street. The small dining room stretched to the bar area, which commanded an unrestricted view of both entertainer and diners, the diners frequently providing more exciting divertissement.

Such as when among the diners present were Tallulah Bankhead and Dorothy Parker.

"Dahling," said Tallulah to a young man standing near their table with his hands in his pockets, "get us another round please."

"I'm not an employee, Miss Bankhead," he said politely.

"Oh, I'm so sorry, darling. You were standing there doing nothing, so I assumed you work here. Well, be a dahling and find our waiter, will you dear?" Mrs. Parker's attention was directed elsewhere. "Who you looking at, Dottie?"

"That old broad across the room there with the two beautiful young men."

Tallulah recognized the woman. "Oh, dahling, don't you know who she is? She's

Rosie Dolly Netcher, the surviving Dolly Sister."

"But all those emerald necklaces around her neck, and those ruby and diamond bracelets."

"I know. We should genuflect. She got it all from the husband, Irving Netcher, Chicago millions. Goddamn it, Dottie, we're two of the smartest girls in the business. Why haven't we snared our millionaire? Why must I work for a living? And why are you always broke?"

"I'm not always broke, Tallulah. I was quite rich these past years in Hollywood. I made a hell of a lot of money."

"So where is it?"

"Oh, Tallulah, darling, life is such a bottomless barrel."

"What the hell does *that* mean?"

"How do I know? I'm not a philosopher."

The waiter brought their refills and said they were from the young man Tallulah had sent to summon him. "Oh, isn't that dahling of him? Where'd he go? Oh, there he is! Young man!" He turned and smiled at her. She lifted her glass in a toast. "Happy hunting!" He winked and resumed conversation with a naval officer at the bar.

"Dottie, you've got to write me a play."

"Tallulah, I meant to tell you earlier, I've agreed to collaborate on a play with Arnaud D'Ussaud, *Ladies of the Corridor*, and, darling, there is no star part. Actually, we're thinking of one of the leading roles, a divorced midwestern housewife living in a hotel for women, for Katharine Cornell."

"Well, she only does star parts, for crying out loud."

"On the contrary, Tallulah. Remember that marvelous revival she did of Chekhov's *Three Sisters?* She was just one of the ensemble. That was truly an all-star cast. I think Katharine Cornell could use my play."

"Katharine Cornell could use a blood transfusion. And I could use a career transfusion. Mene mene tekel. The handwriting's on the wall. I know my radio show's not long for this world, which means the wolves are going to be at my door and howling."

"Don't kid me, Tallulah, you've got plenty of money."

"Money, my dear Mrs. Parker, has a strange way of running out when you're a long time between jobs, and I have had very long times between jobs."

"Why don't you revive *The Little Foxes?*"

"What? Are you mad? Get involved with that Hellman bitch again?"

"She's in bad trouble."

"Is anyone ever in good trouble?"

"I know." She snapped her fingers.

"If you say Clifford Odets, I'll savage you."

"You reading my mind? Joe Savage, he's the one to write a play for you."

"And what exactly is a Joe Savage?"

"A very talented young writer, who, come to think of it, was another one condemned by Lester Miroff."

"Christ, how did Miroff miss fingering the Vienna Boys Choir?"

"They weren't in town. Joseph must be around somewhere. I'll start tracking him down tomorrow. I'm going to bring you two together and that's my mitzvah for the week. He'll write you a marvelous comedy about a star in trouble with the blacklist. Where does that hit you?"

"Too close to home, dahling. And, dahling! There's Lewis Drefuss! Who's he with? Lewis! Lewis!"

Lewis recognized the voice immediately, as who wouldn't, and turned and waved.

"Come join us, dahling! Bring your friend, I'm feeling tolerant."

Seated with the ladies, drinks having been ordered, the friend introduced himself.

"George Baxt?" said Tallulah. "Any relation to Leon Bakst, the great designer?"

"That's B-a-k-s-t. I'm B-a-x-t. Anyway, Leon Bakst is a pseudonym."

"Not really, dahling!"

"Really, dahling," riposted Baxt in a perfect imitation, and she roared with laughter.

Lewis spoke. "George was Abner's agent."

"Oh, darling Mr. Baxt, how sad for you."

"How sad for Abner. I've still got some living numbers, may God have mercy on their souls. And how sad for Martha."

"You knew Martha?"

"Not well, but I'd met her through mutual friends. She was a friend of Jean Muir, who's a good friend of mine."

"Poor Jean," said Mrs. Parker, "what the blacklist did to her."

"She was the first to be shafted," Baxt reminded them.

"She won't be the last, dahling. Well, Lewis, I assume you've heard of Mr. Miroff's late unpleasantness."

"And of all places to get it, gay steam bath."

"I've heard of lots of people getting it in gay steam baths," said Baxt.

Tallulah asked Baxt, "Did Abner or Martha speak much about their son?"

88

"Was there a son? I think I'd once heard mention of a child that was dead, but I don't know the gender. You know anything, Lewis?"

"I only know Miss Bankhead should be heading home for her beauty sleep. She has a picture call tomorrow morning."

"Stop being a spoilsport, Lewis. I'm now involved in detective work. Dottie and I have been helping Jacob Singer in his investigation." She explained to Baxt, "Jacob Singer is a detective, dahling, and Mrs. Parker once assisted him on a case back in nineteen ten . . ."

"Nineteen twenty-six, August to be exact, the day of Rudolph Valentino's funeral . . ."

"That's interesting. Sounds like there might be a book in that," said Baxt. "Why don't you write it, Mrs. Parker?"

Mrs. Parker demurred, feigning modesty. "I'm getting busy with a play."

"George writes," said Lewis.

"Oh really, dahling," said Tallulah, bored.

"What do you write?" asked Mrs. Parker.

"Plays, screenplays, television plays, poison-pen letters."

"Then why are you an agent?" asked Tallulah.

"Because I'm an unsuccessful writer."

"That's not true," said Lewis, "you had a play on tour a couple of years ago."

"Four to be exact," said Baxt, "and Miss Bankhead, it starred your friend Estelle Winwood."

"Good God no, dahling!"

"Good God yes, dahling. It was *Laughter of Ladies.*"

"Of course, dahling," now looking on Baxt in a more favorable light, "her husband directed it."

"That's what he said he was doing," said Baxt dryly, "but he couldn't direct you to a toilet."

Said Mrs. Parker with underlined incredulity. "Estelle Winwood has a husband?"

"Indeed she does, dahling, and don't ask me why." Tallulah was lighting a Craven A and eyeing the waiter for refills.

"She told me why," said Baxt. He had their undivided attention. "She explained at her age she needed someone to call her taxicabs." He appreciated the laughs the line got.

"My dear Tallulah, exactly how *old* is Estelle Winwood?"

Said Baxt, "I'm sure she remembers the *Maine.*"

"Dahling, she not only remembers it, she sailed on it."

Lewis excused himself and went to the men's. Baxt looked at his wristwatch and made small noises about having to leave soon. "Oh, don't go yet," urged Mrs. Parker, "have another drink." He had another drink. He never needed much urging to have another drink. They talked about actors and the blacklist, about suicides and betrayals and murder. "Did you know Lester Miroff?" Mrs. Parker asked Baxt.

"Well, actually, he came by my office a couple of months ago asking if I was interested in representing him. I knew Leona Clystir was his agent and we're old friends. Besides which, I don't client-jump. And especially not a blacklisted client. I'm having enough trouble with some of my own, though so help me Hannah I finally broke it for Axel Dourly. I got him on the Kraft hour next week and I'm sweating out any repercussions. I just hope the show's director stands his ground and refuses to replace him should the demand be made. I didn't like Miroff anyway."

"Dahling, who do you know who might know more about the identity, the fate, possibly the whereabouts of the Walsh child?"

91

Lewis now returned to the table and gave Baxt the high sign it was time they were leaving.

"A few years ago I met someone at Abner and Nanette's Christmas Eve party. Oliver Sholom, he's a director. From the way he and Abner were reminiscing about the good old days, I'm pretty positive the two of them went back a long long time."

"Oliver Sholom, Tallulah," said Dorothy, "at first took the Fifth, but when he couldn't get work, he recanted and spilled his guts."

"He still can't get work," said Lewis. "He's been driving us nuts trying to get a spot with the show."

"Never!" said Tallulah sharply. And then she went strangely silent, even for Tallulah. Oliver Sholom. Perhaps he knew something valuable. She might be a help to Jacob Singer. She liked Jacob Singer. She liked him very much.

"I can see it's time to go home," said Mrs. Parker. "Tallulah has a very silly expression on her face."

"Can I drop anyone?" asked Baxt. "I'm on East Fifty-eighth and Sutton."

"You can drop me, dahling. I'm at the Elysee. Dottie's at the Volney. Lewis, be a dear and see Dottie home. And Dottie, don't forget the Savage person."

"What, dear?"

"The writer. Savage. Play. Me. Tallulah."

"Oh, of course, Joseph. I'll get on it first thing when I wake up tomorrow afternoon."

Jacob Singer was not happy. It was three in the morning and the few people whom he had reached had told him nothing of much use, unless, he wondered, was he getting old, stale, forgetting the fine art he had honed decades ago of listening between the lines. Some were even shocked to learn Lester Miroff had been a homosexual.

One of his associates poked his head in the office. "Wait till you hear this one. A dame on West Fifty-fifth got herself raped by an intruder coming through the window from the fire escape while she's practicing her yoga. It's the first I ever heard of a dame getting fucked in the Lotus position."

Singer waved him away. Somewhere there was someone he should talk to who was not on the list Bankhead and Parker had given him. It was a gut feeling, and his gut was the one thing he could still trust. He yawned and stretched and decided it was time to go home. He wouldn't sleep, he knew that for certain, until his gut gave him permission to do so. He wondered if he dare phone Tallulah Bankhead at this hour and brazenly invite himself over for a drink. The idea and the challenge titillated him, but then out of cowardice he scrubbed it. Singer, he said to himself, you're a chicken-shit detective.

Tallulah reclined on the chaise longue in her bedroom, smoking a Craven A, nursing a scotch and water, and wondering if fantasies were ever fulfilled. If Detective Jacob Singer would phone and invite himself over for a drink. The phone did ring and she leapt for it. "Yes, dahling?" she asked eagerly.

The voice at the other end was faint and disguised. "Miss Bankhead, don't get involved."

Click.

SIX

"HEY, MISS BANKHEAD," asked the gabbier than usual cab driver, "what do I have to do to get into the theater?"

"Take a vow of poverty, dahling."

"I'm studying with Sandy Meisner. Tomorrow I'm doing a scene for him from *Streetcar.*"

"Dahling," said Tallulah at her most bored and deadliest, "I cahn't quite see you as Blanche."

He went mute until they reached Jacob Singer's precinct on West Fifty-fourth Street. For the woman who a few hours earlier had received a death threat, Tallulah was unusually high-spirited and gay, skipping up the steps to the police station like a young girl trysting with her first beau. "I'm not afraid of dying, dahling," she'd said to Singer over the phone when she finally reached him that morning, "I'm afraid of living. What, dahling? Why, I'd adore seeing where you work. I've never seen the inside of a police station, dahling, although I've been threatened with the prospect often enough, God knows. No, I'm not rehearsing today, and no, I'm certainly not attending Lester Miroff's funeral. Noon sounds fine. See you then, dahling."

"A cop!" screeched Patsy. "What are you doing getting mixed up with a cop?"

"Miss Kelly, mind your own business," cautioned Tallulah as she dressed for the noon date. "You volunteered to tidy up my closets and dresser drawers today. Why are you spending so much time opening that bottle of scotch?"

"The cork's stuck, damn it." The phone rang.

"Get that, will you, dahling?"

Patsy crossed to the phone and barked into it. "What?" She listened. "Just a minute." She put her hand over the mouthpiece. "Hey, Tallulah, you know a David Carney?"

"No, what's he selling? The damned switchboard's supposed to screen my calls. So what do I get? A death threat and a David something. Never heard of him!"

"She never heard of you, Mr. Carney." She listened. "Let me ask her. Hey, Tallulah! He's written a play he wants you to read. He says he wrote it just for you."

"I've heard that song before. Oh, tell him to leave it at the desk."

Patsy relayed the message and hung up. "Sounds like another nut case to me." She watched Tallulah arranging a gossamer stole around her shoulders in front of a floor-length mirror. "Say listen, Tallu . . ."

"What, darling?" Tallulah wasn't satisfied with her reflection. She continued fussing with the stole.

"I think you should hire a bodyguard. I

don't like you going out alone in the streets after that nut call last night."

"That was a caution, dahling, not a death threat."

"There's a thin line between the two, Tallu. I'm a street kid. Brought up in Hell's Kitchen. Let me tell you, it's a short walk from a threat to curtains." Her screech softened to the sound of a nail being drawn across corrugated tin. "I love you, girl. I don't like the idea of ever mourning you."

Tallulah stared at Patsy through the mirror and stopped fussing. She was genuinely touched. She left the mirror and went to her friend, put her arms around her, and kissed her cheek. "Patsy, it's at rare moments like this one that I'm not annoyed you're constantly hanging around."

"Don't give me that crap. You begin to get the cold sweats if you're left alone longer than three minutes. And where's Estelle this morning? How come the duchess is not in attendance in your hour of need?"

"Estelle is having her wig vacuumed, or whatever needs doing to that ratty object." The stole was finally draped to the queen's satisfaction. "Now tell me, Patsy, how're you fixed for cash?"

"Don't embarrass me, Tallu." Tallulah deciphered the code immediately. Patsy was broke.

"Dahling, there's a few hundred in my jewelry box. Help yourself." She patted Patsy's cheek as she went past her into the living room. "Don't be stingy. And *don't* get pissed!"

"When you getting back?" Patsy yelled as Tallulah opened the front door.

"I don't know, dahling! It's an open-end booking!"

The Fifty-fourth Street precinct would never be the same again. Hurricane Tallulah was in her element. Here were all assortments of men in blue—thin ones, plump ones, young ones, middle-aged ones, handsome ones, unattractive ones—but men, and after five minutes of Tallulah, they were her slaves. Jacob Singer had taken the trouble to introduce her to each man personally, and Tallulah responded as though she were a politician canvassing votes. "Now tell me, dahling," she said to a goggle-eyed rookie, "is this where you fingerprint your felons? Oh, it is, dahling. Tell me, dahling," she said seductively, "would you like my fingerprints? Tell me where you'd like them, dahling. . . . Oh dahlings, what a cunning camera! Is this

98

where you take those—what do you call them . . . ?"

"Mug shots," provided Singer.

"Mug shots! Now who invents those marvelous expressions! Mug shots? What, dahling? Why, I'd adore to pose for you. Full face and profile? How marvelous, dahling! Do I get a number across my chest? Why you sweet thing, you're blushing!" She patted the photographer's cheek gently. "I'm sure you've got my number, dahling!"

"Jacob dahling, I'm having the most wonderful time. Where's the morgue?"

"The morgue's at Bellevue."

"So far downtown, dahling? *Domage.* I never go below Forty-second Street. What's through here?"

"The holding cells."

"Oh, dahling! Are you holding anyone today? I must pay them a visit. Not to worry, Jacob. I was enchantment itself when I toured for the USO. The recaptured AWOLs adored me." Singer led the way to the cells. "Oh my God, Jacob! Look at that poor boy's face! I suppose this is an example of police brutality!"

"No, Tallulah, this is an example of street brutality."

"Hey, lady," said the prisoner, "you should have seen the other guy."

"Why, dahling?"

Jacob Singer said, "He murdered his brother-in-law."

Aghast, Tallulah said to the prisoner, "Oh no, dahling! Not your brother-in-law! Why, that's incest!"

Singer took her arm. "Come on, Tallulah. I want you to tell me about the phone call in fuller detail."

"There's really little else to tell." It was as though the police officers had formed an honor guard leading to the door of Singer's minuscule office. "Oh, dahlings, you all look so splendid in your uniforms. Are you all New York's finest or does one find better elsewhere?"

Singer shut the door behind them and Tallulah perched on the edge of his desk, torching a Craven A. "Wasn't there anything about the voice you might have recognized?"

"Not a hint, dahling."

"And all he said was, 'Miss Bankhead, don't get involved.' "

"That's all." She exhaled smoke. "Not exactly garrulous, dahling."

"Is it possible it might have been a woman?"

"Well, maybe Sophie Tucker, but we don't know each other well enough to exchange threats."

"This is no joking matter, Tallulah. Lester Miroff was threatened before he was murdered."

"I know that, dahling, and I'm only treating this lightly to keep myself from suffering total collapse. I've been up all night giving it a great deal of thought. It's apparent, isn't it, dahling, that the murderer thinks I know something that's dangerous to him?"

"Well, what do you know?"

"I haven't the vaguest idea, dahling. If I did, I'd tell you, wouldn't I?"

"Would you?"

Tallulah smiled deliciously. "Oh, dahling, a woman is always at her best when she retains an air of mystery about herself, but where there's murder, dahling, I'd keep nothing from you."

"Where did you and Mrs. Parker go last night after I left you?"

"To Tony's for some dinner and to hear Mabel, but Mabel was out ill so we had to make do with some pianist who seemed to have a terror of the black keys."

"Did you meet anyone there? Talk to anyone?"

"Dahling, I'm always meeting people and talking to people. Let me think, there's a young man I mistook for a waiter but he wasn't and he forgave me. In fact, he sent us a round of drinks. And then Lewis Drefuss came in with a friend of his, George something or other . . . oh yes . . . he'd been Abner Walsh's agent, so we chatted at length. As a matter of fact"—she moved from the dest to the chair and sat and crossed her shapely legs—"when I questioned him about the Walshes' child, he said the person who would know more about Abner's marriage to Martha was a director named . . . named . . . now don't give me a hint, let me think a moment . . ."

"Ted Valudni?"

"Oh, no no no . . ."

"Oliver Sholom?"

Tallulah snapped her fingers. "That's it!"

Singer made a note to question this George himself, once he learned his last name. To Tallulah he said, "Sholom phoned me this morning, but I didn't get much out of him."

"Well then, dahling, perhaps you should invite him over for the third degree."

"Tallulah, you've seen too many bad movies."

"I've also starred in too many bad movies,

dahling. Where are you taking me for lunch?"

Singer was still dwelling on the threat. "Lester Miroff was murdered about three in the afternoon. Who'd you talk to besides Mrs. Parker and myself?"

"My usuals. Patsy Kelly, Estelle Winwood, my hairdresser, my couturier, my sister Eugenia, but that was long distance—she's staying with a friend in Maryland. Now let me think who else. Oh yes, Gabriel Darnoff, the actor's son, about his doing a play for me. I've decided to return to the theater, dahling. I'm sure my radio bubble is about to burst and I'm not too enthusiastic about television. I don't get film offers anymore, so what's left but the boards? I'm boring you."

"Not at all. Just keep talking."

"Dahling, you don't have to say *that* to Tallulah!" She chain-smoked a fresh cigarette. "Now let me think, who else? Oh yes. Barry Wren—you've heard of him, I'm sure." Singer nodded. "Trying to talk me into doing a musical with him, the beast. I can assure you I buried him in outrage. Oh yes. Beth Valudni. Ted's wife. They're estranged now and she's doing a sketch with me this Sunday." She was getting tired and thinking about some martinis and some

103

lunch. "And in the hotel, the chambermaid, some bellboys, the switchboard operator, the desk clerk, the doorman . . . that's about it, dahling."

"I'm going to be checking out Martha Walsh's apartment. Care to join me?"

"Dahling, I'd be fascinated. Poor sweetie, she's being cremated or did you know?"

"I didn't."

"The Actor's Fund is paying for it. I offered to do the honors, but it seems Martha had arranged it all herself before her suicide. Now listen, you're not forgetting about lunch, are you? I mean really, dahling, it's past one o'clock and I need a drink, or I'll be experiencing withdrawal symptoms."

In the Golden Cinema Memorabilia Shop on West Forty-second Street, Joseph Savage thanked Dorothy Parker profusely and sincerely, said goodbye, and hung up. "What was *that* all about?" asked the shop's owner, an Ichabod Crane look-alike who was tenderly dusting a framed photograph of former film actress Fifi D'Orsay.

"That was Dorothy Parker."

"Oh, really? And I'm Hoot Gibson."

"So you're Hoot Gibson because that was

Dorothy Parker and she's setting up a meeting for me with Tallulah Bankhead."

Ichabod's look-alike snorted as he moved to a photograph of Esther Ralston. "And what are you supposed to be doing with Tallulah Bankhead?"

The bell over the door jingled "Hooray for Hollywood" as a customer entered.

Joseph was sorting postcard-sized pictures of Douglass Montgomery. "Maybe write a play for her."

"You're not kidding me."

The customer asked with a nasal whine, "Do you have any pictures of Ethelreda Leopold? She used to be a Busby Berkeley girl . . ."

Ichabod drew himself up haughtily and said with words that dripped icicles. "You don't have to tell me anything about Ethelreda. She's in the files in the back under *L*, right next to Leopold and Loeb." To Joseph he said, "I really hope it's a break at last, Joe. I know you've been through hell."

"Thanks. I haven't felt this good since . . . since Lester Miroff was murdered."

"Well, that was only yesterday. Your cup runneth over."

From the back near the files came a shout, "How much for Margaret Lindsay?"

"I don't know, young man," came back a snarled response, "phone her in Hollywood and get the price!"

Lester Miroff's family claimed his body from the morgue shortly after the autopsy was performed. The family, being Orthodox Jews, rushed the body to a funeral parlor and then to a cemetery for burial before sundown. Lester wasn't very good box of-fice. There was just his immediate family in attendance, a few of his parents' friends, two cousins his mother had managed to round up, and three die-hard Miroff fans who owned all his recordings. His obituaries re-minded readers he'd been a cooperative wit-ness for HUAC and was scheduled to star in his own TV show. What they didn't know was that his agent, Leona Clystir, had indus-triously tracked down a faded singing movie star of the mid-thirties, had her lawyers get him signed out of the insane asylum to which he had been committed ten years earlier by his wife—who had been a kiddie in *Our Gang* comedies and now ran a call-girl ser-vice in Santa Barbara—was now flying him to New York under the watchful eyes of two male nurses, and had convinced the execu-tives at CBS he'd be the perfect replacement for Lester Miroff. When told of his unexpected good fortune, the faded singing movie star said, "Crazy, man!" and buried his nose back in a biography of Rudy Vallee.

Gabriel Darnoff lunched with Beth Valudni in a tiny French hideaway in the theater district. She had tracked down Gabriel at the theater where his play was to open, fully expecting him to reject the call, but he knew she'd left her husband and was glad to hear from her. He'd always had a warm spot in his heart for Beth, who had had an affair with his father years ago. Now she and Gabriel were discussing Lester Miroff's murder.

"Who do you think did it?" asked Beth, letting her petite marmite go cold.

"Oh, I should think there's about thirty possible suspects. I'd suspect my father, but Pop's dead. Lester helped kill him. And Barry Wren and . . ." He droned on with a list of those who had been cooperative witnesses until finally Beth put a hand on his and he paused. After a moment's thought, he said, "You know Lester named Barry Wren, so Barry Wren turned around and named Lester. It's almost Laurel and Hardy. I spoke to Tallulah yesterday. I told her I was thinking of doing a play about the black-list and she said, 'It's too soon, dahling.' "

"I think she's right, Gabe. It's too soon to get a perspective on it, and besides, it's far from over. They're serving subpoenas for breakfast every morning. I keep wondering when mine will show up, except Lewis Drefuss at Tallulah's show says he had no trouble clearing me." She spooned some soup, tasted it, made a face, and switched to a piece of crisp French bread and butter. "But murder. That's something else."

"It's going to be an epidemic."

"What do you mean?"

"There are going to be more killings." She stared at him. She had lost her appetite. "Face it, there's an avenger on the loose brandishing a black sword and demanding blood."

"How very gothic and fruity, Gabe. There's never an excuse for cold-blooded murder."

"Lester's was warm-blooded. He got it in a steam room."

"It's not funny, Gabe. I mean if that's why Lester was murdered . . ."

"Why else?"

"Then . . . then . . . damn it, Ted could

be in danger . . . and Barry . . . and all the others . . ."

"Screw them. You're still in love with Ted."

"Of course I am, but I can't live with him."

"I've never heard of people getting a tan from carrying a torch." He was lighting a cigarette. "Do I look a likely suspect, Beth?"

"I don't know. I don't know the look of a suspect."

"I've heard from the police; they've been checking up my whereabouts when Lester was murdered. A certain detective named Jacob Singer." He exhaled smoke. "I don't have an alibi. I was out taking a long walk to forget about my play and the blacklist and the indecency of suicide, and I'm the kind of nondescript-looking guy nobody recognizes or remembers. So I've got no alibi."

"So what's going to happen?" She was genuinely concerned.

He shrugged. "How do I know? I'm not writing this scenario."

Ted Valudni was lunching with his lawyer at the Yale Club. He had hired him at the time he was subpoenaed, firing the one who had been faithful to him through the early struggles when he couldn't pay his fees. This one was a Presbyterian Republican, which Ted considered more politic in light of the touchy situation with HUAC. Armbruster Pershing was a formidable and respected name in the world of law, whose opposition was known to capitulate rather than face the slow torture of being bored to death. His intimates, the two of them, insisted he had a dry sense of humor, but were unable to produce any examples of it.

"I have suffered enough," said Ted Valudni, ignoring his chicken potpie. "I will not tolerate this police harassment."

Armbruster Pershing was mashing one egg fried sunny-side up into his corned beef hash (it was the way he liked it) before adding ketchup; Valudni averted his eyes, fighting rising nausea. "One phone call from a detective is not harassment, Theodore. Did you know this Lester Miroff?"

"Yes."

"Did you know him well?"

"Years ago."

"And he named you to the committee?"

"Yes, among others. But you know all that!"

"Have you ever threatened to kill him?"
Silence. Pershing fixed Valudni with his fa-

mous cold eye. "Have you ever threatened to kill him?"

"Yes. When he first fingered me and got me into this mess."

"Did you make this threat in front of witnesses?"

"My wife."

"And she's left you."

"I'm sure she'll come back."

"Do you want her back?"

"I'm used to her."

"And if she doesn't come back?"

"Then we'll divorce, of course. It's the civilized thing to do."

"Is this a friendly separation?"

"I'm friendly. She's not."

Pershing now fixed him with a wise look. "It's not just the police you're afraid of, is it?"

Valudni pushed his food aside. "No. It's not. I told that Detective Singer. I'm afraid. I'm afraid whoever killed Lester may have a little list."

Pershing's face brightened. "Ah! *The Mikado!*" He sang in a cracked voice, " 'I've got a little list . . .' "

"Armbruster, this is not an occasion for levity. My life may be in danger. What shall I do?"

"Hire a food taster. You're not eating—isn't it any good?"

"I'm not hungry."

"You know, Theodore," the lawyer said, speaking through a mouthful of mess, "if this were a scene from a mystery novel, I might be tempted to think your fear is a camouflage, a red herring to throw me off the scent."

Valudni's palms were sweating. "You think I might have murdered Lester Miroff?"

"Why not?" He laughed his dry laugh. "Oh, now, Theodore, where's your sense of humor? Have some strawberry shortcake. I'm told it's a recipe handed down from Betsy Ross."

Valudni dutifully ordered the shortcake. After one spoonful he decided Betsy should have stuck to her sewing. The lawyer wasn't surprised to notice Valudni's hand trembling.

The members of the dance class that Barry Wren conducted every weekday morning were exhausted. It wasn't from *pliés* or *tour jetés* or fumbled *adagios*, it was from listening to the choreographer's bitchy raillery. Mighty Mouse, as he was referred to behind his back, had obviously had a bad scene before arriving at class. His students swapped gossip about him with the regularity of school-children trading baseball cards. From the grapevine (the ballet class office) they'd heard Barry had been interrogated over the phone by a detective about Lester Miroff's murder.

"He's got no alibi," said one.

"Says he was on the Eighth Avenue subway going up to the Bronx to visit his mother."

"Ha! He never had a mother. They were too poor."

"Bankhead's turned him down. She won't work with a traitor."

"Listen, this I got straight from his assistant."

"Straight, hah!"

"Oh, shut up and listen. Barry's scared shitless. He thinks whoever killed Miroff might be out to get him too."

"Oh, wouldn't that be too divoon, darling? But if you ask me, Mighty Mouse is a perfect suspect."

Barry Wren was screaming. "Will you please concentrate and get on point, goddamn it. You call yourself dancers? You're clumsy and inept and awful and I could kill the whole damn lot of you!"

"See what I mean?" said the dancer who thought Barry a perfect suspect.

SEVEN

WHILE JACOB SINGER spoke to the building superintendent and his son, Tallulah stared solemnly about the living room of Martha Walsh's basement apartment. So neat, so tidy, with no evidence of recent tragedy. Martha had willed the contents to the Salvation Army, who would be sending a van to collect them as soon as the police permitted it. Tallulah walked to the kitchen and marveled at how Martha had made do in such shabby surroundings. There were water leakage stains on the ceiling, a windowpane was cracked; the stove and refrigerator were of an antiquity Tallulah was hard put to categorize. She looked in the refrigerator. It was empty, cleaned out, she assumed, by the janitor's wife.

"Find anything interesting?"

Singer's voice startled her. She clutched her bosom dramatically and growled at him, "Don't ever creep up on me like that again. You almost cost me five years of my life I can ill afford . . . It's really so sad, Jacob. To think she's been living in this hovel for God knows how many years—it's so difficult

114

to conceive of a young girl as enchanting as Martha was when I first met her and Abner ending her years here. But then, God knows what fate has in store for us. Well, at least she's not ending up in a pauper's grave."

"Neither will you, I'm sure." She was following him back to the living room.

"I don't give a damn where I end up, dahling, as long as they don't bury me in a bad play. What's that you're staring at?"

Singer held the photo of Abner, Martha, and the boy that had rested on the mantel. "Family portrait." Tallulah took the photo and studied it.

"Handsome, weren't they?" She fished her spectacles from her handbag for a better look. "Yes, I thought that's what it was."

"What what was?" asked Singer.

"The scar on the boy's left cheek. I wonder if this photo was taken before or after the accident. How remote and distant the boy seems from his parents. See, he's looking to the right, away from them, off into the distance hoping for a glimpse of . . . what?" She handed the picture back to Singer. "I met Abner and Martha . . . let me see," she said as she returned the spectacles to her handbag, "I think it was . . . yes it was in thirty-three. You'll learn, Jacob, that my memory is not the most reliable, except when I'm committing a script to memory I'm always line-perfect, dahling. . . . Where was I?"

"You were back in thirty-three."

"Of course, dahling, I was starring on Broadway in *Forsaking All Others*. A disaster, but I kept it running for over one hundred performances. Not bad in those depression days, and anyway it was my own money." She laughed. "All that gorgeous cash I earned at Paramount Pictures went into that very bad play. Actually it became a rather amusing film with Miss Crawford and Mr. Gable. But that's useless trivia. Thirty-three, yes. Not the best of times for me or for anyone. Talk about useless trivia, Henry Fonda had a small part in the play."

"Let's get back to the Walshes."

"Oh, dahling, I have this awful habit of derailing myself, but you'll get used to it. You have no choice."

"The Walshes."

"Yes yes yes!" She sat at the dining table and lit a Craven A. "Michael Darnoff and I were discussing a revival of *Pygmalion* at the time, but I couldn't quite see myself as Eliza Doolittle nor could I see Darnoff as Henry Higgins. I mean Lear, Iago, and other such;

116

classic heavyweights yes, but Shaw never. Michael was in love with me, but he was perfectly dreadful in bed, constantly upstaging me, dahling." A small rumble of laughter. "No one attempts to upstage Tallulah and survives. Michael took me to a rent party in Greenwich Village. You do remember rent parties, don't you, dahling?" Singer nodded. "Yes, of course you do, how silly of me. It was at this party I met Abner and Martha, my darling darling Nance Liston and . . . of course . . . Gregory and Anya Hagle. They were on a visit from Hollywood and being razzed by the others for their success. I remember being quite put out at that. I mean after all, dahling, we're professionals for artistic fulfillment, true, but Christ, one does have to earn a living. But it was all rather good-natured, and there was a good-sized crowd and the Walshes. . . . It turned out to be their place, a mean little cold-water railroad flat on one of those obscure and quaint Village streets . . . Thompson, Duane, whatever . . . anyway, the Walshes had collected a goodly sum of admission fees and would be able to meet the rent that month." She snapped her fingers. "The boy!"

Singer had long ago recognized that to let her ramble on at her own pace would even-

tually provide a verbal nugget. He was leaning against the fireplace with his arms folded,
lacking only a meerschaum pipe in his mouth
to complete the portrait of a member of the
landed gentry.

"The boy was in one of the bedrooms.
Martha doted on the child and wanted me to
meet him. I do adore children, you know
. . . in their place. She took me to him,
although I remember making small noises
about not waking him at what I assume must
have been quite a late hour. It was after the
theater. But she assured me he was still awake
and he was. Hmmm."

"What's the matter?"

"I feel as though I'm on a psychiatrist's
couch."

"Have you ever been?"

"Just once, dahling, but we were only
necking."

"Let's go back to the boy."

"Is this really helpful?"

"Tallulah, it's more than I could hope
for."

"Oh really, dahling? I mean is this what
detective work is all about?"

"You got it. Listening to people talk and
talk and talk until suddenly what you've been

hoping for is revealed just like that, from out of nowhere."

"Oh, how marvelous! I can't wait to tell Estelle and Patsy."

"Tallulah, the boy."

"What boy?"

"The Walsh boy."

"Oh, Leo."

"Is that his name?"

"What did I say?"

"You said, 'Oh, Leo.' "

"Good heavens and so I did and by God that's the boy's name! Leo! Named for Leo Tolstoi! Oh, dahling, it's so wonderful how this is all coming back to me—think of how I could have helped Sir Arthur Sullivan find his lost chord!" She was, whether Singer recognized it or not, just warming up to the task of recalling the past, and she began pacing the room. For a middle-aged woman, Singer was thinking, she had a remarkably provocative walk.

"Well anyway, Leo was reading a book and was very polite at the interruption. And you know what, by God, it was a collection of Eugene O'Neill plays. He was reading that tiresome one, come to think of it most of O'Neill is tiresome but I'll save that for my next interview. *Mourning Becomes Electra*.

Endless dribble lifted from a Greek classic. I remember telling the boy that Darnoff and I were in the market for something to do together and I remember his somewhat solemnly suggesting we do *The Cherry Orchard*. You *have* heard of it, haven't you, dahling, come to think of it I'd be a divine Arkadina I must give it some thought. I could always dredge up Raymond Massey to co-star but God, dahling, think of consorting with that face through rehearsals the out-of-town tour and eight performances a week. I wonder what Colin Keith Johnson is up to these days?"

"Tallulah, the boy."

"What? Oh, do don't interrupt, Jacob, it's difficult enough as it is, I mean all this was almost twenty years ago, I can't remember what I did twenty minutes ago! Such a handsome little fellow he was—the boy, dahling, not Colin Keith Johnson, except for that ugly jagged scar on his left cheek. Naturally I didn't inquire about it in front of the lad, but Martha later told me he fell off a swing or a seesaw or one of those other deadly things they provide children with in playgrounds. A really strange child he was, don't ask me why, he was so . . . so *old* for his age, that's it, that's what it was, and I don't

120

think he was more than about ten then. It was much later he and Martha were in the train crash out west and the poor thing was tragically crippled and disfigured and Martha was seriously injured but not as bad as the boy. It cost Abner a fortune. The hospitals. The doctors. The sanitorium."

"I love you, Tallulah."

"Why, dahling, it's so early in the day."

"I love you for dredging all this memory up from some hidden well, when yesterday you were completely vague about what had happened to Martha and the boy."

"Well, dahling, you have to give me time. People are always rushing me. I mean if you buy me a beer, dahling, dahling Jacob"—she patted his cheek and wondered why so many men missed patches of stubble when they shaved—"I'll recite one of my favorite poems, "Fellatio at the Bridge."

George Baxt was a relative newcomer as a theatrical agent, having opened his office with a partner, Ethel Wald, less than two years earlier. When Ethel left to marry and migrate to the West Coast, he carried on alone, waiting for the day he would have enough cash to spring himself and resume his career as a writer. As days piled upon days, he found it increasingly difficult to cope with the variety of lunatics who presented themselves at his office in the dubious disguise of actors. One such now sat in his office, Mitchell Zang, haranguing Baxt about the iniquities of the profession, the disgrace of the blacklist, and the tragic loss of his lover, Nance Liston. Mitchell Zang was not blacklisted; he was just an awful actor. Because of his friendship with Nance, Baxt went out of his way to place Zang on some TV shows as a walk-on or extra and, on one or two occasions, got him an under-five-line part. By union rules, these parts were non-commissionable, but out of friendship to Nance Liston, Baxt persevered and kept Zang eating. He was now plotting how to keep Zang out of his office in the future. True, Zang had such a usable face: "That wonderful jagged scar on his left cheek he claims was a bayonet wound," Baxt had explained to his friend Lewis Drefuss. "I'll lay odds he was stabbed by an angry playwright for mauling his lines."

Zang was shouting and Baxt wondered if his secretary was dialing the police. "For chrissakes, cool it, Mitchell!" yelled Baxt. "There are actors waiting in the outer office and you might frighten them into thinking they're talented."

"Fuck 'em."

"I haven't the strength."

Mitchell Zang leaned forward, twisting the beret he held in his hands. "Aren't you glad Lester Miroff was murdered?"

"Glad? Why glad?"

"Didn't he deserve to die? All those fucking informers, don't you agree they should be killed?"

"I'm all for mercy killing, Mitchell"—especially for actors, he diplomatically refrained from adding—"but murder I do not condone, even of people I despise."

"You don't think Barry Wren should be murdered? Ted Valudni?" His list of murder prospects was endless and Baxt ached to hear the sound of a police siren nearing.

"Mitchell, murdering those people won't bring back Nance or Abner Walsh or Michael Darnoff or Mady Christians or—oh, the hell with it, Mitchell, I've got work to do and I've got people waiting and I've got to go hold Nils Asther's hand at a Kraft rehearsal of *Dodsworth,* and why the hell do I dig up jobs for out-of-work old film stars, damn it?"

Mitchell Zang arose slowly. "Whose side are you on anyway?"

"Now really, Mitchell—"

"I'll never come see you again. Never! Never!" Zang fled the office.

Baxt looked at the ceiling and said, "So there really is a God." Then he dialed the Fifty-fourth Street precinct and left a message for Jacob Singer. They'd met a few months earlier when Singer was advising on police procedure for a Philco Playhouse presentation that had starred several Baxt clients, and Baxt was thinking of someday trying his typewriter at writing mysteries. Maybe Zang had just been running off at the mouth as he usually did. But today Zang's anxiety to win approval for the idea of murdering a list of informers made Baxt decide a second opinion was in order. Singer was out and Baxt left a message. Then he shouted to his secretary, "Who's next?"

"James Dean!" she shouted back. Dean's photo composite was at the top of a stack on Baxt's desk. Baxt studied the surly face and thought, oh God, another juvenile. Who the hell needs another juvenile?

Tallulah and Singer were having their beers in a saloon on Ninth Avenue. They sat at the bar because Tallulah enjoyed bantering with bartenders. This one was named Jake and knew she was an actress but couldn't quite place the face, so Tallulah told him she was Ethel Barrymore.

"Sure, Ethel, I'd have known you any-place! What brings you to New York?"

"I've just had my face lifted, dahling. What do you think?"

Jake made an O with his thumb and index finger. "You look great, Ethel, just great." He went to the other end of the bar to break the news to the saloon regulars.

"Poor Jake," said Singer.

"Don't be silly, dahling. He hasn't the vaguest idea who Ethel Barrymore is, let alone me. I've made him very happy. Now what have I helped you accomplish? Are you convinced Leo Walsh is the murderer?"

"Hell no. Who knows where he is? Like you said yesterday, he may be dead. You haven't been much in touch with either of the Walshes, but over the past years have they ever mentioned him?"

"Well, I can't really answer that, dahling. So much is said to me, but I retain so little. Leo became a footnote in Abner's life after he left Martha for Nanette, and I've seen next to nothing of Martha. We lunched a few times, but that was it."

"As of this minute, Miroff's murderer could be anybody. He could be some nut who wandered in unseen off the street and plugged Miroff because he planned to plug the first person he saw."

"Dear God, do such people exist?"

"They exist and they kill and we don't always catch them, and don't start a monologue on perfect crimes either."

"I'm not, dahling, just push that bowl of peanuts in my direction."

While she munched peanuts, Singer said, "X the Unknown could have killed Miroff. Some bleeding heart reads up in the newspapers and the magazines on all these poor souls destroyed by the blacklist and the informers and says to himself or to herself . . . yeah, it could have been a woman, you know. . . ."

"Oh, dahling, don't tell me how lethal women can be, I've been one for years."

"Anyway, our X the Unknown suddenly says, I'm going to kill that bastard. How dare he do this to so many people and get away with it? So out goes anonymous nobody with blood in his or her eye and commits a murder."

"But why would this person threaten me?"

"They think you know something that could lead to them."

"I wish I knew what the hell it was."

"So do I. But I know now all I have to do is let you keep on talking, and sooner or later something worthwhile will pop out."

Tallulah seethed with indignation. "What the hell do you mean sooner or later? I mean really, dahling, you could take every word I say and string them together and put them around your girlfriend's neck and they'll dazzle you—you don't have a girlfriend, do you?" He didn't. "Why, dahling, I'm always being quoted and misquoted and people have been known to drown in the sea of apocrypha attributed to me. Ha-ha-ha-ha-ha! Where are you going, dahling? You're not stiffing me with the tab, are you?"

"I have to check in with the precinct. I'm on a case, you know."

"Yes, dahling, how well I know." Jake brought her another beer. "You know, Jake, you should be on television."

"You think so, Ethel?"

"Yes, I most certainly do think so. My friend Robert Ripley is putting together a show and I must talk to him about you."

"Gee thanks, Ethel, when you need me

I'll be right here. You can always find me here."

"Don't worry, dahling. Ethel will fix everything." Singer was back. "That was quick, dahling."

"An agent we both knew left me a message to call him."

"Oh, which one dahling? Gus Schirmer? Archer King?"

"George Baxt."

"Who? Never heard of him."

"You met him last night at Tony's."

"Oh of course. Him! George what? Never mind, dahling, phone him, and for chrissakes will somebody remove these goddamn peanuts!"

Singer phoned Baxt. He listened attentively to what Baxt had to tell him about Mitchell Zang. When Baxt asked, "Does this make me sound like a fink ratting on the idiot?"

"Hell, no. This is important. I'll put one of the boys on him right away and see if he's got an alibi. Thanks. I appreciate this." He phoned the precinct and assigned an investigator to Mitchell Zang and then returned to Tallulah and told her what he had learned from the agent.

Tallulah groaned. "Not Mitchell Zang.

Oh, not him. I mean the last time he took an IQ test, he owed them thirty-seven points. He was Nance's stud. I don't believe she was in love with him, but he was apparently serviceable and Nance, God rest her soul, had a voracious sexual appetite that required a great deal of servicing. But murder somebody? I find that awfully hard to believe. I can't really see Mitchell Zang as a murderer."

"Tallulah, an actor murdered Lincoln."

"Dahling, I didn't think Walter Huston was all that bad in the part."

Singer asked Jake for the bill while Tallulah repaired her face. She was enjoying herself immensely. She liked detective work. She enjoyed being a help to Singer, and in some way she was being a help to herself. It took her mind off the sword of Damocles hanging over her own head, the stupid threats of guilt by association tossed at her by the two agency stooges. Yes indeed, she liked this detective work and she had a silent plan to continue at it on her own. Mitchell Zang a murderer? Well, he had that sinister scar on his left cheek . . .

"Jacob!" she shouted.

"Christ, you scared the hell out of me!"

"Mitchell Zang!"

"Okay, okay, so if he's innocent, my guy

will check him out. It's only a precaution, Tallulah."

"Jacob, Zang has a very ugly scar on his left cheek."

Not all that much on impulse, Singer kissed her.

"You may want to take that kiss back, dahling."

"Why?"

"Because it suddenly occurs to me, Mitchell might be a bit too old to be the Walsh boy."

"Maybe he just looks that way. He's led a pretty hard life doing all that servicing."

"Tell me, Jacob, and be honest. Don't be afraid of hurting my feelings. Do I have the makings of a good detective?"

"Tallulah, you could be the best of anything you make up your mind to be."

"Really, dahling!" She was terribly pleased. She might have just heard she was to replace Bette Davis in her next picture. "So how come I'm still single?'

Five minutes later, Singer was on his way back to his precinct, albeit reluctant to leave Tallulah unescorted on a street in Hell's Kitchen. She waved away his fears with the excuse that it was such a stunning day, she would take a walk. Luckily he didn't know her well enough to realize that walking was something she did only under threat. Tallulah found a phone booth in a grocery store and looked up an address. The address she sought was in the neighborhood, and a few minutes later she stood in front of a brownstone building on Tenth Avenue, just a few years away from becoming a derelict. A crudely painted sign under the doorbells said BELLS OUT OF ORDER. She found the name she was looking for and went in. As she twisted the knob of the door, she saw the lock was broken. She wondered how people could live in these impoverished circumstances. It never occurred to her to contemplate offering a donation.

She confronted a flight of wooden stairs. The hallway was badly lighted by a single overhead bulb of minimum wattage. The offensive odor almost discouraged her ascent, but she rummaged in her handbag, found a vial of perfume, twisted the cap, and sniffed. Freshly heartened, she began her ascent. She found the door she wanted and knocked. She waited. She knocked again. She could hear the shuffle of feet within. "Hello?" she called out. The door opened a crack. Tallulah mustered her most charming smile. "Oliver Sholom?"

The door opened wider. If this was Oliver Sholom, he was a good deal older than she thought. She was facing a wizened little old man wearing a yarmulke on his head, a tape measure hanging around his neck, a thimble on a finger of his right hand. He was stooped with age and probably a lifetime of disappointment, had probably a week's growth of beard, and was squinting at her through spectacles that were perched precariously at the tip of his nose. Beyond him, she saw a sewing machine, a work table, the accoutrements of a tailor. On the wall, she saw portraits of Lenin and Stalin and Karl Marx. All this while waiting for the man to respond.

He finally spoke. "I am not Oliver Sholom. I am Herbert Sholom, the anarchist. On the next floor in the rear apartment you will find my nephew Oliver Sholom, the informer." He quietly withdrew and shut the door.

I must be mad, thought Tallulah, absolutely mad. What am I doing here? This is hardly wonderland, dahling, but it's where Alice belongs, not Tallulah Bankhead. *Do I have the makings of a good detective?* She could hear Singer's generous reply and it filled her with fresh courage and resolve. She ascended to the next floor, crossed to the door of the rear apartment, and hoped that her efforts would be rewarded. She should have phoned ahead. What if Sholom isn't in? She could certainly never come back to this place again. From behind the door she heard a Chopin étude. The melody was repeating itself. The record was obviously cracked. The needle was stuck. She knocked at the door.

"Who is it?" came a cry behind the door.

"It's Tallulah Bankhead!"

"Oh fuck off!"

Her leonine laugh was unmistakable. Sholom opened the door.

EIGHT

"MAY I come in?" The apartment couldn't be any worse than the hallway, but it wasn't much of an improvement. He stood to one side as she entered, his eyes blinking like semaphores running amok. Tallulah cased the shabbiness in one sweeping look and commented dryly, "Charming."

"It's only temporary. My uncle owns the building. He's letting me use this place until I can find something really suitable."

"You don't have to put on an act for me, Mr. Sholom. I know you're having a bad time of it workwise."

133

"Lifewise, too." He indicated a straight-back chair. "Please sit. This is the most comfortable one."

"Would you for crying out loud do something about that stuck needle, dahling?"

He crossed to the phonograph, an antique upright, and switched it off. "This is a family heirloom."

"If it's worth anything, why don't you hock it, dahling?" She was rooting in her handbag for the necessary Craven A. Now that she was here, she was battling a bad case of nerves. It was worse than opening night five minutes before the curtain would rise. This man was obviously hoping she was here to offer him a job, not digging for information. Now he was holding a match to the cigarette and his hand was trembling. She inhaled, exhaled, said, "Thank you, dahling," and then took the plunge. "Actually, dahling, I'm here hoping you can give me some information I'm after."

He shoved his hands in his pockets and stood staring down at her. "What kind of information? I'm cleared. I can work again, if only someone would offer me a job. I mean, come on, Miss Bankhead, Gadge Kazan and Cliff Odets sang their arias for the committee and they're working. I mean

134

I'm not kidding myself, I never do, I never had a reputation like Kazan's professionally, but my track record's good. I've had a good share of successes, Miss Bankhead, all I need is one break." He ran a hand through his shaggy mop of hair. "You don't know what it's like sitting around here all day waiting for the phone to ring. I can't afford an answering service, so all day long, from nine to six, office hours everywhere else, you know, I sit here waiting for the phone to ring, a job offer, anything. I know I'm not alone. The others who recanted, well, a lot of them can't get work too. But that's their problem."

Dear God, Tallulah was thinking, compared to this man, Raskolnikov was a laugh riot. She thought it wiser not to interrupt his monologue, let him get it off his chest. Surprisingly, she was not unsympathetic.

"And if you could just let me do one show for you, just one show, then I know other doors would start opening for me." He lowered himself onto a footstool, sitting splay-footed with his hands clenched between his legs, looking like a naughty child suffering punishment.

How do I get out of here, Tallulah wondered, then reminded herself she was here as

135

a detective. She was here to find information. "You were once very close to Abner and Martha Walsh, weren't you? Didn't we meet a long time ago in that cold-water flat they were living in in the Village. A rent party?"

She was sounding so friendly, so cozy, he was beginning to feel toasty warm. It was her performance from her Philip Barry flop, *Foolish Notion*. "Yes, of course," he responded eagerly, "how could I forget that?" Now they had something in common; why, they were old friends enjoying a reunion after all these centuries. Of course she was here to rescue him, offer him a job.

"I wonder, Mr. Sholom . . ."

"Please call me Oliver!" He was groveling, pawing the ground, anxious to be thrown a sweet; he was desperate.

"And you call me Miss Bankhead, dahling." The dart sped past him without leaving a mark. His ears were tuned in only to the promise of a job. "I wonder," she resumed, "whatever's become of their son?"

"Who? Whose son?"

"The Walshes, dahling. Leo. Wasn't that his name, Leo?"

"What's that got to do with what we're talking about now?"

136

"Dahling, let me explain." She decided to lie through her teeth. "I'm the executor of Abner's estate. Leo's his heir."

"Lucky Leo."

"Lucky Leo indeed, if he can be located. I met somebody last night, perhaps you know him, he's an agent, George, uh . . . uh . . . Baxt, he suggested you might know Leo's whereabouts."

Sholom leapt to his feet. "I don't give a shit about Leo's whereabouts!" he shouted, and Tallulah wondered how she would defend herself if he came at her with his fists. The only beatings she'd ever experienced in her life had been administered by critics. "Leo Walsh! That's not what he calls himself today!"

He knows him, she thought triumphantly; he knows where Leo is. Jacob Singer will be so proud of me. "What does he call himself?"

Sholom came nearer to her, stooped, and leered into her face. "I'll trade you, Miss Bankhead." She didn't enjoy the sneer in his voice when he spoke her name.

"Trade me for what?"

"I'll give you information in return for an assignment."

"I don't do the hiring on my show, Oliver, Mr. Sholom, whatever."

"You're the star. A very big star. You have influence."

"I could certainly mention it to my producer."

"Not 'mention it,' Miss Bankhead, *demand* it!" He looked like a revolutionary out to spill the Czar's blood. "*Demand* it."

"Now you see here, Oliver, do you know the penalty for obstructing justice?" She certainly didn't.

"I don't give a shit for justice, lady. I got convinced to betray myself and my friends for justice and look how I got paid off!" He made a sweeping gesture. "Tell me, Miss Bankhead, have you ever enjoyed the luxury of poverty? Do you know what it is to cadge quarters from an uncle who despises you? Do you know what it is to have your ego trampled in the mud, completely destroyed?"

"Yes, dahling, when I did Shakespeare's *Cleopatra* . . ." She stopped. Jocularity was wrong. The man was crying.

"Go away, Miss Bankhead. Go away. I'm a dead man. Dead men are no help to anybody. You want Leo Walsh? You go find him. He's out there." He took a dirty handkerchief from his pocket and wiped his eyes. "You think maybe Leo killed Lester Miroff? How do you know it wasn't me?" She had

138

stood up and was walking to the door, but he hurried ahead of her and barred her way. "I was the last person with him, do you know that? I didn't tell that to the police. Screw the police. I was with him in his apartment before he went out to cruise the steam bath. Think about that, Miss Bankhead I might have followed him. I might have followed him and killed him."

Tallulah spoke, but she didn't recognize her own voice. "You should have told that to Detective Singer."

"Oh, do you know Detective Singer?"

"Why, yes, of course. I just had lunch with him."

"And did he send you here? Did he think you could lure information out of me by kidding me into thinking you could get me a job?"

"Why, yes, yes. He knows I'm here right now." She was terrified. How in God's name did tamers survive in a lion's cage?

He said softly, "He knows you're here right now, does he? You're his stoolie, eh, Miss Bankhead? Well," he said magnificently, "that gives us something else in common! We're both stoolies! I'll bet he doesn't know you're here. I'll bet you're doing this on your own. You've never played detective before, have you, Miss Bankhead?"

"Well, actually no, dahling. Now get out of my way. Detective Singer is—"

"Balls, Miss Bankhead, balls!" He moved away from the door. "I hope you're not expecting me to ask for your autograph."

She fled. As she raced down the stairs, she could hear him hurling things around the room. Glass crashing against walls, furniture tumbling over, accompanied by a most hideous wailing, a noise so ghastly she'd heard nothing like it since Judith Anderson's *Medea*. Herbert Sholom was standing at the bottom of the landing.

"What's he doing up there? Has he gone crazy?"

"He's a bit upset, dahling." She was not about to stop for a chat. She hurried out of the building, flagged a taxi, sank into the seat with a sigh of relief, and sought the comfort of a cigarette.

"Where to, lady?"

"Sanctuary."

Oliver Sholom leaned against the door, exhausted. He was crying again. His uncle had been pounding on the door and Oliver shouted for him to go away. The old man looked up to where there was rumored to be a God he didn't believe in, shook his head sadly, wearily, and descended to his own shabby world. Oliver went to the phonograph and, through tear-bleared eyes, searched in the record cabinet and selected a Brahms rhapsody. The turntable revolved, the music soared forth, a melodious balm for his shattered nerves, and he went to the kitchen to seek the solace promised by a half-empty pint bottle of rye. He downed what was left in one long sloppy swig, some of the liquor slopping down onto his chin. A fit of nausea attacked him and he stood over the sink, gagging.

The blow to his head was strong and well-aimed. The person who delivered it had quietly selected the poker from some instruments lying near the unused fireplace. The blow broke skin and cracked skull; blood rivuleted from the wound as Oliver began sinking to the floor. The person struck him again and again until there was little else to strike except bloody pulp. He laid the poker across Sholom's chest as though it were a lily. He examined himself for bloodstains and was satisfied there were none. He returned to the living room, examined his face in the mirror over the fireplace, moistened his lips, and then crossed to the door. He opened it an inch and looked out; the coast was clear. He quietly descended the stairs, past Herbert Sholom's door, from behind which he could hear the whirr of a sewing machine, then down the next flight of stairs and cautiously into the street, where he knew he'd be safely lost in his anonymity.

Back at the Elysee, where Patsy Kelly and Estelle Winwood awaited her like faithful pets, Tallulah surrounded a very dry gin martini and then attacked. She then phoned Singer but he wasn't in, so she left a message embroidered with some chatty banter with the desk sergeant she'd met earlier. She told the ladies of her terribly unpleasant encounter with Oliver Sholom, and Estelle said something about one of these days Tallulah might learn to mind her own business. Tallulah told Estelle to do something that was physically impossible and Estelle suggested Tallulah's mouth needed washing out with soap. Patsy waved a play script at Tallulah.

"What in God's name is that?"

"That play by David Carney."

"What play by David Who?"

"Carney. It's called *Empty Gestures*."

"My life's been full of those. Who's David Carney?"

"For crying out loud, Tallulah, he called this morning and asked you to read the play, and you said I should tell him to leave it at the desk, which he did and I just finished reading it."

"What's it about?"

"It's about a famous stage star who's all washed up and can't get a job no place, so she accepts a tour in a bus-and-truck company of *Streetcar*."

"Sounds loathsome, dahling."

Patsy ploughed onward. "She falls in love with her leading man, who's thirty years younger—"

"Thirty!"

"—but he rejects her—"

"How dare he!"

"—because she's much too old for him."

"Nonsense! He's undoubtedly gay."

"No, he ain't gay."

"He has to be, dahling, if he's touring in a bus-and-truck company."

"Do you want to hear the rest of this?"

Estelle was playing solitaire and wondering how one goes about becoming a mass murderer.

"Is it any good?"

"It's absolutely awful. I wouldn't wrap fish in it."

"Is there a phone number for this person?"

"A phone number and a note saying only you can play this part, and if you don't he'll kill himself."

"How thoughtful." She was mixing herself another martini.

Estelle said, "The poor boy must be mad, sending a play about an aging actress to an aging actress."

"Put a note in it suggesting he get it to Miriam Hopkins. I hear all she's getting these days are threatening letters from her butcher." She sipped. "Be a dear, Patsy, and leave it for him at the desk."

When Jacob Singer returned to the precinct, he found waiting for him Tallulah's message and Mitchell Zang.

"Are you Singer? I'm Mitchell Zang."

"Come on into my office."

Zang followed him twisting his beret nervously.

"Sit down," said Singer. "I'll be with you in a minute." He dialed the Elysee and was put through to Tallulah immediately.

"Dahling, you'll never guess what I've been up to."

"I'm not good at guessing games, Tallulah."

"I've been playing detective!" Patsy shot her a look as she left for the lobby to deposit the Carney script at the desk. He'd been most unpleasant when she'd phoned to say Tallulah wasn't interested.

"One doesn't play detective, Tallulah. What have you been up to?"

She told him in detail, while Singer's hold on the phone tightened and the veins stood out on his head and his blood simmered and he did his best not to to shout at her. When she got to the part about Sholom barring her exit while he continued to harangue her, Singer exploded.

"You damn fool, he could have taken a poke at you!"

"Now really, dahling, that's hardly an excuse to call me a damn fool! At least I got out of him he does know Leo Walsh and probably knows where he is! Now all you have to do is bring him in and hit him with a rubber hose, dahling." Silence. "Jacob, are you there, dahling?" She didn't wait for a reply. She knew he hadn't hung up on her because she didn't hear a dial tone. "Well, at least he did admit to me he was with Miroff before he went off to be killed. You could at least thank me for that. Why, for crying out loud, dahling, he might well be the murderer!"

"And if he is, you're lucky he didn't add you to his list of victims while he so conveniently had you in his own apartment."

"Oh." Her voice rose an octave. "Oh! That never occurred to me. Oh well, what the hell, dahling, he didn't murder me and here I am safe and sound, so tell me you're not mad at me. Now come on, Jacob, I was only trying to help."

He conceded to himself that Sholom had made some important admissions to her, but he was not about to tell her that. He said, "Thank you, Tallulah. Now I have to hang up. I've got somebody with me."

"Of course, Jacob," said Tallulah coldly, and hung up. "The lout!"

"Does that mark finis to Detective Singer?" piped Estelle as she shuffled the cards.

"The man's a boor. I can't understand what Dottie Parker sees in him. Well, Dottie was never exactly celebrated for her taste in men. The first husband was a sot and the one she's married to now is better in the kitchen than he is in bed, and as for her affairs, God, what she put up with!"

Patsy returned brandishing a newspaper and screeching. "Guess what actor's dead at sixty-nine!"

"Dahling, I knew a lot of actors who were dead at sixty-nine." The phone rang. "You answer it, Patsy. If it's Jacob Singer, tell him I died and I'm being cremated in the morning. Omit flowers."

Patsy held the phone out to Tallulah. "It's Lillian Hellman."

Tallulah's expression changed. It was glacial. Her voice was basso profundo. "Lillian who?"

"Aw, come on now, Tallu, stop doing a number on me!"

Estelle interjected, "She *did* write the greatest hit of your career, Tallulah. Surely even you can't carry a grudge this long."

Tallulah took the phone and said in a monotone, "Hello, Lillie, how nice to hear from you after all these years what do you want?"

Lillian Hellman was in the Elysee lobby speaking into a house phone. She was tempted to slam the phone down, having a temper as notoriously vicious as Bankhead's. But she was a woman in desperate trouble and she needed the actress. "I'm sorry to pop in on you from out of the blue like this, after all these years, but it's important I talk to you. I sounded out Dottie Parker first before planning the invasion and it was she who suggested I come directly to you at the hotel. Would you let me buy you a drink?"

Tallulah mulled the offer for a moment. "I'd invite you up, but we can't talk privately—I have friends here."

"Well, we could always take a powder, Tally," screeched Patsy. "Come on, Estelle, let's go to a bar and attack sailors."

Tallulah said into the phone, "We can have a drink in the Monkey Bar. Go in and get a table and I'll be down in a few moments." The Monkey Bar was just off the lobby. Hellman went in, found a secluded booth, and ordered a scotch on the rocks.

Tallulah changed her dress and shoes, re-did her makeup, and swallowed a sedative. Estelle had come into the room as Tallulah popped the pills.

"Tallulah, I thought you swore off those things!"

"Dahling, I use these in times of stress. How do I look?"

"Better than she will."

"Estelle, dahling, you should have been a diplomat."

"I am, Tallulah, that's why we remain friends."

Tallulah swept into the Monkey Bar tossing hello's in all directions, the greetings striking bartender and waiters as she paused dramatically in the doorway. When she was sure she was the cynosure of everyone in the room, she acknowledged Hellman, whom she had of course spotted when she first entered, and joined her in the booth.

"Well, Lillie, it's been a long time. How's Dash?"

"Not good." Dashiell Hammett and Hellman had been enduring a stormy relationship for close to two decades. "Jail wrecked him. His health's never been too good to begin with."

"I'm sorry to hear that. Waiter! A very dry gin martini, straight up, and leave out the garbage. I'm sorry he had to go to jail."

"For Dash, there was no choice. He certainly had no intention of ever being a cooperative witness. In his spot, would you?"

"I'd name Lassie, Flicka, and Thunderhead, son of Flicka. I gather you've heard they're thinking of training their guns on me?"

"Little do they know what they're letting themselves in for, if they do." They both laughed but not enthustically. "You're look-ing wonderfully fit, Tallulah."

"So do you, dahling." Hellman looked aw-ful. "A bit drawn, of course." Tallulah kindly refrained from adding, "And quartered."

Hellman leaned forward. "Tallulah, I'm having a bad time. I'm desperate."

"You must be, dahling, if you're coming to me. After all those bricks we hurled at each other during *Foxes*. Are you broke?"

"I'm hurting, but I'm not asking for money. Dash has cost me a small fortune. He's been living off me for years, and what the hell, that's what an affair is all about, they tell me."

"Never trust them who tell, dahling, they're free with words and little else. How come the committee hasn't been after you? I mean really, dahling, you lean so far to the left you make the Tower of Pisa look upright."

"They're getting to me. They do it in sections. Let's hit some big guns today, and then fill the next couple of months with the little guys who mean nothing. The sort of names the newspapers bury on the back pages. But when they can get a Julie Gar-field, a Freddie March . . ."

"And Tallulah, if they dare."

"You'd be very big box office for them. Very big. Calling it disgraceful is being kind. I can't think of an adjective awful enough to describe what's going on. Look, I won't waste any more time . . ." She waited while the waiter served the martini. After he left, she continued. "Would you take *Little Foxes* out on tour?"

"Revive it *now?*"

"Why not? I've spoken to Kermit Bloomgarten"—a respected Broadway producer who had mounted other Hellman plays—"and he'll go for it if you do it."

"Oh, dahling, to go back to it again after all these years. I mean really, Lillie, what more could I do with the part? Looking back, it seems as though I played it for a hundred years."

"There's a whole new generation out there across the country who've never seen you."

Tallulah said, "Yes, there's that to consider, isn't there? What a treat it would be for them."

"Then you'll do it?"

"Now listen, Lillie, you know I can't be sledgehammered into anything. I mean really, dahling, if we're burying the hatchet, why don't we bury it over a new play? Write something new for me. We could stand Broadway on its ear!"

Hellman leaned back. "I haven't got a new play in me. Not right now. Maybe later. After this mess is over and done with. Tallulah, when they call me, I shall certainly not cooperate. Supposing they put me in jail?"

"They wouldn't dare!"

"That's what Dash thought when they nailed him."

"Lillie, I know you need one, but I can't give you an answer just yet. I'm involved in too much. I'm still committed to my radio show for another month, and then there's this damn mess with Lester Miroff's murder and Christ, why don't I find myself a convent somewhere and take a long rest. I suppose if I did, those nuns would be hopping over the walls in trios."

"Dottie's told me about you and this detective."

"Don't believe a word of it!"

"You mean already poor Dottie's behind the times?"

"I'm sure she'll find it preferable to being behind the eight ball."

"Poor Lester Miroff. He knew not what

he did, the sad bastard. He wasn't really all that bad a guy, you know."

Tallulah was almost touched by this rare display of empathy on Hellman's part. She said, "It's amazing, Lillie, how death improves people."

"Dottie says you received a death threat."

"I knew I shouldn't have told her!" said Tallulah, seething. "I suppose now it's all over town. But really, dahling, one receives death threats so infrequently, I suppose I couldn't resist phoning her this morning. I heard you're just back from Mexico. How was it?"

"Tallulah, it was so quiet, you could hear a peon drop."

Tallulah told the waiter to put the drinks on her house bill while Hellman demurred, insisting it was she who had asked Tallulah. "Nonsense, dahling, I've owed you a drink for years. Now, Lillie, don't look so solemn. Your life doesn't hang by my positive response. Don't let me think that, Lillie, I'm carrying enough guilt as it is." Hellman reassured her.

After they parted, Tallulah rang her suite and told Patsy she was going for a walk. She needed air. She needed to think. She left the hotel and headed north to Central Park.

She wasn't aware she was being followed.

NINE

As FAR as Jacob Singer was concerned, Mitchell Zang had only one thing going for him, the ugly scar on his left cheek. He had diarrhea of the mouth, which was fine by Singer, who preferred too much talk to no talk at all. After thirty minutes of Zang, Singer was fairly positive Zang wasn't Leo Walsh, but he was a likely candidate for nomination as a murder suspect. Zang hated Lester Miroff; he hated this one and that one who were somehow involved in the blacklist, whether accusers or victims. He particularly hated Barry Wren for leading Nance Liston to her destruction, though it was also pretty unfair of Nance to die intestate. Now Zang really had to look for work.

"What about yesterday afternoon?" asked Singer, tapping his pencil lightly on the desk.

"What about it?"

Singer reminded him of the probable time during which Lester Miroff was murdered at the Everhard.

"Say listen, I don't go to no places like that there. No way, man, no way. I'm strictly a pussy man. I mean them guys can do what they like, y'know? Live and let live. I'm very big with tolerance, that was Nance's influence. Y'know? I don't call niggers niggers anymore or kikes kikes. I mean I wouldn't want one of them to marry my sister—"

Singer interrupted sharply. "Between about half past two and half past four, where were you yesterday?"

Zang screwed up his face and looked at the ceiling. Singer was almost sorry he was causing Zang to tax his brain. "Half past two and half past four? I guess I was making the rounds, y'know, visiting agents, casting directors, oh yeah, I dropped into Walgreen's, y'know, the one on Broadway and Forty-fourth, the actor's hangout, y'know, we trade tips there. There was nothing doing, so I think I went home."

"Where's home?"

"I'm still living in Nance's place down on Saint Mark's." He gave him the address; Singer already had his phone number and the number where he could be reached at the Actor's Service.

"Can you tell me the names of some people who would remember seeing you between those hours?"

155

The face screwed up again in agony, convincing Singer that here was the original who couldn't chew gum and cross a street at the same time. This cretin was what Nance Liston had found attractive. Well, what the hell, somebody once married Mussolini. Zang's lips moved and some names erupted from his mouth. Singer wrote them down. They were unfamiliar to him. The detritus of Broadway hopefuls, the walking wounded, the ones who lived on hopes and fantasies and by waiting on table or clerking in supermarkets or selling their bodies. The percentage who achieved anything was close to zero, but they continued making rounds, taking lessons, acting, singing, dancing, fencing, but never enrolling in a class that taught reality. It probably didn't exist. "What?" he asked sharply.

"I mean isn't this enough, already? I got an audition for a monster in *Bats*."

"What's *Bats?*"

"A musical version of *Dracula*. It's for a summer tour, I think starring Leo Gorcey, I'm not sure."

Singer released him with the usual admonition not to leave town. Zang fitted the beret over his head, which made him look like the nipple on a baby's bottle. Zang wasn't gone twenty seconds when all hell broke loose. "Jake!" shouted the desk sergeant, "Delaney's found a stiff!"

Detective Oscar Delaney, only recently promoted, found Oliver Sholom and lost his lunch. When he phoned the precinct, he could barely speak. When he started to describe the condition of the body, he suffered dry heaves.

"Is it Sholom or isn't it?" shouted Singer when he appropriated the phone from the sergeant.

"Who can tell?" gasped Delaney. "Christ, Jake, it's cranberry jelly."

"I'll be right over."

Delaney hung up and leaned against the wall. He noticed a movement out of the corner of his eye and reached for his gun.

"What's going on here?" asked Herbert Sholom.

Delaney sized up the little man and decided the gun wasn't necessary. "Who are you?"

"I own this building. This apartment is mine, too. My nephew lives here. Where is he? I was in the hall to empty the garbage and saw his door open and heard you talking on the phone. What's cranberry jelly?"

Delaney had a sadistic streak. "On the floor in the kitchen."

The little man went to the kitchen. Delaney stared at the yarmulke on his head, the measuring tape draped around his neck, the shabby, not terribly clean clothes, the slow shuffle, bent over as though he had only recently relinquished the weight of the world back to Atlas. He stopped in the doorway of the kitchen. He said "Oy vay" or something that sounded like it and turned away in revulsion.

"Is that your nephew?" asked Delaney, figuring the uncle might make an identification from the clothes the body was wearing. But the old man said nothing. His hands covered his face, his shoulders shook, and the sobs emerging from the depths of his being were heartrending. Delaney went to the old man and solicitously started to lead him to a chair. The old man shook him away.

"I'm sorry, sir," said Delaney.

"Sorry for what?" asked Herbert Sholom, wiping his eyes with a cloth swatch he pulled from a trouser pocket.

"I mean . . . your nephew? Is that your nephew?"

"It must be. He lives here. He's been

home all day. So it must be Oliver. That's his sweater he's wearing. I recognize the pants, I sewed them up myself. Those are my stitches along the seams, very fine stitches, such stitches you'll see nowhere else." He sighed. "The rotten bastard. Somebody should have killed him a long time ago and maybe spared all the agony he caused."

"Excuse me, but if you feel that way about him, why were you crying?"

"He's a relative." The man's hands were outstretched, palms upward. "For a relative you cry. It's expected!"

Tallulah Bankhead visiting the Central Park Zoo deserved consideration as a television special. She was wearing her dark glasses and swinging her handbag like a schoolgirl whose books were tied by a strap. In the other hand she held the inevitable Craven A, and whether she was recognized or not, she had a smile for everyone. She had no idea why these sudden high spirits after a dispiriting day with Oliver Sholom, Jacob Singer on the phone, and Lillian Hellman at the Monkey Bar. She knew she'd never do the tour for Hellman, not out of malice but out of her occasionally sound theatrical judgment. There was nothing more she could bring to the part of Regina Giddons. Perhaps if she had gotten the movie, but no. Sam Goldwyn, who produced it, didn't think she was movie box office, and probably Hellman agreed. They were in the midst of their celebrated vendetta then. Hellman must have had a hand in kayoing her. When cajoled into seeing the finished film by Estelle Winwood, Tallulah begrudgingly admitted that Bette Davis's interpretation of Regina was an interesting one, despite her mannerisms and despite the play being "opened out" with a series of extraneous scenes that only served to prolong the waits between drama. Tallulah had even ventured out to the Flatbush Theater in Brooklyn one Saturday afternoon to see and admire Ruth Chatterton in the play, Chatterton touring what was known as the Subway Circuit, where tired Broadway hits went to die.

Tallulah had sworn years ago she would never become one of those actors who toured eternally in their one celebrated vehicle, never venturing into anything else, never going for the stretch the way she had tried and succeeded superbly in *The Skin of Our Teeth* and then later tried and failed dismally in *The Eagle Has Two Heads*. But that's what acting was all about, she had learned from her British peers in the seven or eight years she had spent in the London theater during the 1920s; try anything, but at least try it. It's why the London audiences adored her, though most of her vehicles there were pot-boilers, save for Sidney Howard's *They Knew What They Wanted*, which failed despite its brilliant American reputation.

She had to do something else. Maybe Gabriel Darnoff would come through with something, perhaps this unknown quantity, Joseph Savage, and oh God I told Patsy to call him and have him up for a drink at six. It was almost that now. Well, she was Tallulah, he certainly wouldn't expect her to be punctual. She was standing in front of the elephants. "Hello, dahlings. You brutes." She felt whimsical. "Don't you remember me, dahlings? Me Jane!"

She turned around, intending to get back to the hotel, and was confronted by a maniac. He was a weird-looking man of about thirty or thereabouts clutching a manila envelope in one hand that obviously contained a script. With the other he was waving his fist in Tallulah's face. His skin was cratered with pockmarks, and his thinning hair hung down below his ears like tired strings of wisteria. His nose was running and there was spittle bubbling in the corners of his mouth.

"You didn't read it! I know you didn't read it! I only left it for you this morning, so I know you didn't read it so soon. I know it! You're rude and thoughtless like all them other bigshots. You enjoy walking over downtrodden war veterans like me. Korea I fought in! Korea! I fought to make the world safe for you, Tallulah Bankhead. Don't deny it! You're Tallulah Bankhead! I followed you from the hotel and now I'm going to kill you!"

Tallulah didn't cry out, she didn't back away, she didn't try to run. She was too paralyzed with fear either to move or to notice the heavyset man who came up behind the playwright and swiftly locked him in a stranglehold.

"Don't be afraid, Miss Bankhead. There'll be a patrol car along in a few minutes."

Tallulah found her voice, which she had sorely missed. "I'm absolutely flabbergasted! Who is this maniac? And who are you, dahling, thank you so much for coming to my rescue, don't you think you've got too tight a hold on him, dahling, his skin's turning blue, his tongue's hanging out, and his eyes are beginning to pop." She was able to read the name on the envelope, recognizing Patsy's childish scrawl. David Carney. "Oh my God, the play. The aging actress play." The heavyset man relaxed his grip a bit when he felt Carney beginning to slump. "Dahling, I think he needs artificial respiration."

"He needs psychiatric treatment."

"Well, after all, dahling, if he did serve in Korea, he's probably suffering shellshock or brainwashing or gonorrhea or whatever it is they get in those absurd places even missionaries never heard of." Dawn suddenly spread a rosy glow in her brain. "Are you a detective, dahling?"

The man smiled. "Adam Todd. Jake Singer put me on your tail."

"Oh, dahling, surely you can rephrase that. Oh, do relax your grip. Why, the poor boy's crying." Todd eased his hold a bit, and Carney could feel air returning to his lungs. Tallulah saw the patrol car approaching and wished that the small crowd that had gathered would disperse. She hoped she wouldn't be asked to give a statement or an autograph, as she now was really awfully late for her appointment with Joseph Savage, and oh God, another playwright who would probably in time be out for her blood. She had this strange effect on playwrights.

"Oh, do stop crying, Mr. Carney, it's unbecoming. It's your own fault you're one of Todd's chosen people." She asked the detective, "Dahling, you're not by any chance a relative of Mike Todd's are you? He's been wanting me to play Catherine of Russia in some dreadful pageant he's trying to put together, but I've already done her on film in *A Royal Scandal*, which was a disaster, dahling, though I thought I was quite good in it and then Mae West's already done the empress for Mike and that also nose-dived. And here's the patrol car. Oh, isn't the driver dahling, dahling, he looks like John Hodiak. We were in *Lifeboat*. Hodiak, that is dahling, not the driver. Now, dahling, I have to rush, I have a playwright waiting at my hotel . . ."

"Oh my God!" cried David Carney.

"Dahling, I'm so sorry. I mean I haven't read a thing this other playwright's written, but then, dahling, if you're not prepared to endure the pain, you should find another profession. Have you ever tried composing greeting cards?"

David Carney was exhausted. He was led docilely to the patrol car and deposited in the backseat. "I say, Adam Todd. Couldn't those dahlings give us a lift back to the hotel? I mean I assume you'll be continuing on my tail, what a vulgar expression, and . . ."

With siren shrieking, Tallulah Bankhead was borne to the Hotel Elysee by two of New York's finest, while David Carney decided it was time for another complete breakdown. It was easier than writing a play.

Joseph Savage was thirty-one years old, attractive, intelligent, talented, blacklisted, and having a perfectly lovely time waiting for Tallulah Bankhead to return from her walk. Patsy Kelly was flying high. She'd had a phone call from the celebrated director John Murray Anderson, inquiring if she was available for a possible revue he might be doing.

"I knew the wheel'd spin back to me!" she bellowed as she added more scotch to her half-filled glass. "Me in a John Murray Anderson revue!"

"Now Patsy, dear"—there was caution in Estelle Winwood's voice—"he said a *possible* revue he *might* be doing. Patsy, you shouldn't drink on an empty promise."

"Now don't you go throwing cold water on it, Estelle! I'm going to see my name in lights!" She screeched "lights."

"You'll see your name in lights, Patsy, when you change it to 'Exit.' "

"You're just jealous because you've got no offers from nobody!"

"Patsy, don't you think you'd be happier remaining in obscurity?"

"Have another drink, Joe," cried Patsy to Savage, "you look thirsty."

"Oh, I'm fine. I don't drink very much."

"There's no such thing as drinking very much." Patsy executed a time step, interrupted by Tallulah's entrance.

"God, what an experience I've just been through! Attacked by that David Carney maniac in the Central Park Zoo, rescued by a brick shithouse assigned to my tail by Singer but the drive back here in the patrol car was absolutely marvelous. Is this Mr. Savage? Do forgive me, John—"

"Joseph," said Savage.

"Of course, dahling, you most certainly know your own name." She had flung handbag and gloves and anything else flingable helter skelter as Patsy followed in her wake retrieving them. "Estelle, I need a very large vodka martini immediately . . ."

"No gin?" chirruped Estelle as she went to the bar.

"No, dahling, gin works too fast and

there's the evening still ahead of me." She plopped onto the sofa next to Savage. "Why must being a celebrity be so exhausting?" She flung her arms wide and then turned to Savage with one of her more brilliant smiles. "Dottie Parker thinks the world of you. Have I seen anything of yours? Oh ha-ha-ha! Forgive me, dahling, that sounded so forward, I meant of course anything of yours you've written."

"My most successful film was *The Ladies Are Waiting.*"

Tallulah was scratching her head. "Did I see that?"

"I did," said Estelle as she gave Tallulah the martini. "It was absolutely charming. Terribly funny, Tallulah, he writes marvelous dialogue."

"Oh, well, then, that's marvelous, dahling. Really, Joseph, there are so few writers today who can do truly superb dialogue. Of course there's Noël, though he gets a bit tired now and then, and in films there's Joe Mankiewicz, even if he did slander me in *All About Eve,* and in television there's absolutely nobody. Tell me, Joseph, have you something in mind for me? I'm perfectly willing to commission a play." She leaned over and patted his hand. "I'm sure you could use the money, dahling."

"That's one of the reasons I'm here."

"What's the other?"

"I wanted to meet you. I've admired you for a long time."

"Don't you dare tell me your mother held you in her arms when you saw *Foxes.*"

"No, it was *Something Gay.*"

"Oh God, *that* one. Have a drink, your glass is empty."

"No, I've really had enough."

"There's no such thing." Patsy took his glass and went to the bar. "Now, dahling, do you have something in mind for me?"

He told her his idea in a few brief, well-spoken sentences. He knew how to tell and sell a story, with the emphasis on the character he had in mind for her. She liked the idea immediately and said so. "Patsy, bring me my checkbook." Savage said a silent prayer of thanks.

Estelle said, "Oh dear, off with my head. I forgot to tell you, Tallulah." Tallulah waited. "Your detective friend is going to drop in on you. There's been another murder."

Tallulah jumped to her feet and stormed.

"How the hell can you forget another murder!"

"Oh, do don't shout at me, Tallulah. You know it jars my nerves. And I hate murder and murderers and the police make me edgy. Why don't you ever contemplate an affair with someone calm and serene like a clergyman?"

"Estelle! Who got murdered?"

"That guy you visited today," screeched Patsy, "that Oliver guy." She put the checkbook on the end table next to the sofa and handed a pen to Tallulah.

"Oliver Sholom was murdered?" Tallulah was aghast. She heard a sharp intake of breath and it took her a few minutes to realize it had come from Joseph Savage. She looked at the pen, went to the end table, hastily scribbled a check, tore it out of the book, and handed it to Savage. She was startled to realize his face was chalk white. Joseph Savage, the blacklisted playwright now freshly in from left field. A friend of Dottie's and blacklisted. She wondered . . . He folded the check and put it in his inside pocket without looking at the sum written there. It was a generous five hundred dollars. "You look shocked, Joseph, did you know Oliver?"

"Yes, he directed my play." He spoke

169

softly. "Miss Bankhead, he's also the reason I'm blacklisted. It's knowledge easily available."

"You knew Lester Miroff?"

"I met him once. Whatever you're thinking, Miss Bankhead, I didn't. But I wish I had." He stood up. "Thanks for the job. I'll do my very best for you."

Tallulah mustered a smile as she took the hand he held out to her. "I'm sure you will, dahling. Oh, do I have your phone number in case I need to contact you?"

He took a card from his wallet and gave it to her. "This is the best place to get me. I work here."

Tallulah glanced at the card and commented, "Movie memorabilia. How fascinating."

"It's a hobby and thank God it's now a living. Goodbye. Goodbye, ladies." After he left, Tallulah walked to the window, deep in thought, anxious for Singer's arrival. Seven words were echoing inside her head, over and over and over.

I didn't, but I wish I had.

TEN

"LEWIS DREFUSS is on his way up," announced Patsy. Tallulah stirred and walked away from the window. There was a lot of high kicking going on in her mind, and the choreography was much too slapdash for Tallulah's taste. Victims and backstabbers were jockeying for position in the center spotlight, but there was stiff competition from Lester Miroff and Oliver Sholom. Making their way down a grand staircase which would have won Florenz Ziegfeld's approval were Gabriel Darnoff, Joe Savage, David Carney, Barry Wren, Mitchell Zang, and a few others who were either longshots or time wasters. The trouble was, Tallulah wasn't quite sure whom to eliminate. And there was that troublesome character waiting in the wings, the one with no face. If only she could create the face. There was something else nibbling away at the back of her mind. Something that had happened, something she heard, something somebody did, something that was all wrong and out of character, something that to a professional detective might have been a dead giveaway. Oh, the hell with it. The professionals were always slipping up—why the hell couldn't she?

"Tallulah," said Estelle while cheating at solitaire, "you're talking to yourself again."

Tallulah was mixing a martini. "Dahling, it's the only time I get intelligent answers."

Patsy opened the door for Lewis Drefuss. "Sorry to barge in on you like this, Tallulah, but there are some changes in this Sunday's show and I thought you ought to have them."

"I'm always delighted to see you, dahling. But be warned that at any moment Jacob Singer will be arriving and I have the feeling this place will be under siege. *What* changes?"

"Meredith thinks it would be fun if you did a duet with Ethel Merman."

"Me and Merman? I'll be down for the count by the second note. That's like pitting a piccolo against a Wurlitzer. What song's he chosen?"

"Bye Bye Blackbird."

"I'd prefer 'Bye Bye Blacklist.' And what other choice goodies do you have for me?" They sat next to each other on the sofa. She put on her spectacles while he rifled through the script. Tallulah's mind wandered away on its own after just a few seconds and Lewis wasn't aware he had lost her attention. She nodded every time he paused, second nature to her onstage, when she tired of a long run and thanks to her superb training always knew when to jump in on cue. Helen Hayes had once told her she did a whole act of a play preparing the menu for a party she was planning for her children without hearing the other actors or mistiming any of her own lines. She was thoroughly astonished when the curtain came down and she heard bravos coming from out front. She thought the matinee ladies were approving the menu she had finally decided on.

"You've heard Oliver Sholom was murdered?"

"I what, dahling?" Lewis repeated the sentence. "Oh yes, dahling, Singer told me. How'd you find out?"

"It was on the news."

"It seems I missed meeting the same fate by just a few moments."

"What do you mean?"

"I was there, dahling. I was with Sholom. I was trying to be a detective." And by golly Singer had begrudgingly admitted she got Sholom to spill a few important beans in his hysteria, but she didn't tell that to Lewis. She was saving it to throw in Singer's face in case it became necessary.

Estelle piped up, "Tallulah has a death wish, Lewis, didn't you know that?"

"Oh shut up and cheat, Estelle."

"I will not shut up. Tallulah's got this strange streak of masochism in her, she loves to suffer. That's why she makes so many poor choices. Now take John Emery . . ."

Tallulah had crossed a leg over the other and was swinging it, a sure sign of an impending blowup to those who knew her well. "You take John Emery, dahling." Had the words struck anyone, they would have been lethal. She said to Lewis, "He was my one short trip down the aisle."

Estelle choo-choo'd ownward, unfazed. "We all told her, if you must get mixed up with an actor, then have an affair and be done with it. But no, Tallulah decides to marry this person of a small but not unpleasant talent, confer on him co-starring billing with little hope of challenging the Lunts."

"*What* Lunts?"

"It didn't work, of course, because talent alone does not suffice. One must have magic, that elusive quality that so few in the theater possess. Now Tallulah has magic, but magic needs to be fortified, especially in the theater. To really ascend to Olympian heights, magic must be wedded to magic as Lynn and Alfred have done, but no, not our girl here sitting and waving her leg at me and stop that, Tallulah, it's making me dizzy!"

"That's not what's making you dizzy, dahling."

Estelle directed her mouth back to Lewis. Patsy was reading a paperback although little was sinking in. "Our girl here weds herself to a profile. Now that's one thing John Emery has on Alfred Lunt. John has a profile."

"I thought he was gorgeous," Tallulah told Lewis.

"You think Victor McLaglen's gorgeous," snapped Patsy.

Tallulah's eyes narrowed briefly into slits but she said nothing. Regardless of what Patsy said, it usually lost something in the translation. There were times when Tallulah wished Patsy's conversation was complemented by subtitles.

Estelle continued, "But one soon tires of a profile and so Mr. Emery was sent packing."

"He's doing damn well in pictures, dahling."

"Well, of course he is, dear. That's where profiles belong."

"Oh, for crying out loud, can I help it if I'm a sucker for a gorgeous side view?" She said to Lewis, "I was just a babe in his arms when John Barrymore tried to rape me in his room at the Algonquin. I had to kick him in the crotch to make my escape. Poor darling, he was a genius, you know. A true genius. But the poor darling rarely bathed. Soap and water were anathema to him. How those wives put up with it I'll never know."

"More masochists," stated Estelle flatly while stealing a forbidden peek at a hidden card. "People with death wishes should form a society like Alcoholics Anonymous."

Tallulah decided to ignore her friend and said to Lewis, "Anyway, dahling, there I was in that poor bastard's grubby little apartment and I ended up throwing him into a temper tantrum the likes of which you've never seen. I mean really, dahling, I've created some beauts of my own, but Mr. Sholom certainly put me to shame. Still, it was no reason to put him to death." She was on her feet and pacing. "Come to think of it, why the hell *was* he murdered?"

On cue, Jacob Singer knocked heavily on the door.

"I'm sure that's not opportunity. Patsy, let old 'Heavy heavy hangs over my head' make his entrance." To Lewis she said, "Stick around, dahling. I find the sight of you comforting. By the way, don't you ever find me sexy?"

Lewis's chin dropped, while Tallulah flung her arms wide in a theatrical gesture frequently copied by others but rarely with the Bankhead effect. "Dahling Jacob, what kept you?" He never had a chance to answer. He was trapped in the center of a Bankhead offensive, a speck in the eye of a hurricane. "Dahling, I expected you to enter like some ferocious insurgent wielding a machete, but here you are all freshly shaved and scrubbed and is that the scent of Yardley I detect? No, it must be something else, some formula reserved for the exclusive use of brilliant lawmen." Over her shoulder to Lewis, who had finally closed his mouth, she said, "Jacob is a genius and much too modest. Jacob, I'm sure one day you'll write your book and stagger all of us. The way Lewis Lawes did with his *Twenty Thousand Years in Sing Sing.* You've heard of Lawes, haven't you, Lewis dahling?" Lewis hadn't. "He was the warden at Sing Sing. I did a Sunday-night performance there once, dahling, and they didn't want me to leave!"

"Was it that bad?" squawked Patsy.

"Patsy," the voice threatening, "pour drinks. Now what was I saying . . ."

"Everything," said Singer.

"Now, Jacob, if you're going to be unpleasant and surly and this is Lewis Drefuss without whom my program would be a disaster I can't be sure if you've met before or if either of you cares and what are you drinking dahlings tell Patsy so Jacob I don't especially expect you to purr like a pussycat but I also don't . . ."

Singer had his hands up to try to stem the flow of traffic from the Bankhead mouth.

"Dahling, this is hardly the time for exercising—"

"Ho, lady, ho!"

"Ho indeed, dahling, and why?" She gasped. "Don't tell me there's been another murder!"

"There are always murders, Tallulah. So far none of them connect with this case." He said to Lewis, "I assume you know what case I'm referring to." Lewis said he did while Patsy interrupted and asked for their drink orders. Once that was out of the way, Tallulah told Singer to sit down and she then phoned room service for hors d'oeuvres. During the ensuing conversation she managed to go to her bedroom and change into a Balenciaga hostess gown without missing a word or a cue.

"I hope you realize you came dangerously close to co-starring with Sholom this afternoon."

"I most certainly do and you don't have to raise your voice. I can hear you quite clearly. Have you visited the scene of the crime?"

He couldn't resist. With great relish he described the condition of the corpse and the kitchen while Tallulah, unresponsive, shouted to Patsy to hurry up with her drink. Singer wondered if the actress ever admitted defeat.

"Jacob, I adore that marvelous man you've assigned to guard me. Is he downstairs in the lobby? Let's have him up. Has he told you he saved my life today? Oh God, I forgot to tell the girls, I think. Or if I did I don't remember. That playwright attacked me in the zoo!"

"What playwright?" screeched Patsy while bringing Tallulah her martini.

"What's his name now?" wondered Tallulah for a second.

"How do *I* know? He attacked you, not me."

"Really, Patsy, you're no help at all. Carney. That's his name. Art Carney."

"Art Carney doesn't write plays."

"Who's Art Carney? Do I know him? When did we meet?"

Jacob literally gulped his scotch. He then said, "David Carney."

"That's the man. *David* Carney." She called after Patsy's retreating figure. "Art Carney's an impostor."

"Oh, him again." She explained to Estelle, "The play about the aging actress. Tallu should have attacked *him*."

Tallulah spent five minutes on her attack and rescue and returned to the others as the waiter arrived with the hors d'oeuvres. Tallulah was looking good and she knew it. She signed the bill while almost dahlinging the waiter to death (the Elysee staff had long since grown immune to the Bankhead affectations) and then examined the tray. "Oh, good, no anchovies. I *loathe* anchovies." She popped an hors d'oeuvre into her mouth and chewed wolfishly. "I haven't the vaguest idea what this is I'm eating and don't anyone dare venture a guess. It's really quite good. Patsy, do offer the things around."

Patsy wearily crossed to the tray and lifted it. "When do you want me to do the windows?"

"Patsy dahling, I've more than enough irony in my fire."

180

"Tallulah," said Jacob, swooping into a welcome pause, "you might have been murdered."

"Dahling, I've said it before and I'll say it again, death holds no fear for me. I've died so many deaths at the hands of the critics. I appreciate your concern, Jacob."

"Keeping a man assigned to you is not inexpensive. I'd prefer that from here on in you'd stick out."

She said to Lewis, "Don't you adore police argot?" She suddenly erupted into song, her ghastly baritone set to Gershwin's music, "Argot rhythm, argot music, argot my man, who could ask for anything more?" She'd have loved to ask for a hell of a lot more, but she was too proud. She said to Jacob, who was still wincing at the sound of her singing, "You said yourself I managed to get some information out of Sholom that he'd succeeded in concealing when you questioned him after Miroff's murder." She suddenly turned to Lewis, the recipient of her new train of thought. "You were friendly with Abner Walsh, dahling. Did he ever mention his son, Leo?"

"I didn't know he had a son."

"Oh, didn't you, dahling? I don't know

why I'm surprised. A lot of others have professed ignorance on the subject."

Lewis asked Singer, "How's his son connected to these killings?"

Jacob shifted in his seat after asking for a fresh drink, with which the intrepid Patsy obliged. "Well, Leo's just a long shot. Stop me if I begin to bore you. You see, in most cases of murder sooner or later something turns up in your favor. Maybe a clue, maybe somebody happens to say something that helps lift the fog. Sometimes an informer turns up offering us a bargain. But we've had nothing much with both these killings. Like the guy who found Miroff's body. No help whatsoever. The murderer's had nothing but luck on his side. Nobody sees him coming in or out of the baths because he's damned lucky. It was the right time of day. Business is slack, so the attendants goof off. They're in a back room making coffee or whacking each other off or whatever the hell the employees do in a gay beehive. Same thing with Sholom.

"Nobody sees him enter or leave the building. Sholom's uncle lives on the floor below. He's a tailor, he operates out of his place. He says he's hard of hearing, so he heard nothing. And it's even worse when he's at his sewing machine, because it's old and it clatters. All he remembers is Tallulah."

"Well really, dahling, I *am* memorable."

Singer ignored her. He was too appreciative of Lewis's undivided attention. He liked the guy. When Lewis was interested, he showed it. And he hadn't yawned yet. "Taking it a step further, all we can round up is a cab driver who remembers picking up Tallulah and bringing her here."

"All right, dahling, I confess. I murdered them."

"Don't joke about it, lady. Maybe you did." Her laughter made the wall shake. "So you see, Lewis . . . you don't mind me calling you Lewis . . ." Lewis said of course not and Singer continued. "So you see . . . all we've got is a long list of possible suspects. You know, the ones he fingered, relatives of those who committed suicide or those who died of heart attacks and stuff like that, maybe brought on by the stress of the blacklist. I'm sorry if I sound so cold-blooded, but that's what a murder investigation is all about. So to continue and to make a long story short—"

"Too late," growled Tallulah. She wanted her spotlight back and would pout until she got it.

"—this brings us to the offspring of these suicides, et cetera. Maybe one of them did it. They've got the motive. Hatred. Revenge. It boils inside and then finally erupts. Some people scream and hit their fists against a wall or go out on a bender or beat up their wives. But there's always the one guy who explodes with murder. Well, I suppose if there wasn't I'd be out of business. So the only offspring that's a missing link is this Leo Walsh."

Tallulah leapt in. "Dahling, has it occurred to you he might have changed his name?"

"It has most certainly occurred to me." He explained to Lewis, "All we've got to go on is that he's got this ugly scar on his left cheek."

"He might have had plastic surgery," suggested Lewis.

Singer smiled. "That disheartening thought has also occurred to me."

The phone rang and it was Dorothy Parker. Tallulah said to her, "Of course, dahling. Don't be depressed and please don't think about committing suicide until after dinner, dahling. I'll meet you there in an hour." She hung up and said to the others, "That was Dottie Parker and she's suicidal which," she said to Lewis, "is chronic with

184

her. Her miserable Pekinese died in her arms a couple of hours ago. Apparently no last bark with which to comfort Dottie. Care to join us at Tony's dahling?" she asked Singer.

"Sorry, I got a lot of paperwork to do tonight. I'm trying to catch up with this Barry Wren guy, but his answering service keeps telling me he'll be home later. You'd think at least a guy in show business would pick up his messages."

Lewis asked, "I know Barry Wren. Is he a suspect?"

"Lewis," said Singer, accepting Tallulah's offer of another drink, "everybody's a suspect right now. I might even think of admitting you to the club. Or Patsy here or even Estelle."

"Don't be ridiculous, dahling. The only thing Estelle ever murders is another actor's laugh."

Estelle said nothing; she'd heard the line too often in the past. Bankhead constantly repeated herself, to the delight of some and the chagrin of most.

"What are you up to tonight, Lewis dahling? Would you care to join us? Of course it'll undoubtedly be a bit depressing, but then Tony's might be fun and perhaps

185

Mabel's gotten over her cold and will be singing. Have you ever heard Mabel Mercer sing, Jacob?" He couldn't squeeze in a reply; Tallulah left him no space. "She's absolutely unique. Her phrasing is something you'll never hear anywhere else except perhaps from Sinatra and Sylvia Syms, who admit they worship her and copy her. I mean full marks for anyone who copied from the best and of course, dahlings, I have dozens of imitators except none of them ever really get me right except on occasion Miss Bette Davis as in whatever became of but then of course the best other Tallulah in show business is T.C. Jones and he's a female impersonator, dahling, but of course I freely admit I've copied from Ethel that's Barrymore not Merman or Waters what were you trying to say, Lewis, dahling?"

"I can't make it. I'd love to. But I can't. I've got a date uptown."

"Oh, dahling, is uptown becoming fashionable again? I suppose the trend'll be back to Harlem soon. I gather the murder rate up there is on the increase and why doesn't Harry Truman do something about racial tensions and forget about Margaret's dreadful voice? Lewis is the White House still pushing to get us to use Margaret as in may

God have mercy." She snapped her fingers. "Sayyyy! There's the solution! I'll trade Harry Margaret for getting that bloody HUAC off my back. Maybe I can be nice about it and throw in Lillie Hellman did I tell you we had a delightful drink together and sort of buried the hatchet that is until I tell her I just can't go touring in *Foxes* again I've had it up to here with Regina Giddons though God knows I'm one of the few troupers left in the business who adores trouping audiences on the road are so generous and giving except in Detroit where they're a collective pain in the backside which I strongly suspect has something to do with assembly lines but Jacob I thought you questioned Barry Wren thoroughly after Miroff was murdered I could have sworn you told me that!"

"I had this talk with Zero Mostel, which is why I was delayed getting here . . ."

"Poor dahling Zero, how is he managing to survive?"

"By the skin of his teeth. Sweet guy if a little eccentric. Anyway, I found some notes about him in Sholom's apartment, so I asked him over to see me. True, when he entered the station he waved his cane and yelled 'Storm Troopers! Fascists,' which didn't immediately endear him to anyone. In fact he offered to stand trial for the murders because he hated both guys and could use the publicity. I don't mind telling you I almost agreed to go along with him." He chuckled at the memory of Mostel. "Anyway, he loathes Wren even more, but he thought Wren might know Leo Walsh's whereabouts. Mostel thinks that at the time he was out there doing a picture at Metro, before the blacklist, of course, Wren was there trying to get a foot in edgewise since Metro you know does all them big musicals. You see, Mostel remembers Abner Walsh was out there at the time, doing some guest shot in some Abbott and Costello looney tune and all them of course were still chummy. Mostel's pretty positive the Walsh boy was there too, he thinks trying a shot at acting. So you see, maybe there's a chance the kid kept in touch with Wren after he made it big on Broadway. Who the hell knows? I can't pass up anybody. Who knows when I'll draw the lucky buck?"

"Poor Jacob," sympathized Tallulah, "you sound so frustrated."

"Tallulah, I don't mind admitting, I haven't been this frustrated since Helen Morgan refused to sleep with me."

Tallulah smiled. "Well, dahling, it was probably easier for her to sing "My Bill" than "My Jacob." She tried it. "See, it doesn't work."

"Doesn't it, Tallulah?"

The innuendo embraced her gently. For the first time in years, Tallulah Bankhead blushed.

Barry Wren had bought his town house in the East Seventies at a time when real estate in the area was depreciating and town houses were going begging. With his occasional luck, the East Side was on the rise again and he now resided in a very valuable property, a property he knew he'd have had to unload at a beggar's price had he not cooperated with the inquisition. Oh, what the hell, J. Edgar Hoover himself had Barry in for a secret session and convinced him he was doing the right thing. So what if it had made Barry nervous that the head of the FBI sat there shamelessly holding hands with the man who lived with him?

It was after nine o'clock when Barry let himself in through the front door and then chained and bolted it. He was frightened. He'd been frightened when Lester Miroff was murdered. Oliver Sholom's brutal murder added fuel to Barry's flames of fear. He checked his answering service after turning on all the lights downstairs, and there was another message from Jacob Singer. He sat down and mulled over the idea of seeing Singer in the morning and cooperating with him in return for protection. He was truly gifted at cooperating and there was no reason not to provide Singer with a taste. There was a draft in the room. Damn that woman, meaning his housekeeper. I warned her to lock all the windows carefully when she left. He found the open window in the kitchen at the back of the house. He slammed it shut and tried to latch it. The latch was broken.

Damn.

He thought for a moment. What to do to dissuade any possible invader? He lined up several empty bottles on the sill and when he was done felt proudly creative. They'd make enough of a racket if anyone tried to enter. He turned off the lights and went upstairs to run a bath. He was bone weary, brain weary, and conscience weary.

And he was lonely. He was frighteningly lonely. A few months ago there'd have been a dozen messages with his answering service. Tonight, just Jacob Singer, persistent bastard. Barry turned on all the lights of the second floor, which consisted of the guest bedroom and bath in the front and his own mammoth-sized bedroom and bathroom in the back. He threw his knapsack on the bed, the trademark that held his rehearsal slippers, costume, miscellanea, and a box of Oreo cookies. He went to the bathroom designed especially for him by Elsie de Wolfe, the celebrated Lady Mendl, who'd made a fortune doing interior decoration in between standing on her head at parties. He was lavish with the bath salts imported especially from Paris and then returned to the bedroom, where he turned on the television full blast, the better to hear it when he was in his bath. It occasionally occurred to him to position the set so he could see it from the tub. He did this now. He stripped to the buff and then lay down on the floor where he exercised his legs for a few moments. He heard a comedian's joke and he laughed, not because he found it funny but occasionally these days when he was alone he liked to remind himself he hadn't gone mute. The commercial was on and he loathed tap-dancing beer cans and so went into the bedroom. He tested the water and found the temperature suitable. He turned off the taps and slowly lowered himself into the water. Once stretched out, he lay still, the water and the salts soothing him.

His eyes were closed. Little beads of perspiration were forming on his bald head. He stroked his genitals to make sure they were still there. He could hear one of his favorite women singers doing wonderful things with "I'll Be Seeing You." Barry Wren never saw anything again. The powerful hands weighed down on him and forced him under the water. Every nerve in his body shrieked and pleaded for rescue. His legs thrashed and his hands tried to wrench those powerful hands away, but he was no match for his killer.

The killer was hoping it would be considered death by accidental drowning, which is why he tidied up the bathroom before leaving it and going out the back window, which he had entered by jimmying open the lock. It was an easy climb over the backyard fence into the yard of the tenement on the other side. Then he thought of where to eat.

Killing people gave him a ferocious appetite.

ELEVEN

WITH HANDS shoved deeply into his trouser pockets, Gabriel Darnoff walked into the lobby of the Belasco Theater. It was almost eleven P.M. and the curtain should be coming down soon on the third act of his play. He went into the theater and stood in the back, where his nervous producers were pacing back and forth. The two men had been behind his earlier two hits and out of loyalty had gone along with Gabriel's new one. The one who was first to voice a lack of faith in the script had commented to his partner, "Abe, loyalty is bad business." Gabriel was prepared to be destroyed by the critics. A strong star performance might have rescued it, but strong stars had turned it down. His producers had refused to gamble on his father for the lead because in the months following his blacklisting, Michael Darnoff had been gradually falling apart, drinking heavily and causing embarrassing scenes in public. To assuage his own guilt, Gabriel had convinced the producers to offer his father a smaller role, but Darnoff the elder was no fool. He knew the appearance of a star such as he in a supporting role would upset the balance of the play, not that there was much balance to upset.

Abe whispered to Gabriel, "Where you been? Why'd you disappear when the curtain went up?"

"How's it going?" asked the playwright.

"It's gone," replied Abe glumly. The other partner, Webster by name, was sucking on his teeth, a sure sign the ship was sinking and don't bother radioing for help.

Webster said to Gabriel, "Your mother loves the play."

That confirmed it was a disaster. Everything his mother loved turned to dust, especially his father. Had his mother hated the play, he'd have gone out and invested in a fresh mistress. The curtain came down slowly. There was an embarrassing pause and then at last the applause began.

"They're applauding," said Webster.

"Probably because their hands went dead," replied Abe. "Come on, Gabe," he said to Darnoff, "failure isn't the end of the world. You're entitled. That's the trouble with this goddamn business, they don't allow you to fail. On the other hand they're dying to see you fail, they hate it when you're successful.

Oh God, why don't I go back to ladies' pajamas!"

Bella Darnoff, coming up the aisle, saw her son and waved with enthusiasm. She threw her arms around him and cried, "It's your best yet! I'm so thrilled and so proud to be your mother. Oh, if only your father was here tonight, that he should have missed this triumph." Triumph, thought Gabriel, it's worse than I thought. "Smile, darling! What's the matter with you? You look like you just killed somebody!"

David Carney was washing his hands for possibly the tenth time that night. The police had held him only a few hours and finally released him when the only two witnesses to the zoo incident who came forward swore, albeit reluctantly, because they were positive Carney should be modeling straitjackets, that he had never laid a hand on Tallulah Bankhead. Bankhead, they were assured by Jacob Singer, would not press charges. Carney was released with a severe reprimand and a warning, and when he got home he washed his hands. Over and over he soaped them and rinsed them and then he'd soap and rinse them again. It was almost a religious ritual, or the action of a surgeon preparing to operate.

I could kill her. Like I killed the others, I could kill her.

The phone rang. It was his sister Audrey. "So what trouble did you get into today?" She knew her brother well. He told her about accosting Bankhead. "*Tallulah* Bankhead?"

"Yes, Tallulah Shithead. I should have killed the bitch, like I killed the others."

"That's right, honey, you go out and kill somebody." With her hand over the mouthpiece, she said to her husband, a celebrated crooked stockbroker, "Davey's thinking of another killing spree."

"I wish you wouldn't joke about that," said her husband. "I wouldn't put it past that kookieboo."

"What was that, Davey dear?"

"When I kill, I kill to set things right. There is so much injustice in this world, so much corruption, I mean somebody's got to go out there and set things right. Don't you agree?"

Audrey said cosily, "Davey, do we ever disagree? Didn't we both like *Sunset Boulevard?*"

"Yes, but that's because Gloria Swanson was right to shoot her cheating lover."

"But she was crazy," said Audrey, tactfully refraining from adding "too."

"I have to hang up, Audrey. I have to go out. There's someone I'm going to kill tonight."

"Well, it's a nice night, sweetie. Now remember to get something to eat."

"Oh, I always eat after I kill. Killing makes me so hungry."

"And Davey . . ."

"What?"

"Don't kill anybody nice. Did you get the check we sent you?"

"Yes, thank you. Thank you very much."

"Well, like I promised Momma and Poppa on their deathbeds, I'll always look after you."

He broke into a sob. "I didn't mean to kill them, Audrey, honest I didn't."

"I know you didn't and I'm sure they know you didn't. Wherever they are, Davey, I'm sure they forgive you." To her husband, "For God's sake turn the sound down!" He was fiddling the dial on the television set.

"I'm glad you think they forgive me. The others won't forgive me. The one I killed yesterday and the one I killed the day before and the one I'm going to kill tonight . . ."

"Davey, do us both a favor. Don't go to

197

the police and confess. I mean after your incident with Tallulah, they might be a little hard on you. You know what I mean? Maybe you should stay home and write another play."

"I will never write another play! Twenty-three unproduced plays is enough! Rejections rejections rejections! God! I must kill George Abbott and Joshua Logan and those schmucks at the Theater Guild! Goodbye, Audrey, don't ever forget me!"

When Audrey heard the dial tone, she put the phone down, folded her arms around herself, and sat biting her lower lip.

"Why do you phone him so often?" whined her husband. "He always depresses you."

"I'm not depressed, I'm thinking."

"That's worse."

"I'm thinking about all those murders he insists he's committed. Honey . . ."

"What?"

"Supposing he really did them?"

"Oh shit, Aud, there you go giving me nightmares again." She returned to her thoughts when he returned to the television set, and neither of them was happy.

Joseph Savage sat in the rear of a Fifth Avenue bus that was heading down to Washington Square. He looked at his wristwatch. Eleven o'clock. He'd eaten a hearty dinner, in fact he had been unusually ravenous. Tallulah's check was for an amount larger than he had hoped for. He would deposit it in the morning and maybe treat himself to a new jacket and trousers and a new pair of shoes. Most of the department stores were featuring spring sales. It was the first he had thought of himself all night.

He'd been dwelling on murder. On murder involving Tallulah. It was the idea for the play for her he'd been mulling in his mind after leaving her. He had walked and walked and it wasn't long before he found himself on the Upper East Side, standing outside Barry Wren's town house and contemplating murder. Lester Miroff was dead and Oliver Sholom had been knocked off, and why not Barry Wren? He was one of the worst of the lot. He was rich, Joseph knew that. He owned a town house and a house on Fire Island and he got lots of offers.

Joseph had salvaged very little from the recent unpleasantness. He didn't have all that much in the first place, but at least there'd been some script offers for television. Dottie Parker had urged him to come to Hollywood, where she was positive he'd do well, but now that was all cloud-cuckoo-land for him, for her, Dalton Trumbo, Albert Maltz, so many fine talents condemned to oblivion by former friends and associates. Joseph and just about everybody else knew that the FBI had a list of informers supplying them with names. Mostly actors and actresses and writers and directors who had never made it big or were no longer in demand and jealous of those who were. Everyone knew for sure that Ronald Reagan and that miserable bitch columnist Hedda Hopper cooperated with the FBI and turned in names. Here in New York a gang of vindictive has-beens were behind the publication of *Aware!*—a tipsheet that named names of supposed communists. It was a disgrace and a dishonor and it had brought about betrayals and deceptions and murder.

Murder.

Yes, Joseph was now positive, Barry Wren should be the next victim. And why not? Show business deaths always happen in threes. One, Lester Miroff, two, Oliver Sholom, three, Barry Wren.

And now in the bus, well-fed and self-satisfied, he couldn't wait to get home and commit his idea to paper. Tallulah as an amateur detective solving the murders of three jackals. He was positive she'd be pleased.

Tallulah was humming along with Mabel Mercer, who was pleading in song to be flown to the moon. It was her second encore, and the elderly singer was anxious to call it a night and get home to the man with whom she shared her life. After all these decades of singing abroad and at home, the voice had gotten a bit shaky. She had trouble with her top notes and at the other end of the scale had perfected a sort of melodious growl that helped her slide over difficult passages. Yet she remained a nonpareil, a brilliant stylist. Strangely enough, this late in life and in her career, she'd become a bestseller on record albums for the connoisseur. There was even a spillover beginning, with her albums now appearing in stores other than the specialty shops. Tonight she was pleased there were a number of celebrities in the club. It helped future business if word got around that Tallulah Bankhead and Dorothy Parker had been in, and George Baxt had been bringing in some of his better-known clients such as Oscar Homolka and Signe Hasso. Several of the other agents were doing the same, and Tony Soma was delighted that Mabel continued to be a successful money spinner. Tony's was one of the few clubs in New York that now attracted gays and straights in equal numbers and everyone got along just fine.

Mabel was finished wanting to fly to the moon and live among the stars, and she was regally walking from the spotlight to her dressing room behind the bar. Tallulah was standing and clapping her hands, shouting, "Brava! Brava! More, dahling, just one more dahling. Oh, Mabel, do do 'Run Into the Roundhouse, Nellie, He Can't Corner You There!' " Tallulah was always lavishly generous with praise for those chosen few she genuinely admired. "Isn't she marvelous, Dottie? Dottie, drop that knife!"

"I'm only going to butter a biscuit," said Dottie, positive her voice wasn't cutting through the din. She liked Mabel Mercer's singing but she wished she'd go away. Always leave them hungry, Mabel, a philosophy she'd learned to practice in her numerous affairs.

Mabel didn't return. She too was a practitioner of the don't-give-them-too-much school. The uproar in the club settled down to a din and eventually became a hum, and

Tallulah and Mrs. Parker picked up the conversation they had put on hold when Miss Mercer had come out to sing.

"What's with Joseph Savage?" Tallulah asked Mrs. Parker.

"Didn't you see him today?"

"Of course I did. And I like him very much. I gave him a retainer to write me a play."

"Now, Tallulah, that's really nice! That's really really nice! You've saved his life."

"Perhaps, dahling. Do you think he's capable of taking any?"

"What do you mean? Was he particularly vindictive about his situation? I'd be surprised if he was. Joe's kept a low profile about the lousy spot he's in. He never discusses it. He keeps it all inside."

"That's far from admirable, dahling. One of these days he'll explode and then watch out!"

"Maybe. What makes you think so?"

She told Mrs. Parker of Savage's comment about not having killed Miroff and Sholom but being sorry he hadn't, or, as Tallulah said, words more or less to that effect.

"Well, come to think of it, Tallulah, I frequently of late think of committing a few homicides. It's lucky Moses isn't around today, the committee would be after him for parting the Red Sea."

"Did you ever have an affair with Jacob Singer?" The busboy was clearing the table and hooked by the question. He worked slowly so he could hear as much of their conversation as possible. He was hoping some day to write a celebrity exposé.

"Why?"

"Why not?"

"He never interested me sexually. Does he interest you?"

"Well, dahling," replied Tallulah with a wicked smile, "there's not too much of that kind of traffic threatening me these days." To the dawdling busboy she said, "Would you care to join us, dahling, because if you do, it'll be separate checks." He hurried away. "Waiter! Dahling." The waiter arrived. "Coffee and brandies. Will that be all right, Dottie?"

"A B&B for me," she said.

"Make mine Cointreau, dahling. Make them both doubles. Christ, all this awful cigarette smoke," she said as she lit a Craven A. Then, "What do you think of my death threat?"

"What does Jacob think of your death threat?"

"He's assigned me a bodyguard."

"That's what *I* think of your death threat."

"In fact, I think I've got more than one. The one who rescued me at the zoo from that madman whatsisname Carney seems to have been replaced by another who resembles Jack Oakie."

Mrs. Parker was repairing her face and stopped to ask Tallulah, "Carney? David Carney?"

"You know him?"

"I know about him."

"You sound morbid. You're about to tell me something I'm going to regret hearing. Tell me."

"It was in all the papers about five or six years ago."

"I rarely read the papers, dahling, you know that. I mean I occasionally check the sports section to see how my favorite ball team is doing and God knows I refuse to read my notices unless I'm told they're superlative tell me about Carney."

"I knew his mother and father, Elsa and Isaac. They were hard-core communists back in the good old days when communism was fun and games and a threat to nobody but the communists themselves. They had two kids. The oldest, a girl, I forget her name, married young and remained in the background. David is the youngest. He was brilliant. A genius. He wrote like a dream."

"He doesn't anymore, according to Patsy. She read the play he wanted me to do and said it was a bummer."

"How can you trust the judgment of anyone who starred in Hal Roach comedies?"

"Believe me, Dottie, Patsy's not the fool she makes herself out to be. Her still waters run deep."

"I wouldn't care to go wading in them." The waiter served the coffee and brandies and Tallulah waved him away impatiently. "Anyway, back to David Carney. He was about twenty or so when he was published in *Esquire*."

"Really!"

"Then he began being published all over the place. Hollywood was after him. Elsa and Isaac were against Hollywood, they said it would corrupt him. David was devoted to his parents. He worshiped Elsa. Then David had some kind of accident, I'm not sure what it was. It brought about a personality change. It seems there'd been another accident in which he'd been badly banged up when he was kid." She had Tallulah's undivided attention. "No comment on his being accident-prone?"

"No, I want to hear the rest. What about the personality change? Did it turn him into a Jekyll and Hyde?"

"Whose story is this?" It was a rare and treasured moment in which Bankhead said nothing. "It turned him into a Jekyll and Hyde. He started writing plays. And Patsy's right, they were perfectly awful. There was no sign of his earlier genius. It was gone. Then one day the sister got sore at him, something like that, I'm not sure. She told him he'd been adopted." Tallulah was leaning on the table, fascinated, her hands propping up her head, ashes from the cigarette in her mouth dropping onto the tablecloth. "He went berserk."

"Was it true or was she being bitchy the way only a sibling can be bitchy like when my darling sister Eugenia uses me for dart practice?"

"No, it was true. And what's more, she told him both parents had incurable cancers."

"Oh, don't tell me, don't tell me. I know what's coming. I can't stand it. Well, tell me!"

"He killed them. Poison. He said they

asked him to. Are you sure you haven't heard about this before?"

"Oh God, dahling, I hear so much, how do you expect me to retain it all and juggle a lover and learn my lines at the same time! How did he get away with it?"

"He didn't. He was judged insane and put away."

"Well, he's loose now. Say, wait a minute, does Jacob Singer know all this?"

"I should think so. Why?"

"He told me not to press charges against him. That madman might have killed me!"

"He's harmless."

Tallulah leaned forward and said with intensity, "Dahling, I have seen your harmless Mr. Carney in a rage, and let me tell you, I haven't seen such an unpleasant sight since I saw Kate Smith stripping in her dressing room. Hmmm."

"What?"

"I wonder, I just wonder. Adopted, you say? It isn't likely the Walshes would have put their son Leo up for adoption at some point, is it?"

"Only if they found him unpleasant, I should think. You knew them better than I did."

"Yes, but you find out more about people than I do."

"Jacob's much better at it than I am."

"Well, that's part of his profession to find out things other people don't find out. What's he told you he hasn't told me now come on out with it when did you see Jacob?"

"This afternoon, before he dropped in on you."

"And was that what made you feel suicidal?"

"No, dear, it was just my bi-monthly attack of the gloms. What have I done with my life, it's too late to improve it, old age is just around the corner and leering—"

"Stop that, Dottie, you're depressing me. What has Jacob told you that he hasn't told me and why?"

"Because he wants you to stop this amateur sleuthing. That phone threat has him really worried."

"If he's all that worried, why doesn't he confine me to quarters?"

"Because he knows there's no confining you to anything."

"For God's sake, weren't you in danger when you worked with him on that Lacey something business?"

"Oh yes, I thought Lacey was going to

dump me out of his private plane at one point. But the hell with Lacey, he's dead."

"So's the theater."

"I wouldn't mind seeing some theater in town. What's on that's good?"

"There's supposed to be a rather good revival of *Coriolanus*."

"I said theater, not Shakespeare."

"Dottie, you have deliberately changed the subject. You learned something about the Walshes from Jacob Singer. Waiter! Two brandy stingers! And we're not parting company tonight until I've heard every last word."

Mrs. Parker sighed the sigh she reserved for times of total defeat and reluctant capitulation. "What Jacob's dug up was some interesting information about Martha Walsh and the boy."

"He works fast, doesn't he?" Tallulah's admiration pleased Mrs. Parker. She had great respect for Jacob Singer.

"That's why he's one of the best. Tallulah, you remember shortly after you met them at that rent party, Abner scraped together enough cash to get him to Hollywood to try his luck in pictures. Musicals were coming back thanks to the success of that campy *Forty-Second Street* and just about anybody

210

who could carry a tune or do a time step was in demand. Abner had some luck and sent for Martha and the boy. There was that awful train crash. Somehow, Martha survived with minor injuries, but the boy was almost killed." The waiter served their stingers and Mrs. Parker thanked her rescuer, her throat was that parched. After a healthy swallow, she continued. It wasn't often that anyone had Tallulah Bankhead mesmerized, and Mrs. Parker was never one to relax her grip on an opportunity.

"Just about every bone in his poor little body was broken. And his face was mangled, *that* on top of that awful scar."

"The poor little bugger."

"Financially, of course, Abner now has his back against the wall and the miracle happens, he gets a recording deal. Then a radio show, some guest shots in the movies, you know, the usual B-movie routine that almost plunged Universal Pictures into bankruptcy. Abner and Martha place the boy into some rehabilitation center in Arizona. His bones mend, his by then very disturbed mind *tries* to mend—"

"Well, I told you he was terribly strange and withdrawn when I first saw him . . ."

"—and he underwent extensive plastic surgery."

Tallulah banged her fist on the table. "So that damn scar's probably gone!"

"Exactly, dear. Wherever Leo Walsh is today, there isn't a blemish on him."

"And here Jacob lets me go on thinking I have to find a man with an ugly scar, like that Mitchell Zang person."

"Oh, I know Mitchell Zang. Wasn't he Nance's boyfriend?"

"Yes, that's him."

"I've heard nothing but unpleasant things about him."

"Such as?"

"He takes money from women."

"So does Macy's."

"He has an ungovernable temper. I'd heard he'd beaten up on Nance a few times."

"The brute! Probably got his scar in a knife fight."

"After the plastic surgery."

"For God's sake, he isn't Leo Walsh, is he?"

Mrs. Parker shrugged. "Why not keep him as a suspect? Leo Walsh's surgery took place almost twenty years ago. A lot could have happened to him since then. After all, a lot happened to Abner and Martha. Abner met Nanette in New York while Martha was at the rehab center with the boy, and so goodbye Martha and Leo, hello Nanette."

"I wonder what she knows."

"Nanette? Why don't you ask her?"

"You know where to reach her?"

"She's probably at her studio in the Village. She lives and works in a converted carriage house on Duane Street. She's in the phone book."

"I suppose Jacob's already been to see her."

"Not that I know of. And besides, if he has, what difference does it make? You might get something out of her that he didn't succeed in getting. Look how good you were with Oliver Sholom, if I can believe you."

"Really, Dottie, when have you known me to lie? I mean I do exaggerate a bit and color my stories, but that's for entertainment's sake. I'm going to look up Nanette Walsh. She sculpts, doesn't she?"

"I've heard she wields a mean chisel, and I've known some pretty mean chiselers in my day."

"What about her politics?"

"The lady is tinted a rather light shade of parlor pink."

Tallulah thought for a moment while Mrs.

Parker stifled a yawn and entertained the possibility of another stinger. "Dottie, do things ever get lost in your mind?"

"Oh yes. People too. Mostly people, and with any luck, they stay lost."

"That isn't exactly what I mean, dahling. There's something elusive hidden in my mind, something I either heard or saw the past couple of days that I think just might unlock the door to the solution of these crimes. How do I dig it out?"

"Tallulah, if it's a good swimmer, it's bound to surface sooner or later. Try talking it over with Jacob."

"I did. I told him about Joe Savage's strange remark, of course, but he didn't react."

"Tallulah, believe me, it's filed away in his head. Jacob has a stone face Buster Keaton would appreciate."

"For his own reasons, I suppose, he didn't dwell much on either David Carney or Mitchell Zang. Or Gabriel Darnoff for that matter."

"Well, for sure *he's* not Leo Walsh. I wonder how his play went tonight. I hear it's a dog."

"Dottie, it doesn't necessarily wash if we find Leo Walsh we've found the murderer of

Miroff and Sholom. There must be dozens of people in the immediate vicinity with reasonable motives for murdering them."

"And there's always the possibility the murderer will never be apprehended. Let's have another round of stingers and to hell with the rest." Mrs. Parker signaled the waiter, who was wishing they'd go home. Tony's was almost deserted. There were a few diehards at the bar and only one other table was occupied by a young couple who sat holding hands and saying nothing, just staring into each other's vacant eyes. Mrs. Parker noticed them and commented, "Those boys probably met a couple of hours ago and they're still faithful to each other."

"Dottie, about Nanette Walsh."

"What about her?"

"She dumped Abner when he was blacklisted, didn't she?"

"It wasn't quite that way. They were washed up ages before he was fingered. Actually, she stood by him through the entire mess and *then* she dumped him."

"Leo Walsh, wherever he is, must hate her guts."

"Wherever he is," said Mrs. Parker as her eyes sparkled at the sight of the new stingers the waiter was delivering, "I wonder if he knows he's being traced and if he does, how cleverly is he covering his tracks."

"Frankly, dahling, I'm wondering why he hasn't come forward. Why he didn't appear after Abner and Martha died?" She sipped her drink. "That sort of behavior makes it a strong case to suppose he's the guilty party."

"It could also mean that for reasons we don't know about and may never learn about, he'd had a falling out with them and just didn't give a damn. Or else he may be dead."

"I somehow don't believe he's dead. And I think that is linked to that elusive piece of information I've got sequestered in my brain." She raised her glass. "To Leo Walsh. I'm falling in love with him."

TWELVE

NANETTE WALSH was a woman of eloquent silences. More often brutally blunt and out-spoken, she became awe-inspiring in her moments of quiet introspection when she was examining a person, an idea, a suspicion, an inspiration, or coming to a decision. Now at two in the morning, she was still at work on a bust of Abner Walsh, a work she had begun several years ago. She had abandoned it, then returned to it, then abandoned it again, her inspiration fluctuating with her emotional attitude toward her late husband. With his death, she was drawn back to it. Perhaps out of guilt, perhaps out of sorrow, no one would know. Nanette herself did not know. She had loved Abner in her fashion the way she had loved others, a devoted friend, an ardent and passionate partner in sex, but had never been able to give totally of herself. She admitted only to herself, and then reluctantly, that she had given up Abner because whatever he'd had to offer her in the past was spent. There was no chance of the reservoir refilling, and if it did, Nanette was disinterested in its contents. Nanette stood by him when he needed her, but she had long ceased feeling a part of him.

And she was no longer a part of the oaf who sat sprawled in an easy chair chugalugging from a bottle of beer. Mitchell Zang's stream of consciousness defied damming. Months before Nance Liston's suicide, Zang had taken to dropping in on Nanette's carriage house for the occasional sexual nosh. Nanette had to admit he was a superior bedroom athlete, and so what if it cost her the occasional handout? She was not a person who picked up dates in singles bars.

But like everything and everyone else in Nanette's life, once it had served its purpose, she was anxious to be rid of Mitchell Zang.

"I tell you, Nannie, there ain't no justice." Her grip tightened on the mallet she was wielding, albeit gently. She was working on Abner's nose and she had always treated his nose gently. "How the hell Arlen Stayne got to where he is today, I'll never know." She knew Arlen Stayne, a bad actor who had managed to wheedle his way into the position of casting director, and had since unseated a well-known television producer and now reigned in his place. "I mean I knew him in the old days and today I can't even get in to see him. How the hell does he do it?"

Nanette finally spoke. "He has never been terribly particular about where he places his lips."

"Let's go to bed."

"Go home. It's after two."

"I want to stay here."

"You're not staying here."

"Come on, stop being a cold bitch. I've had a rough night."

She stopped working and turned to him. "Mitchell, to be perfectly frank, when you go home, I want you to stay there."

218

He sat up. "And what the hell does *that* mean?"

"That means that tonight finishes it. I'm not the future in your future and it's time to call it quits."

He leapt to his feet. The innocent beer bottle threatened to become a dangerous weapon. "Like hell it is."

Her face turned ugly. "I make my own decisions, boy. Now go on home and tomorrow you can start prowling around for another meal ticket."

"You ain't dumping me like I'm a bag of garbage." She tactfully refrained from seconding the analogy. "I'd like to punch you in the mouth."

"Try it!" She raised the mallet, holding it with both her hands. "Just try it! You'll have a dented skull to go with that scar!"

With a hideous cry, he leapt at her. She brought the mallet down, missing his skull and grazing his shoulder. His fist connected with her face and she fell back against a sideboard. She struggled to keep her balance as he circled to hit her again. She lifted the mallet again and this time was successful. 'Ha!" she yelled as she brought it down on his head with all her strength. He sank to his knees while she ran to the door, fled out of the carriage house into the street, and blessed God for sending a cruising patrol car in her direction.

Tallulah Bankhead and Dorothy Parker were feeling no pain. Not that any was being inflicted upon them, but a series of stingers had left them nearly immobilized. They were joined by the two young men from the nearby table, and found out they weren't lovers at all. One of the young men, Mervyn, claimed to be psychic and had been "reading" his companion, whose name was Lorenzo.

"Lorenzo?" questioned Tallulah, as she examined the young man, who she thought was more a Ronald or a William, but never a Lorenzo. "How marvelously classical. Lorenzo!"

"I was named after a cat," said Lorenzo. "He was my mother's favorite pet when she was a child, if she was ever a child."

"Don't you like your mother, dahling?"

"I have to. She's my role model."

Mrs. Parker was trying to remember what country she was in and stayed silent. Tallulah turned to Mervyn. "So you're psychic."

"Yes. I can tell you a great deal about yourself, Miss Bankhead."

"Don't be presumptuous, young man, unless you prove to be amusing."

"I see you in another life."

"I've led many lives, dahling, not all of them mine."

"Many centuries ago, you were a very powerful Egyptian monarch. You had vast estates and were incredibly rich."

"Really? So where the hell's all the money now?"

"Devalued."

"Dottie, you're not paying attention."

"Where are we, dear?" asked Mrs. Parker sweetly. "And who are these four young gentlemen?"

"There are only two, dahling, and one of them's going to be an angel and get us a cab." Lorenzo volunteered. "And, dahling, there should be a detective waiting outside. Tell him we can all share the cab!" She smiled at Mervyn. "I must have you at one of my parties . . . um . . . what was your name again, dear?"

"Mervyn."

"Of course. Waiter! The bill!"

The waiter politely told her she'd already paid it.

"Oh, have I, dahling? Mervyn, would you

help me get Mrs. Parker out of here? Dottie, it's time for beddy-bye."

"Yes, dear, but where?"

While others were nursing hangovers the following morning, and still others were trying to solve murder cases, while Nanette Walsh pressed cold compresses against a bruise on her cheek and Mitchell Zang, lying in bed in Nance Liston's apartment, cursed all women and casting directors, a formidable woman of two hundred and some-odd pounds was letting herself into Barry Wren's town house. Annabel Forsythe, who had been given the option of living in or living out, had chosen out so as to spend some time with her common-law husband and four children, two of whom she was positive were his.

Annabel was in particularly good mood this morning. Today was the last time her man Ike would have to report to his parole officer (assault, petty theft, and fraud) and then he'd be free to go back to his old bad habits, which sometimes turned a neat profit. She was humming her favorite spiritual, "Ezekiel Saw the Wheel," while she went to the kitchen to see if there was any tidying up necessary from the night before. Mr. Wren was an immaculate choreographer and performer and an absolute slob. Annabel was positive the exterminator was sending his son through college on his earnings from Barry Wren.

There was no dirty dishes, no pots with charred bottoms, no spillages on the floor. Annabel frowned when she realized the oven was still lit. She'd left a stew for Barry Wren. She looked in the oven. He hadn't eaten any of it and the stew was just almost burned out. Annabel thought of the starving children of India and then decided "Fuck 'em," it's every kid for himself. She turned off the oven, used pot holders to transfer the stew to the sink, and then left it to soak in hot water and suds.

In the hallway, she could hear the television set blasting in Barry's bedroom. So he's up, good. Maybe he's getting out early and I can give that room a really good going-over. Annabel adored housework. She was to broom and rag what Michelangelo had been to brush and paint. She cleaned and scrubbed exquisitely, a jewel among semiprecious stones. One would be hard put to recognize her as one of the long-limbed cocoa-skinned showgirls who had paraded around the old Cotton Club in Harlem.

She entered the bedroom, where there was

no sign of Barry. Probably in the john. She crossed to the blaring television set and lowered the sound. If that annoyed Mr. Wren, who liked things noisy, she knew he'd yell, but there was no sound from the bathroom. She became absorbed in the old western on the screen. A weatherbeaten old fort was besieged by hordes of Indians. An army officer was frantically shouting. "There's Sioux and Chippewa and Iowas, and my God, all the Indian nations have assembled to attack us!" It was a very early talkie and his voice squeaked. "Look! There's Arapahos and Dakotas and Saginaws . . ."

His subordinate said, "There must be a Pawnee."

Annabel lost interest. She went to the bed to straighten it. It didn't need straightening. It hadn't been slept in. All she saw was Wren's knapsack. Funny, she thought, very funny. Maybe he'd slept in the guest room. The door to the bathroom was open and she now realized that Barry had positioned the television set so he would see the screen from the tub. Hands on hips, still humming, she entered the bathroom.

She didn't scream. She bent down and tried to lift Barry from the tub. She knew at once he was dead; she'd seen death often

224

enough. He was too heavy. The body slipped back into the tub. Annabel thought, as she hurried to the telephone, sheeee-it, now I've got to hunt me another position, and I might never find another one as cushy as this one. Sheeee-it, he never noticed how I screwed around the household accounts. The household money. It was kept in a jar in one of the kitchen closets. As soon as she dialed the police, she'd do the tidying up in the kitchen.

Now how the hell do you drown in a bathtub? she wondered. Oh well, let the fuzz figure that one out.

Detective Oscar Delaney, who had found Oliver Sholom's body, accompanied Jacob Singer and the other officers to Barry Wren's town house. He'd never been in a town house before. He'd heard about them and read about them and in the movies they were mostly occupied by Katharine Hepburn and Ronald Colman, but he never dreamt that he himself would set foot in one. Jacob Singer seemed very blasé about it, but then, Jacob Singer was a man of the world, or so Delaney was led to believe by some of the company he kept. Tallulah Bankhead. Dorothy Parker, whoever she was, Delaney being rather remiss where American literature was concerned. The mountain of a woman who opened the door guided them to the bath-room upstairs. Delaney marveled how some-one her size could bound up the stairs like an ibex hopping from alp to alp. Jacob Singer had said, "Bingo," when told Barry Wren's body had been discovered. Tallulah had claimed they die in threes and by golly here was the third.

Jacob was rather pleased with himself. He had figured the most likely candidate for third victim would be Barry Wren, though there'd always been the prospect of a dark-horse entrant. Delaney wondered why Singer was smiling. There was a dead body awaiting them, how could he be so cold-blooded? Singer was surprised to see the coronor had preceded them and was already busy with the body.

"How'd you get here so soon?" asked Jacob.

"Slow morning."

"So what have we got?"

"One dead dancer. Drowned."

"Accidental?" Singer was sure it was a foolish query, but he always had the same routine with coroners. It was like Abbott and Costello's "Who's on First"—tired, familiar, but expected.

"He's got bruises on his shoulders, and

unless he's been low man in a team of acrobats, he was held under water until he was dead."

From the doorway, Annabel told them she'd found the latch on one of the kitchen windows broken while tidying up down there. "Looks like it was jimmied to me," said Annabel knowledgeably. She was a jimmied window maven. Singer sent an officer to the kitchen to examine it.

Singer led Annabel back to the bedroom. "What's your name?"

"Annabel Forsythe." She smiled as she sat on the bed. "We're the North Carolina Forsythes."

Singer liked her at once. "When'd you last see Mr. Wren alive?"

"Yesterday morning when he went off to class. He teaches ballet and—"

Singer told her he was well aware of Barry Wren's celebrity.

Annabel told him, "He said he was going to be in last night and would I fix him some dinner and leave it in the oven, which I did. I fixed him my Stew Annabel, which is a recipe I got from an old admirer, my grandmother. I fixed enough for two in case he might invite someone to join him, he is . . . was . . . a very lonely person. I don't think he had any friends at all no more, well, at least not since he grassed to the Feds. You know what I mean."

"I know."

"The food wasn't touched. The oven was on when I got here, the stew and the pot a mess. I've got the pot soaking in the sink right now, except I suppose why bother?"

"Does he have any family?"

"I know he has a mother in the Bronx. I never heard him talk about anybody else. You'll find it in his book of phone numbers in the desk over there."

Singer found the phone book and little else of value or interest. Singer told Delaney to try to locate the mother and break the news before she heard it from the media. Reporters and photographers were already swarming around on the sidewalk waiting to get in, which they wouldn't until the police photographer and the others had finished their jobs. "Annabel, was he mixed up with anybody? Girlfriend, boyfriend?"

"No, sir, he freelanced, but there wasn't much of that lately. Mr. Wren, he was one frightened dude. The locks and bolts on the front door are brand-new. And he'd caution me to make sure every window was locked tight before I left. I think he knew his name was on somebody's list." She shrugged. "I heard what the man told you. Murdered. Well, I had no complaints. He was always good to me." She looked as if she expected additional questions, but Singer went instead to the telephone.

Tallulah had demolished her usual hangover breakfast of a pint of vanilla ice cream and a jug of vichysoisse sent over from "21," the club on West Fifty-second Street. Lewis Drefuss was with her, having arrived at the same time as the waiter from the club, and so made himself busy serving the ice cream and cold soup.

"Really, dahling, I don't know how Dottie does it and survives. I mean, dahling, how that woman can *drink!*" Lewis maintained a straight face with difficulty. "I mean I gave up counting the Jack Roses when she switched to brandy, and then stingers, my dear, stingers, I mean what's more lethal than stingers God this vichysoisse is hitting the spot and that psychic who told me I was an Egyptian somebody once upon a time how old do you think Mabel Mercer is?"

The phone came to Lewis's rescue. Hand over the mouthpiece, he asked Tallulah, "Do you want to speak to Jacob Singer?"

"Isn't everybody an early bird this morning? As you know, I can never sleep more than a few hours but I mean here's you at this hour and where do you get all that energy though I suppose at your age what's the trick and I suppose the Bobbsey Twins will descend on me any moment now and do you wonder why Patsy screeches so much it must be hereditary Good morning Jacob dahling so bright and early to what do I attribute the honor?" She listened. "Oh my God no! My God no! Drowned in his own bathtub. Stewed so to speak in his own juices. Are you sure it's murder? I'll bet the murderer hoped it would look like an accident. Maybe tripped in the tub, hit his head, knocked himself out, and drowned." She let Jacob talk, briefly. "Ha-ha-ha-ha-ha! What? Oh, dahling, how clever of you to remember!" To Lewis she said, "All showbiz deaths come in threes and I predicted there'd be a third and by God here it is, how thoughtful of Barry Wren I hope the wretch is frying in hell. What, dahling? I'm talking to Lewis Drefuss. He arrived early to harass me. Actually, we're going to record Sunday's program this afternoon, so now I'm free on Sunday which is a blessing, No, dahling, I never go to church, I have it sent in, Ha-ha-

230

ha-ha-ha. What?" She listened while spooning some vichysoisse. "I should think whoever held him under the water must possess a great deal of strength." She playfully squeezed Lewis's arm. He resisted the desire to jerk his arm away. "I suppose that eliminates any woman suspect, unless he was done in by Cheryl Crawford. What? No, I don't want any more bodyguards. The ones I have are enough. I need more protection like Eleanor Powell needs more teeth. Yes, dahling, by all means go back to your sleuthing. I must call Dottie at once and tell her. What, dahling?" She was raptly attentive. "You're joking! Is Zang still in the pokey? The poor bastard, I'm glad they let him go, he's such a loser. But, Jacob, I've heard he has a history of abusing women. I don't know Nanette Walsh"—she almost added "yet"—"but all my sympathy's with her. Thanks for telling me, dahling, and oh, dahling, wait . . . wait . . . about what time was Barry Wren murdered?" She listened. "Well then, dahling, you'd better start checking up on alibis. Goodbye, dahling." She handed the phone to Lewis, who placed it in the cradle and polished off the rest of the cold soup.

After a few seconds of meditation, she said, "I suppose that conversation with Mr.

231

Singer sounded somewhat cold-blooded to you."

"I don't think anything of the sort. It's a shock to hear there's been another murder and that it's Barry Wren. I didn't know you had bodyguards. Why should you be in danger?"

"Didn't you, dahling? I thought you did. I thought you gathered that yesterday when I . . . oh, the hell with it, it doesn't matter. I'm in danger because I'm supposed to perhaps know something and I'll be damned if I can remember what it is I'm supposed to know. Bit of a Chinese puzzle, isn't it, dahling, you were too young to have seen me in one of my Paramount fiascos *The Cheat* in which I played the mistress of a Chinese sadist who brands me with an iron and that was Sessue Hayakawa who is Japanese which is typical of Hollywood and he and his wife were so sweet I hope they survived Hiroshima though God knows what they would have been doing in Hiroshima and Dottie oh God yes I must phone Dottie be a dear Lewis and tell the operator to get Dottie at her hotel, she'll know the number she's dialed it often enough what time's the runthrough before the recording and God I'll never be able to get through that duet with Merman . . ."

Three hours later while Tallulah was at the studio for the rehearsal and runthrough, Barry Wren's murder was the lead topic on coast-to-coast newscasts. At the Golden Cinema Memorabilia Shop, while helping a customer locate the Marjorie Weaver file, Joseph Savage heard the news on the radio and felt lightheaded. He wondered if anyone had seen him near Barry Wren's house the night before. The newscaster didn't say what time Wren had been murdered, only that he'd been murdered last night. Maybe somebody who'd been on the Fifth Avenue bus last night would remember him. One of the part-time employees, a young woman named Lorena Duncan who was taking night classes at New York University in filmography and would two decades later be running a major Hollywood studio, asked if he felt ill.

"What? What? Do I look ill?"

"You've turned white as a ghost."

"I didn't get much sleep last night. I'm working on a new play." He told her about the Bankhead job, and she was pleased at his good news and congratulated him.

"Look, Joe, it's not busy right now. Why don't you go in the back and lie down on the cot for a while?"

"No, no, I'm fine. I'm fine." He stared at an eight-by-ten glossy of Henry Armetta he didn't remember picking up. *I'm just dandy. Last night I predicted to myself Barry Wren would be the next murder victim. I'm just dandy.*

Gabriel Darnoff was having a perfectly awful day. He didn't know which was worse, the unanimous verdict of the newspaper critics that his new play was positively dreadful, or the news of Barry Wren's murder. This early in the afternoon, still wearing his bathrobe, still not shaved or bathed, drinking his seventh cup of unsweetened black coffee, seated in a wing chair and puffing on a cigarillo, he was plagued by the memory of having been near Barry Wren's house the previous night. He'd left the theater when the curtain went up and hadn't returned until it was about to come down. *Would anyone believe that all he did during those three hours was walk? Of course not. Oh, Poppa, did you have to commit suicide? Because of you I'm a murder suspect. A murder suspect.*

He paced the room. *Murder suspect. Through circumstances beyond his control, a man becomes a murder suspect, and what's more, there's every likelihood he did the* killings. Say, that's not a bad idea. Wait a minute. Wait a minute. Maybe it should be a woman. It might be just right for Tallulah. So what if she's getting a bit long in the tooth, she's still a draw and she could use a hit badly. They could all use a hit badly. Gabriel Darnoff could use a hit . . .

His mother was on the phone. "A black curse on all the critics! They should grow like onions with their heads in the ground. But at least every cloud has a silver lining, my sweet child. Barry Wren is murdered! Such a mitzvah! Your father must be dancing in heaven!"

Gabriel smiled, "Mama, I hope for your sake there's a life after death, so you'll be reunited with Poppa."

"Gabriel darling, if there's a life after death, he's remarried."

Mitchell Zang flung a vase and it crashed against a wall and shattered into dangerous-looking fragments. What kind of a life is this? How much longer do I go on this way? Bit parts, walk-ons, rejection upon rejection, no friends, no woman to pay my bills, and now that bedbug Wren has to go and get himself murdered. I wonder if he was killed when they were holding me at the station, or when I was with Nanette—that fucking whore; I'm not through with her. Not by a long shot. Christ, the way those cops tackled me and held my arms twisted behind my back, I could have been crippled for life. I should have broken her nose. I should have stomped on her and broken her ribs. Damn it! Why didn't I wreck the bust of Abner Walsh she's working on, that would have served her right. He prowled around the room searching, searching for something left to hock. The pawn shop on Broadway had a window chockablock with all of Nance Liston's redeemables; there couldn't possibly be anything left in the apartment. Maybe he could sell the furniture, but that could get him into a heap of trouble he didn't need. Maybe . . .

Just maybe there was a way to get Tallulah Bankhead interested in him. He'd heard she went for younger guys. She had money. She was always picking up the tab. Nance told him she was always giving money to friends. Maybe I'll call her up, he thought, tell her there's something Nance wanted her to have and maybe I could bring it around and maybe we'll have a drink and then maybe dinner and later a little kadiddle from which she'll barely recover I'll be so sensational and then

. . . He stopped. Does one dare take a sock at Tallulah Bankhead?

The phone interrupted his fantasy. It was George Baxt, the agent.

Baxt was never very good at disguising the loathing in his voice, so he was quick. "Marion Dougherty has a bit on next Wednesday's Kraft, a longshoreman—believe it or not, it's over five lines, two hundred and twenty-five. They'll only need you the two days before air time. Are you free?" Is he free? The beast should be on exhibit in the Bronx Zoo or in a jar in a laboratory.

Zang's heart sang. Rescue was at hand. He wheedled a fifty-dollar advance from Baxt. He'd be in his office in an hour to get it.

"You know what I'd like to serve Mitchell Zang?" Baxt told his secretary. "A poisoned prostitute."

David Carney looked at himself in the mirror in his bedroom. There was pride in his voice as he said to his image, "You're aces, kid! You're right up there with the best of them! Barry Wren! Now he's *really* the big time. Oh, you can't really sniff at Lester Miroff and Oliver Sholom, they weren't so famous, but still . . . you shouldn't be so modest, Davey."

"You shouldn't be so modest," Elsa Carney had said to him when he sold his first short story. "That's what it's all about, isn't it, when you've got talent? Success, money, adulation . . . !"

Fine talk, he thought at the time, coming from a left-winger who promoted a philosophy of share the wealth. Well, she and Isaac certainly shared in his. Oh, to hell with them. They're always haunting me. They're so damned pushy. Why didn't they do something about that awful acne when I was a kid, leaving me with these ugly pockmarks? Why didn't they get me the plastic surgery they were always talking about? The hell with them. The hell with everybody.

Aloud to his reflection in the mirror, he inquired while rubbing his hands together in greedy expectation, "Now who shall I kill next?"

THIRTEEN

ARMBRUSTER PERSHING was not your everyday run-of-the-mill theatrical attorney. Although he represented a fair share of show-business heavyweights, he kept his own profile as low as celebrity could permit. Saving Ted Valudni from the threat of foreclosure on his career was a matter of one phone call to Washington, D.C., and then agreeing to a bargain that satisfied both parties. But here Armbruster Pershing was facing a perplexing dilemma. How, Ted Valudni asked him, how do I prevent a killer from using me as a target? Who do I call for protection? On the afternoon of Tallulah's recording, Valudni phoned Pershing from the apartment he hadn't ventured from in two days. Fear had immobilized him. Not only was he a possible victim, on Jacob Singer's list he was a possible perpetrator. His defected wife Beth was no comfort whatsoever. To add insult to injury, within two days of decamping, she was already at work doing a sketch with Tallulah. After years of retirement, she sallies forth and conquers. Hell, luck was always on Beth's side. She was lucky she'd married Ted and shared his success and wealth and position, instead of marrying the novelist she was engaged to when Ted first met her. He was one of those writers who wrote tender little tales about growing up in the Deep South with his wonderful mammy who called him "my own little chile" and his grandpa

239

who took him fishin' (barefoot, of course) and his Uncle Jizzum who drank sumthin' fierce, and there were characters with names like Jenny Bess, and Cora Belle and Bobby Jack and of course a dog named Yeller. The writer had a small but loyal following and was popular in remainder, but he never made a dime worth envying.

"Beth," Ted said to her when he tracked her down at the studio during a break, "how can you throw twenty years of marriage out the window?"

"It's easy."

"What's happened to you?" he yelled. "When did you become so callous? My life is in danger and it means nothing to you?"

"Is the insurance paid up?"

"I see. It boils down to that. I never dreamt the day would come when I'd say I have no one left to turn to."

"Or to turn in."

"It's not enough you have mortally wounded me with a stab wound, do you have to twist the hilt?"

"Teddy, who are you kidding? Do you think I didn't know about all your affairs?" He was staring at the telephone with loathing. Even the telephone had turned on him. "Do you think I don't know about the hidden bank accounts in Martinique and Montenegro?" She was watching Tallulah deep in conversation with Lewis Drefuss and wondering what was wrong. Now Tallulah was having one of her coughing fits, a beaut. Ethel Merman was rehearsing at the top of her lungs; her pianist wore earmuffs and an angelic smile. Beth said into the mouthpiece, "For years since you made it big in Hollywood, our marriage has been a one-sided secret controlled by you. Teddy, darling, I'm no longer a marionette. I've seen my lawyer and he'll be in touch with Pershing. And Ted"—it was a tone of voice he recognized, the dangerous one: Plead and cajole as he might, there was no hope of appeasing her— "don't be stingy."

After she hung up, she went in search of the container of coffee she had deposited on somebody's work table. Tallulah was lighting a Craven A while coughing, and waved Beth over. "Who was that on the phone? You look as though you've been invited to a funeral."

"It was Ted."

"That says it all, dahling."

"I suppose I should be feeling sorry for him. He's frightened."

"As well he should be, dahling. I'm sur-

241

prised he's still among the living, what with the rise in the mortality rate among his sort. Probably with his luck the murderer's beginning to get bored with all this activity. Perhaps what we've been experiencing is a sudden outburst of hyperthyroid activity. Which reminds me, where's my watchdog? Oh, there he is, dahling, isn't he attractive, near the water cooler, the large man yawning."

Beth agreed Adam Todd was attractive. Then she was caught off guard by Tallulah's next question.

"Beth, strictly between us girls, you know Ted better than any of us. Could he be committing these murders?"

"But, Tallulah, he's turned the apartment into a fortress. He hasn't left it since the murders began."

"How do you know?"

"He told me."

"He could tell you anything he likes. Do you always believe it?"

"Believe me, Tallulah, Ted is frightened. He was never a good actor."

"I know lots of actors who were never very good and then all of a sudden they give a masterful performance from out of nowhere. Well, Jacob Singer says the staff haven't seen him come or go for the past forty-eight hours. Of course there could be ways he knows of getting in or out without being detected."

"Why are you so positive the killer's a man?"

Merman was doing her vocal exercises and they heard a glass break.

"Dahling, a very strong woman had to hold Barry Wren under water and bash Oliver Sholom's head to pulp. I don't know anyone right for the part, do you?"

"Hope Emerson."

"Oh, God, dahling, aren't you divine! Ha-ha-ha! Hope Emerson! Wasn't she divine as the warden in *Caged?* That marvelous moment when she phones her boyfriend and says seductively"—she did a superb imitation of Emerson's voice—"Hellooooo, Thornnnntonnn . . ." She ran her fingers through her thick mane of hair. "Oh, God, when are we going to get to record this bloody show? Lewis, is it me you're signaling?"

"Mrs. Parker's on the phone."

"Excuse me, Beth." She went to Lewis and took the phone. "Dottie, dahling, don't tell me you're just getting up!"

"Tallulah, dear, I've been thinking, you've got to do something about your drinking."

Armbruster Pershing took his fourth phone call of the day from Ted Valudni. He listened to the frantic man and then advised him, "You can't leave town, Ted. Not without the police's permission."

"Oh, screw the police!" Valudni was celebrated for his nasty temper and uncontrollable displays of anger, and now he was in pique condition. "They can't force me to stay here! They've got nothing on me! I've got to be in Hollywood for meetings—"

"That's a month off."

"So I go early! I need to find a place to live, don't I?"

"Skipping town could be interpreted as an admission of guilt."

"Whose side are you on, anyway?"

Pershing was the soul of patience. "You pay me for advice and I'm advising you. Don't leave town. Don't even think of it. I could drop in for a drink around six-thirty or so if you like? I prefer reasoning this face to face."

Ted pouted. "Well, yes, that would be nice. Do you mind stopping in at Gristede's and picking me up some lamb chops, a container of milk, a container of orange juice, a loaf of rye bread, a couple of cans of Bumble Bee white-meat tuna, and a box of Ebinger's chocolate-covered whole-wheat doughnuts . . ."

As Pershing listened, he stared out the window, his cheeks puffed out and his head shaking, not from palsy but from disbelief. Why, he wondered, why hadn't he listened to his father and gone into animal husbandry?

In his office at the precinct, Jacob Singer reread the autopsy report on Barry Wren. The murderer should have waited and let fate do the job for him. Wren had an advanced cancer of the colon. According to the coroner, the best he could have hoped for was another year, give or take a month, so in being murdered last night, he really wasn't missing much. Oliver Delaney had been assigned to round up the usual suspects and Gabriel Darnoff was the first to be announced. Singer knew his play was a bomb, Dorothy Parker having read him *The New York Times* review with great relish: "His earlier plays were written with lightning. Last night's offering has to be the work of a limp strand of spaghetti."

"I don't have an alibi," said Darnoff, blunt

and to the point and winning Singer's admiration.

"In my book, Mr. Darnoff, that scores points for you. No karfuffling around, no looking at the fly specks on the ceiling, no hostility—you didn't even bring your lawyer."

"He's a bore."

"You weren't at the theater last night?"

"No. Wasn't I lucky?"

"The audience wasn't."

"Score points for you."

"Dorothy Parker read me the notices."

"She read them to me, too."

Singer smiled. "So what are you going to tell me?"

"I left the theater when the curtain went up, and in between the curtain coming down, when I returned, I walked miles and miles and miles. I walked the length and breadth of New York City. I didn't drop into a bar for a drink or sit on a bench in the park and I was somewhere near Barry Wren's house at some point and I don't remember murdering him. Anyway, I read how he was killed and if I had done it, I can assure you I would have been drenched with bath water because I'm a very sloppy person and my clothes would have been very damp when I returned to the theater."

"The murderer could have stripped off his clothes before the murder and then put them back on after the job was done."

"Gee, I wish I had an alibi."

"Me too. I don't think playwrights should be murderers. They have so much other *tsurris* to put up with."

"You've met my mother."

"How's she bearing up?"

"Pop's suicide was a blow, but she's strong peasant stock. She'll remarry."

"You were very close to your father."

"I worshiped him."

"He was a brilliant actor. I'll never forget his *Lear*."

"That isn't why I worshiped him." Singer looked at the playwright and realized he was fighting tears. Singer didn't hurry him. "It's funny, Mr. Singer, I can put emotions down on paper, but when it comes to verbalizing them, I'm tongue-tied. I can't explain my feelings for my father. I can only say that he was never not supportive, that he never allowed me to accept defeat, that he taught me to be kind to my fellow man and to very bad actors who have to be fired out of town. He taught me not to throw sticks at dogs and to view those less fortunate, such as theater critics and those who denounce their friends to save their own skins, with a philosophical 'There but for the Grace of God go I.' He never let me wallow in self-pity, and he wanted his epitaph to read, 'I hope I'm not too early.' " He sat back in his chair and applied a match to a cigarillo. "I'll never forgive the robbers who stole him from me. So that's all I've got to tell you. I could have phoned it in."

"I learn more looking at you while you're talking. Tell me, Mr. Darnoff, were you ever an actor?"

Five minutes later, Gabriel Darnoff was replaced by Joseph Savage, who kept lacing his fingers together and then unlacing them. Singer said to him, "There were an awful lot of people out taking long walks last night."

"I have no reason to lie to you, Mr. Singer. That's exactly what I was doing. I had a lot of thinking to do, and I think best on my feet. You see, a very nice lady handed me some hope yesterday." He told him about the commission from Tallulah to write a play.

Singer said, "That is a very nice thing for a very nice lady to do. In fact, it's a thumb in the eye to the committee. You know they're out to nail her."

"Everybody knows." He laughed.

"So she hires a blacklisted writer to write her a play. Did you come up with an idea?"

"Yes, thank God. Please don't ask me to tell you what it is. I consider it bad luck to discuss a work in progress."

"It's also bad luck to get murdered in a bathtub. I don't suppose at some point you were in the vicinity of Wren's town house."

"I'm sorry to say I was."

"About what time?"

"I don't know. I'm sorry this isn't London. I might have heard Big Ben chime."

Singer hoped he'd write better jokes for Tallulah.

"I did take the Fifth Avenue bus home, if that's any help."

"You're the one who needs the help, Mr. Savage. I suppose you can't remember what time that was either."

"Well, it was latish."

"How latish?"

"Maybe after ten or so."

"Do you remember what number bus you took?"

"I live in the Village, so it would have to be one of the two buses that go down to Eighth Street."

"Do you suppose somebody might remember seeing you on the bus?"

"I doubt it. I'm always well behaved in public."

Joseph Savage gladly gave way to David Carney. "Been behaving yourself, David?" asked Singer, watching Carney sitting and rubbing the palms of his hands back and forth on his thighs."

"I've been behaving as usual. A murder here, a murder there."

"Who'd you murder last night?"

"I don't have to tell you, you know that. I murdered Barry Wren."

"How did you murder him?"

"It's in the papers. Don't you read the papers? That was a very nice picture of you in the *Mirror*. You look like John Wayne. Who was that big black lady with you?"

"My mistress. David, I want you to tell me how you murdered Barry Wren."

"You're sure it won't bore you?"

"Not at all. I've read Evelyn Waugh and survived."

"I think Waugh is hell."

"This is a police station, David, not the New School. Tell me how you murdered Barry Wren."

Carney was beginning to get agitated. "I drowned him, for God's sake."

"How did you drown him?"

"With my hands, how else?"

"You don't have to shout."

"You don't have to be so dense!"

Singer held up his hands. "Truce, David, truce."

"Indeed. Truce or consequences."

"You mustn't threaten me, David."

"I don't threaten, I act."

Bingo, thought Singer. He doesn't threaten, he acts. "So you didn't make those phone threats to Lester Miroff and Miss Bankhead?"

"Her! I'd like to wring her neck. I'd like to tie her to a post and shoot arrows into her! She's a mean, rotten, despicable liar." He examined a fingernail. "She's tragic. She's afraid to grow old. That's why she won't do my play, which I'm sure she never read. Old actresses don't like to do plays about old actresses."

"So why write them?"

Carney drew himself up haughtily. "An artist must follow the dictates of his muse. Anyway, I'm no longer writing plays."

"What are you doing instead?"

"I'm murdering people, you nitwit, doesn't *anything* sink in?"

"Don't be abusive, David."

"You better watch your step, mister. You don't want to get on my list."

"Who's next on your list, David?"

With hands on hips he said, "That's for me to know and you to find out!"

"Pretty please?"

"Pretty please my ass!"

After Carney left, Oscar Delaney, who'd overheard it all, came into the office with an indescribable expression on his face and asked Singer, "You are letting that nutcase loose? You aren't putting him in a straitjacket and throwing him in a cell at Bellevue and conveniently losing the key?"

Singer was sitting with his head in his hands, weary. "Oscar, there's no way I can put him away legally. We could have held him yesterday when he had at Bankhead in the zoo, but he never touched her. There were witnesses. And fiddle-dee-dee, I'm too tired to think about it. Oscar?"

"What?"

"Why did they name you Oscar?"

"There was an actor named Oscar Apfel my mother admired and—"

"That's enough, Oscar. Who's waiting?"

252

"Last night's star attraction in a return appearance by popular demand. I wish he'd buy himself a new beret."

Mitchell Zang came bouncing into the room. "Gee, I've had some great news!"

"I wish I did," said Singer.

"I'm starring on a Kraft Theater in a couple of weeks. Terrific script. And what a supporting cast. John Newland, John Baragrey, John Fiedler—"

"That's an awful lot of Johns."

"—and Reba Tassell."

"What an anticlimax. Okay, Zang, you know why you're here. Where were you last night?"

"Right here! You saw me yourself!"

"That was in the wee hours. Where were you before you exercised your fists on Mrs. Walsh?"

"Like what time?"

"Like about when Barry Wren was playing bathing beauty."

"What time was that?"

Mitchell Zang was big and easily twenty years younger than Singer, but the detective knew he could deck the son of a bitch with one well-aimed and well-timed blow. He resisted the temptation, but he promised himself that someday, in the very near future, he would find a reason to let Mitchell Zang provoke him.

"It was sometime between nine and ten."

"I was having a drink at the Circus Bar."

Too quick, thought Singer. He said, "That's an actor's hangout on West Forty-fifth, right?"

"Just off Eighth, before the Imperial Theater."

And long after the Renaissance. "Witnesses?"

"Well, gee, I don't know. It was so crowded."

Jacob fixed him with a devastating look. "Mitchell, the Circus Bar does not come to life until after eleven o'clock, when working actors and footsore gypsies who can afford the price of a beer converge there. So don't give me any of your bullshit. Be honest with me and I'll believe you're starring on a TV show."

The interview lasted another fifteen minutes. Zang might be an idiot, but he was a genius at double-talk. He had no alibi was what it all boiled down to. Singer threatened him with deportation.

"But I'm a citizen!" protested Zang.

"I'll find the loophole."

Zang left, mentally wrecked. Ted Valudni

entered with Armbruster Pershing. Oliver Delaney had to bring in another chair. After the other two were seated, he thought that if Singer tried to squeeze a fourth into the office, he'd have to use KY. Valudni wore a Trilby hat and a long trailing scarf around his neck that partially concealed the lower part of his face.

"We meet at last, Mr. Valudni," said Singer. "I trust you're over the flu you've been pleading the past two times you've been asked to make an appearance."

"I will not be victimized! I will not tolerate police brutality! You know I'm endangering my life by appearing here! This is my attorney, Armbruster Pershing. Tell him, Armbruster!"

"What do you want me to tell him?"

"Why do I pay you!"

"Gentlemen," said Singer, "peace. You were with Mr. Valudni, Mr. Pershing, when I sent the officer to pick him up?"

"Yes, wasn't that convenient?"

Singer was surprised that he had such an honest face; it was so rare in lawyers.

"Why haven't I been given police protection?"

Singer loathed Valudni. He even hated himself for having liked some of Valudni's pictures. What was worse, he hated himself for having paid to see them.

"Mr. Valudni," said Singer with exaggerated patience, "if everybody in this city who thought they needed protection were given protection, the city would go broke before the weekend. I appreciate your bravery in coming here. Where were you last night between nine and ten?"

"I was at home cowering with fear."

"Why? You saw a mouse?"

"Three friends of mine were murdered—"

"How'd you know about the third then?"

"I didn't! Well, you know what I mean!"

"No, I don't, tell me."

"Well, these murders have me petrified. I'm not a brave man, I can't afford to be one."

"I know. I read your testimony."

Valudni was deflated. Pershing said to Singer, "My client feels threatened and I'm sure you understand why he does. These murders have a pattern in which he could fit and that's why he's afraid to leave his house."

"He'd be safer in public. Barry Wren had locks and bolts and a fat lot of good it did him. Mr. Valudni, you got a back door?"

"Of course I have a back door, for deliveries, for people you wouldn't admit through your front door."

"And you were a communist?"

"You're harassing me! Armbruster, do I have to put up with this?"

Pershing said, "Tell the man what you did, and then I think he'll let you go home."

"Why must he harp on things like my back door!"

"I'm sitting right here, Valudni, you don't have to keep referring to me in the third person! You're not on the back lot at Twentieth directing Marlon Brando!"

Valudni asked gently, "What about my back door?"

"It can be easily jimmied and broken into and you could be murdered in your living room, and the way you've got yourself barricaded in, nobody would know you're dead until some neighbor smelled your decay. Was anyone with you last night?"

"No, I was alone. But I never left the apartment. I can prove it! Ask the night staff! The doorman."

"How many doormen are there?"

"How many do we need? There's just one door."

"So there's just one doorman. Does he have eyes in the back of his head?"

"I never look at the back of his head."

"He'd have to have eyes there to see what's going on if he's helping somebody in or out of a cab, wouldn't he? You could slip past him then, couldn't you?"

"I didn't!"

"You could go out your back door and down the service elevator and out through the alley that leads to the next street."

"I didn't!"

"What did you do?"

"I told you. I stayed at home, frightened. Well, I did watch a movie I did when I was an actor a long time ago with—"

"Oh, cut the horseshit, Valudni. You had every reason to murder those three guys. Each one of them put you in the hot seat, if I have to say so myself, it's justifiable homicide. Now come on, Valudni, confess." Pershing wanted to laugh, but didn't dare. "If you confess, I can go have dinner with Tallulah Bankhead instead of being here with you, which I wish I wasn't." He said to Pershing, "No offense."

"None taken."

"So I bid you good night, gentlemen," he said while glaring at Valudni, "and I use the term gentlemen advisedly."

258

Tallulah Bankhead was examining the numbers on Nanette Walsh's carriage house. The recording of her Sunday program had gone smoothly, which was a blessing, and she was free sooner than she had expected. She thought the carriage house adorable. So this is where a sculptor sculpts, and also gets a sock in the face from a part-time lover. *Chacun* et cetera. She walked to the door and put her hand on the knocker.

Here I am, dahling, Tallulah Bankhead as Caesar about to cross the Rubicon.

FOURTEEN

SHE COULD hear the sound of the knocker resounding from within while inside her head her private phonograph was playing the Quaalude in C-sharp Minor. She had downed enough tranquilizers that day to drug a football squad. She attacked the knocker again. Nanette Walsh had agreed to see her at six and it was six and Tallulah was punctual, which called for a historical plaque to be affixed to the building. From the corner of her right eye she could see a subtle movement at the window and then the corner of a drape falling back into place. Tallulah knocked again. Come on, dahling, stop trying for an effect, this isn't opportunity, it's Tallulah.

The door opened. The handsome woman with badly disguised bruises on her face smiled without opening her mouth. "Well, Tallulah, we meet again."

Tallulah pushed the door aside and swept past Nanette into the impressively oversized room. "We've met before, dahling? You'll have to forgive me, my memory's a sieve. When did we meet?"

Nanette shut the door and shot its bolt into place. I suppose bolts are now the fashion, thought Tallulah, thanks to some nuts. "With Abner at some parties, a long time ago."

"Dahling, in my life a long time ago is this morning."

"Can I get you a drink?"

"Not too soon. A very dry vodka martini with lots of rocks."

"Lemon peel? Olive? Onions?"

"No fruit, dahling. Too much acid." Nanette went to the bar and Tallulah gave the room her own special brand of microscopic examination. Her house in Bedford Village, decorated by an aspiring young man who worshiped at her throne, Tallulah de-

260

scribed as being decorated in early acolyte. Nanette's studio she would describe as decorated in passé Bohemia. It was the sort of Greenwich Village decor Tallulah would have admired in 1920, when she was still young and impressionable. Velvet drapes hung from a balcony and lacked only Douglas Fairbanks Senior swooping down, brandishing a saber and flashing his grand-piano teeth while laughing with devil-may-care insouciance, a memory courtesy of his film *The Black Pirate*. There was much agonizing in the subjects of the paintings hung scatter fashion on the walls. Käthe Kollwitz-type women and children with their mouths open, presumably caught in mid-howl, and she suspected at least one of them might be an authentic Kollwitz, a legacy from Abner Walsh. Kollwitz would have been his taste.

There was even a grand piano, may God have mercy, and thrown across it a somewhat beautiful Spanish shawl. On the piano were a number of autographed photographs of friends and celebrities. Among these were George Gershwin, Igor Stravinsky, Max Ernst, Salvador Dali, Jacob Epstein, and Zelma O'Neil. The furniture was large and overstuffed and in need of a cleaning. What did impress Tallulah was the magnificent skylight two stories overhead, under which in center spot was Nanette's work in progress, the bust of Abner Walsh. This was really good, and Tallulah said so. Nanette thanked her with appropriate modesty as she gave her the martini. Tallulah sipped it and complimented Nanette again, whereupon Nanette thanked her once more with a tone of ersatz affection that caused Tallulah to remind herself only two letters separated affection from affectation.

"Now, Tallulah," said Nanette as she sank onto an ottoman and crossed her legs, revealing the trim ankles of which she was justly proud, "shall we stop beating around the bush?"

"Of course, dahling." She positioned herself on the sofa, martini in the left hand, blazing Craven A in the right. "It's so pointless not to come to the point."

"You're here for information involving the murders."

"Dahling, you are clever, so precious and prescient."

"I had nothing to do with them."

"I didn't think you did, except indirectly." She indicated Nanette's bruised face with a gentle wave of a hand. "I assume those are the legacies left you by Mr. Zang. Dahling, you'd do better to use Max Factor eight. It does wonders for bruises and miracles for black eyes. I got that tip from Mayo Methot." She provided in an aside, "Bogart's penultimate wife."

Nanette, who hadn't poured herself a drink, changed her mind. She went to the bar and mixed a rye and ginger ale, the type of concoction that was known to send Tallulah into a fit of the vapors, she found it that noxious. "The police can tell you more about that rat fink Zang than I can."

"Don't be so modest, dahling. It's Leo Walsh I'm interested in."

"Wouldn't he love to hear that? He never generated much interest from anyone other than his parents."

"Then you know where he is?"

"I know he's in New York."

Tallulah leaned forward. "Are you sure?"

"Do you want a blood oath?"

"No, dahling, there's been enough bloodshed lately. Where can I find Leo?"

"I haven't the vaguest. My attachment to the name Walsh began with Abner and ended there. I never met his first wife and the boy because I didn't want to and I never wanted to and no, I was never curious about them. When Abner left them for me, they were out

263

in Arizona and that was twenty years ago. I suppose you know what Arizona was all about."

"More or less."

"That, I must say, was a horror story."

Good God, thought Tallulah, a glimmer of heart.

Nanette interpreted Tallulah's look correctly. "I'm not a cold-blooded person, Tallulah. I'm not the wicked other woman who stole Abner from Martha while she was off somewhere nursing their badly injured son. I'm sure you don't picture me as the siren of the Rhine sitting on a rock combing my blonde tresses while luring sailors to their doom in song."

"Hardly, dahling, that's a role more suited to Carol Channing."

"Abner did the chasing. He came after me. I was young, I was just getting started, I'd sold my first piece for fifty dollars and thought I was a millionaire. I met Abner at a vernissage—"

"Verna who, dahling? I mean I remember vaguely some film actress named Verna Hillie . . ."

"Vernissage is a preview of an art exhibit. Why, I'm surprised, Tallulah, you're such a woman of the world."

"Only this world, dahling. Now let's not interrupt ourselves."

"Abner was headed for the top. He had records and a radio program and offers from Hollywood and I was giddy from his attention. I didn't know a thing about Martha and Leo until I was so thoroughly hooked by Abner, so completely in love with him, that when he finally told me, I didn't give a damn. I wanted Abner and I got him."

"Bravo, dahling. Men are such fools and we girls adore fooling them, I keep telling myself. Abner divorced Martha right away?"

"Not fast enough to suit me. He went to Arizona to break it to Martha, and of course when he saw the boy, body encased in plaster, face covered with bandages"—she walked slowly to the piano, posing dramatically against it, reminding Tallulah of Helen Gahagan in *Tonight or Never*—"he almost canceled the divorce."

"I'm glad to hear that. I'd hate to think he was a total shit."

"You're another one who thinks Abner deserving of sainthood. Let me tell you, Tallulah, Abner wore his halo at a rakish angle."

"I know, dahling, I know. But he did leave them, that's history."

"Martha didn't make it easy for him. She buried him in guilt and whatever else she could use as a weapon."

"Especially Leo."

"Leo hated my guts. Hates my guts."

"Are you sure? He's older now, possibly wiser . . ." Probably a homicidal maniac, so watch out, Nanette.

"You knew Martha, didn't you?"

"She had her suicide note hand-delivered to me."

"Did you like her?"

"When she wasn't dwelling on the past. Other people's yesterdays bore me. I didn't see much of her after the divorce. She seemed to have disappeared into poverty."

"Poverty, my ass!" Tallulah thought she might have prudently alluded to a less spectacular part of her anatomy. "Abner sent her a check every month on the dot, a very generous sum. It was when she got back from the West Coast that she did her Little Match Girl bit, moving into that basement apartment to the accompaniment of 'Heart and Flowers.' "

"Leo moved back with her?" Something was nagging at Tallulah, something to do with that piece of hidden information she couldn't dislodge from her bank of memory.

266

"No, Leo went to Los Angeles. That was about ten years ago. He was twenty, I think Abner said, I'm so vague about dates." Happily, she wasn't vague about the Walshes. "They'd stayed in Arizona for a very long time, while Leo was an outpatient. He had to have years of therapy to restore the use of his body, numerous plastic operations."

"Meaning it was hell on earth for him." Poor little bastard, thought Tallulah, that kind of experience could unhinge anyone.

Nanette sighed and then mixed fresh drinks. She was glad Tallulah was there. She dreaded being alone in the house. She feared Mitchell Zang, even though the police had warned him away from her, and she dreaded the murderer, and worse, she dreaded her own company. "Strangely enough, Leo didn't bear his father any animosity. They corresponded regularly. Leo wrote poetry and short stories. They were young poems, young stories, but they were filled with love and hope. He'd always send a note with them, 'When this you see, remember me.' "

"I can see he was not about to be forgotten." He's certainly memorable today. "Abner must have told you what Leo was up to in Los Angeles."

"Oh yes, he went there to try his hand at acting."

"Really!"

"Abner sent him to Barry Wren and what's his name the director . . ."

"Oliver Sholom?"

"Oliver Sholom. He got him introductions to some others. Lester Miroff . . . let me think . . . Eddie Dmytryk . . . Albert Dekker . . . Gustav Von Seyffertitz . . ."

"Is that a name or a condition?"

"Leo didn't do too well there as an actor. I don't think he used many of those contacts. Abner said he was shy, he behaved as though the plastic surgery hadn't completely rehabilitated his looks at all. Abner had this picture of him . . ."

Tallulah was on her feet. "Where is it? Where's this picture?"

Nanette was afraid Tallulah would spring at her. "I . . . I . . . I . . ." she stammered, "I packed it along with Abner's other things I put in storage."

"You must get me that picture!"

"But it's in storage!"

"Well, you can get to it, can't you? You can call the storage people and tell them you need to find it. I'm sure they'll be most cooperative! Nanette, it is essential we get

268

that photograph for the police." She colored her voice dramatically to underline the urgency for Nanette. "Dahling, Leo Walsh could be the murderer." Nanette's hand flew to her throat, reminding Tallulah of Elissa Landi in *The Yellow Ticket*. "You say he's here, here in New York, and we must find him. Right now he could be the invisible man moving among us and murdering the people who betrayed his father. Leo's lost Abner, he's lost Martha, the two people he loved the most in this worst of all possible worlds."

"But how can you be sure he's the killer? Do you have proof?"

Tallulah's voice dropped several octaves. "Dahling, don't be a wet blanket. Consider this, Nanette. If Leo *is* the murderer and you've seen that photograph and can identify him, then, dahling, you could be the next one up at bat." Tallulah drew a finger across her throat.

"Oh, Christ," gasped Nanette.

"Now you go to that phone and call that storage company."

"It's too late. They're bound to be closed."

"Damn it, you're right. The first thing in the morning! Scout's honor and honor bright.

This is essential, Nanette. For want of a better cliché it's a matter of life or death."

"You're not going, are you?" Tallulah was gathering her handbag and scarf.

"I must, dahling. I've a dinner date with Jacob Singer, the detective on the case, a really dear friend but hardly a mad impetuous youth. I'm sure he'll be eager to learn what you've told me and my triumph of triumphs, the photo of Leo Walsh. I'll prove to Mr. smart-ass Singer what a terrific sleuth I am. Why, dahling, what's wrong?"

"I'm frightened."

"Oh, dahling, do forgive me. Perhaps I was bit too vehement. I get that way toward the end of a run. I didn't mean that about Leo. I'm sure he's forgotten he sent it to Abner, it was so long ago or else he'd have laid siege to this dahling little house by now." She paused. "I didn't mean that. Come on, Nanette, you're made of sterner stuff. Look at those hands of yours! They're so big and strong, all these years of wielding gavels and chisels and mallets and . . . and . . . they *are* so strong, aren't they, dahling."

Nanette held her hands out and looked at them admiringly, fear of being murdered briefly pigeonholed while she basked in the glow of Tallulah's compliment. "Abner said they looked as though I could strangle a horse."

"And did you?"

Nanette laughed. "What do you think of this bust I'm doing of Abner?" Tallulah was positive she'd paid the expected compliment earlier, but like a good sport and a better actress, she gushed the words she knew Nanette wanted to hear. "Thank you, Tallulah. It's a bit difficult working from memory, but then who knew him better than I did?"

"Martha." Tallulah smiled. "After all, dahling, she was there first."

"You're making me regret not knowing her."

"I'm glad you said that. Now, dahling, I really must fly. I have to get back and change. Remember, first thing in the morning and then phone me at the Elysee." Impulsively, she pecked Nanette's cheek and left. Outside, she heard the door being bolted, and then hurried in search of a taxi.

In Tallulah's apartment while she changed for her date with Singer, Patsy screeched, "I'm so flat broke I may soon have to take to the streets!"

"Dahling, if you take to the streets, all

271

you'll succeed in accomplishing is ruining a good pair of shoes."

"Thanks for the vote of confidence!"

"Tell me, dahling, have you ever slept with a man?"

"I slept with my father."

"Patsy!"

"I was six months old, don't give yourself a hemorrhage. Hey, Estelle, what are you doing out there, trying to remember your affair with Teddy Roosevelt?"

In the living room, Estelle was at a mirror putting little bows in her wig. "I never met Teddy Roosevelt," Estelle shouted back in her crow's caw, "but I once waltzed with Sir Henry Irving."

"Who led?" Patsy had entered, going to the bar, a bird dog on a mission of retrieval.

"Why do you make so much of my age, Patsy? I don't deny I'm in my seventies. I mean it was perfectly ludicrous when I played Lynn Fontanne's mother in *The Pirate*, she being approximately five years younger than I."

"Yeah, but she had better face-lifts."

"She never had face-lifts. She had face peels. She'd lie for hours under a sunlamp until her face was completely baked, and then the doctor would peel off the layer until what was revealed was unlined skin as smooth and beautiful as a baby's behind."

Tallulah entered. "Talking about Dietrich?" She looked at the clock on the desk. "Jacob's late and I've got so much to tell him." She had her handbag open. "You ladies will of course make yourselves scarce on his arrival." She handed some banknotes to Patsy.

"Oh no," demurred Patsy, "I couldn't."

"Force yourself."

Estelle left the mirror and walked daintily to the bar, where she poured her favorite tipple, a dry sherry. "Tallulah dear. I'm going to a birthday party tomorrow for a very wealthy gentleman. What do you give the man who has everything?"

"The woman who has everything."

"Impossible. They're married."

"Tallulah," said Patsy, "you know what I need?"

"Protective custody."

"I need a really good agent. What about this Baxt kid?"

"That's an idea. Phone him in the morning. He adores faded movie names."

"Whaddya mean faded!"

"I'm sorry, dahling, I meant feted." She locked eyes with Estelle and then exhaled with relief. "Who's going to mix me a vodka martini?"

"Why, one of your favorite old-timers, of course, Tallu, good old Patsy Kelly, the kid who God forgot, a back number in mint condition who could use a mint."

"I find your sarcasm unbecoming, Patsy. I've suffered slips of the tongue since I was a slip of a girl. Call Baxt, he *has* worked wonders for some of those who have been unkindly forgotten or mislaid. He's been getting work for Wynne Gibson and Luella Gear and dear Dorothy Peterson, and he even dredged up poor old Janet Beecher for a Lux Theater. Of course the poor dahling was under sedation and oxygen for the following two weeks, but he does persist."

"How do you know all this, for crying out loud!"

"Lewis Drefuss told me today at the studio. Lewis is terribly fond of him. Oh, why doesn't Singer get here!"

"Dorothy Peterson, eh?" mused Patsy. "You could count her successes on one finger."

The phone rang, and Jacob Singer was announced. Tallulah checked the tray of hors d'oeuvres that had been delivered earlier and fixed Patsy with an accusing eye. "How many of these have you eaten, Miss Kelly?"

"Only three. Well, you guys can't eat 'em all!"

"That's beside the point! You've spoiled the symmetry! You know the chef fusses to give me symmetry!"

Estelle was getting into her coat. "Tallulah, must you always create a crisis over small matters? Don't you ever give a thought to the war in Korea?"

"I never played Korea!"

Estelle said, "Come, Patsy, I'll buy you a lovely dinner."

"Oh, yeah? Then can we go dancing at Roseland?"

In the hall they met Singer, who politely hoped they weren't leaving on his account, and Estelle said, "No, on Tallulah's."

Tallulah greeted him with a kiss, put his hat on a table, poured him a scotch and water, then mixed herself another martini while babbling about nothing in particular, which was one of her greatest gifts. Singer watched her, wondering how old she was—which had to be somewhere in her fifties (she was exactly fifty)—though he thought she looked younger.

Tallulah said as she crossed to him with

his drink, "Why, Jacob Singer, what a lascivious expression on your face!"

"I was thinking you're one hell of a woman."

"Even that will improve when you hear what I've got to tell you, dahling."

She made a banquet of her meeting with Nanette Walsh. She described the interior of the cottage precisely and with her usual good humor. She then recited the Martha and Leo story, saving the existence of Leo's photograph until a beautifully timed, climactic moment. Singer's mind never had a ghost of a chance of wandering. Tallulah's narrative held it in a viselike grip, and Tallulah recognized the faint smile on his face as a reflection not of cynicism but of admiration with a soupçon of respect. Then after a dramatic pause which gave her time to mix another round of drinks, Tallulah described the incident of Nanette's powerful hands. Jacob made a mental note to have Nanette Walsh brought in for additional questioning, and heard Tallulah say maybe Nanette could use a bodyguard.

"How about that lovely young black officer you introduced me to when I visited you at the precinct? The one who called me 'Tallulah cat.'"

"That was Pharaoh Love, but I can't spare him. He's too busy doing entrapment. He's a genius at it."

"Entrapment? What do you mean entrapment?"

"Well, he goes out to tea houses . . ."

"Tea houses? Where the hell in New York are there tea houses?"

Singer wished he didn't have to, but he explained: "Tea houses . . . public toilets . . . we call them tea houses . . ."

"How terribly quaint, dahling, if terribly inappropriate. And what does Mr. Love do in these tea houses?"

"He sets himself up as a target for homos. He stands at a urinal and fondles his ding dong and when one of the boys bites at the bait—"

"How vulgar!"

"—he collars them for soliciting."

"Why, that's perfectly dreadful! Why, why, why, it's unconstitutional! I've never heard anything so scandalous in my life! My God! You mean you dahling upholders of the law send officers out to deliberately trap those poor unfortunates . . . ! I never . . . I just never . . . I shall phone the President of the United States at once!"

"Sit down, Tallulah, it's been going on for

decades and it'll go on for decades long after we're gone." She sat down, while still fussing and fuming and making squawking noises like a hen who's misplaced her brood. "Anyway, Love's not available and I can't assign anyone to Mrs. Walsh because I'm too damn short of hands as it is. Now how'd you leave it with her?"

"I told you! She'll be in touch with the storage company in the morning and phone me when she has the photograph in hand. And I for one can't wait to see it." She suddenly deflated. "Oh God, I suppose it'll turn out to be someone neither one of us has ever seen before, and I suppose that'll open a fresh can of beans. He probably lives in some suburb like West Seventieth Street with a toothy wife and a passel of sniveling brats and is guilty of something so deadly as cheating on his income tax."

"Where would you like to have dinner?"

Tallulah ignored the question. "Still, I'd like to meet him. I'd like to know him. He's suffered so much, poor dahling. Think of it, Jacob, the misery and suffering that poor lad has undergone. It's such an injustice! The pain, the agony, the suffering . . ."

"Quit it, Tallulah, I'll be weeping into the booze."

"You don't fool me one bit, Jacob Singer. Under that granite exterior there beats the heart of a poet." He knew he was being seduced with words. "There's a little of Robert Browning in you, a touch of Lord Byron, a smidgen of Omar Khayyám . . . garnished with too much Robert Service. But nevertheless, let me tell you, Jacob Singer, if Leo Walsh turns out to be the killer, I shall personally finance his defense."

Singer put his drink down, took her drink from her hand and placed it next to his drink, and then surprisingly gently took her in his arms and cemented his lips to hers. When she came up for air, Tallulah looked into his eyes and said huskily, "Jacob Singer dahling, this is so seldom."

They had a very late dinner.

The next morning Tallulah was gurgling over the phone to Dorothy Parker, while Lewis Drefuss waited to consult her with a list of potential guests for the next radio show, which was to be the last of the season. He was unembarrassed, more amused, by Tallulah's graphic description of her conquest of Jacob Singer. Mrs. Parker likened it to the fall of Troy but refrained from any prurient reference to the Trojan Horse, though it was tempting.

"Tallulah dear," said Mrs. Parker dryly between sips of her morning coffee, "I'm picturing you with your hair braided and braces on your teeth."

"Dahling, I'm not carrying on like a schoolgirl, am I? I can't be, I haven't the vaguest idea how schoolgirls carry on. I don't remember ever being one. I mean I can't even recall the first three times I lost my virginity. Lewis, you're blushing, oh dahling, it so becomes you. Lewis Drefuss, Dottie, you've met, he coordinates the talent for my program. Although he's practically the producer, believe me, we'd be dead without him my God look at the time it's past noon and Lewis and I have so much to do! Operator! How many times have I told you never to interrupt me unless it's essential? Oh my God, it's Nanette Walsh! I have to talk to her! Dottie, I'll call you right back. Operator, connect Mrs. Walsh." To Lewis, she said excitedly, "I think this is the break we've been waiting for! Nanette dahling!" She listened and her face flushed at the news she heard. "Good girl! I'll send someone for it right away! His name's Lewis Drefuss, he's sitting right here, and he'll be down there pronto." She hung up.

"Lewis dahling, this is an emergency!" She explained the errand and with his usual good nature he agreed to run it for her. She pressed two ten-dollar bills on him for cab fare down and back, and though he tried to refuse it, she insisted with her famous show of strength. "Hurry, Lewis dahling, hurry." He left and she sat down on the sofa, every nerve in her body tingling. Then in a quick-silver burst of enthusiasm she flung her arms up and shouted to the ceiling, "Oh God dahling, what hath Tallulah wrought!"

FIFTEEN

WHILE WAITING for Tallulah to call back, Mrs. Parker dipped into a paperback collection of new voices in poetry. She was appalled by some, depressed by some, deplored a great many, and begrudgingly admired one or two. She hadn't composed a poem in too long a time but was now overwhelmed with sudden inspiration. She wrote on the flyleaf:

I'm up to my ath
In Sylvia Plath.

Under this she wrote, "No future." The phone rang and it was Tallulah, who babbled the latest turn of events in the case. Mrs. Parker commented, "I think you should let Jacob Singer know all this. It's his case, dear."

"I know, dahling, but I can't resist springing this on him. I know he hasn't been taking seriously my detective work, but I think I've been doing damn well. The trouble with Jacob, like so many other people I know, is they overestimate themselves while underestimating me."

"I still think an officer should have gone for the photograph." She thought about something. "Tallulah?"

"Yes, dahling?"

"Supposing it's a photograph of a plump little baby Leo on a bearskin rug."

"I'll kill Nanette."

Nanette Walsh and Oliver Sholom had never had anything in common until today. Her skull had been crushed. The weapon, a mallet, lay on the floor near her, matted with blood and skin and shards of skull. The murderer had even less respect for womanhood than he had for his male victims. Yet

Nanette was recognizable. She had been attacked from behind; her face had not been touched. She was sprawled prone on the floor, a very stern and disapproving look on her face. She obviously hadn't cared one bit for the mode of departure assigned her.

Lewis Drefuss was trembling. He found the kitchen and drank a glass of water. There was a phone extension on the wall and he dialed the Elysee. Tallulah's line was engaged, but Lewis convinced the operator it was an emergency. Once again, Mrs. Parker was cut off in her prime and Tallulah barked, "What's the problem? Do you have the photograph?"

"I found her dead."

"What!"

"She's been murdered."

"Jesus! Where's the photograph?"

"There isn't any. What shall I do?"

"I'm coming right down. Don't touch a thing." Tallulah would never forget one of Singer's lectures on proper police procedure. "The place has to be dusted for fingerprints."

"Shouldn't I call the police?"

"The police! Jacob! Of course, dahling. You'd better let me do it. Jacob Singer will be furious, but I know how to handle him. Oh my God! Nanette Walsh! A dark horse when all the while my money's been on Ted Valudni. God, I choose murder victims like I choose most of my plays, very badly. Don't let anyone in until the police or I arrive. And, dahling, if she's too ghastly a sight, cover her with that dreadful Spanish shawl draped across the grand piano. Remove the photographs first, of course; wreckage would only confuse the police."

She dialed the precinct and was told Singer was in conference. She told the sergeant to tell Singer there was another murder. Singer grabbed for the phone and shouted, "Are you all right?"

"I'm just dandy, dahling, Nanette Walsh isn't." She told him rapidly the morning's events. He shouted at her. She shouted back. "If I had a gun, Jacob Singer, I'd kill you!"

"You don't need a gun, you've got your mouth!" He slammed the phone down.

"Son of a bitch!" shouted Tallulah at the dial tone. The rapidity with which she dressed, flew from the apartment, flagged a cab, and arrived at Nanette Walsh's carriage house should have been entered in the *Guinness Book of Records*. Jacob Singer was getting out of a patrol car followed by Oscar Delaney and three other plainclothesmen. A cab screeched to a halt behind Tallulah's, and Adam Todd got out, very angry, and very red in the face as he fumbled for his wallet to pay the fare.

Tallulah saw him and said, "Oh dahling! I forgot all about you! We could have shared one down here!"

"What's going on?" he asked as he hurried after her.

"There's been another murder, dahling. From the distaff side for variety's sake."

Nanette Walsh was covered with a bed sheet Lewis had found in a cupboard. Lewis was sitting on the piano bench, his hands folded in his lap, looking forlorn and ill. Tallulah went to him and put her arms around his shoulders. "Oh, dahling, had I known the errand would end this ghoulishly, I'd never have sent you!"

"How were you to know?"

"True. Would you like a glass of water?"

"I've had three."

"Have another. It's very good for you. It flushes the system." The coroner arrived and with a grunt that passed for a greeting went immediately to work. Singer crossed to Lewis and Tallulah.

Tallulah's eyes flashed a warning, the kind that sent ingenues seeking a different profession. Jacob just shook his head and then directed his attention to Lewis. "You found the body, Lewis?"

"Yes."

"What were you doing down here?"

"I sent him," said Tallulah.

"I'm asking Lewis."

"Well, if you don't mind, Mr. Singer"—she bore down on the *Mr.* as though she were crushing out a cigarette with her shoe—"the story begins with me." And I hope it doesn't end with me.

"All right, let's hear it."

"Well, dahling, yesterday after recording the show I came down here for a drink with Nanette and . . ." She recounted the events swiftly and—surprisingly for Tallulah Bankhead—lucidly. She always told a story well and this was one of her better performances. Singer didn't make notes as she spoke, but Oscar Delaney did. Oscar was so precise as to be almost prissy. He not only dotted *i*'s and crossed *t*'s, he was very big on colons, parentheses, and underlinings. He would one day publish a very good book on police procedures, and then never be heard from again, like a former Vice President. Tallulah was winding down while lighting her fifth Craven A ". . . and so, dahling, I sent Lewis here to collect the photograph."

"You should have told me about it." Singer's voice wasn't friendly.

"You're quite right, Jacob, you are very very right, and I'll never forgive myself. But you will, won't you, dahling?"

"Okay, Lewis. It's your turn." He warned Tallulah, "And don't you coach or interrupt!"

Tallulah glowered and exhaled smoke like the dragon contemplating St. George.

Lewis spoke slowly and deliberately. He wanted to get the story right and only have to tell it once. He wanted to get the hell out of there, into fresh air, away from death and law officers and the police photographer who had arrived while Tallulah was talking, and was wondering if there would be a right time to ask for her autograph.

"When I got here, I used the door knocker. But the door was open." Tallulah listened carefully, something she did brilliantly in performance if not otherwise. This was one occasion when she knew it was important to listen with all her concentration. "When I knocked, it just opened further. I called out her name. After a while, I decided to go in. The light wasn't very good, there were no lamps lighted, not anything, just what light was coming from the skylight. I kept shout-

287

ing her name, thinking maybe she was up-stairs or in the kitchen. Hell, I don't know, I was spooked. I could feel something was wrong. And then I saw her lying there."

"The mallet was in the position you see it now?"

"Yes. I didn't touch anything. I was so shocked, it was such a revolting sight, I went to the kitchen for a glass of water. Oh! My fingerprints!"

Singer said, "Then what did you do?"

"I phoned Tallulah."

"Why didn't you phone the police?"

Tallulah finally spoke up. "Because I al-ways get top billing, dahling, and don't jump down my throat. He was correct in calling me because I got him into this mess, albeit inadvertently. And I was glad he did because I knew I had to be the one to break it to you and take the rap for not having told you about the photograph in the first place! I don't suppose I can pour myself a drink—she has a very good bar."

"Don't you touch a goddamn thing." His attention returned to Lewis. "Was there any sign of the photograph?"

"Oh God, it didn't even occur to me to look. I'm sorry."

"It's okay." He assigned Adam Todd and

two other officers to look for Leo Walsh's picture. He asked Lewis, "When you got here, none of the downstairs windows were open, just the door?"

"I didn't notice."

"No, there would be no reason to."

Tallulah squeezed Lewis's shoulder and he gave her a look of gratification. "I hope he's not too angry with you."

"Don't let it bother you, dahling. I've never been all that respectful of authority. By the way, dahling, is there anything protruding from between my shoulder blades?"

Jacob had left them and was wandering about the room, his hands plunged in his trouser pockets. To an untutored eye, he looked bored. His associates knew he was hard at work. His eyes examined everything. He didn't like the bust of Abner Walsh but didn't say so. He examined furniture and looked under chairs. That had already been done by the others, but he liked to cover their tracks. They found nothing that would prove to be of any help. They didn't find the photograph. His eyes met Tallulah's across the room and he read her correctly. She needed to talk to him alone, away from the scene of the crime. He went to her and Lewis. He spoke to Lewis. "You don't have

289

to hang around, Lewis." Lewis made a move and Jacob thought he was going to kiss his hand in gratitude. Lewis got up.

He asked Tallulah, "Do you want a lift uptown?"

"No thank you, dahling. I don't think Detective Singer is finished with me." *If he is, there's that dahling musician who plays piano weekends at the Famous Door.*

Singer was speaking to Lewis. "We'll need you to sign your statement." Lewis told him where he could be reached and left. Singer conferred in a low voice with his colleagues and then took Tallulah by the arm and steered her out to the street.

"Oh my God, dahling! Look at this mob!" Word of the murder and the unscheduled appearance of a great star had spread through the area faster than a social disease at an overseas army camp. The media was represented by television, radio, and the newspapers. Photographers descended like a plague of locusts, and microphones were shoved in their faces.

"No comment!" shouted Jacob. "No comment!"

"Dahlings, how lovely to be here," said Tallulah into the array of microphones, trying loyally to favor NBC's.

"Miss Bankhead!" shouted NBC. "What's your connection to the murder?"

"The poor unfortunate victim and I were in the roller derby years ago. We'd meet annually to toast our dead buddies."

"Come on, Tallulah, level with us. We're always good to you!" shouted CBS.

"Oh really, dahlings. Did you ever read my notices for *Anthony and Cleopatra?*"

"What's Mrs. Walsh's connection to the other three murders?"

"Dahling, that's for the police to say. After all, dahlings, I'm an actress, not a detective."

"You said it, I didn't."

Tallulah glared at Singer. Ten minutes later they were sitting in the booth of a quaint Greenwich Village coffee shop. They ordered sandwiches and coffee from a waiter dressed, Tallulah finally deduced, as Peter Pan.

"You *are* supposed to be Peter Pan, aren't you, dahling?"

"That's right, Miss Bankhead." She was never not recognized. "Didn't you notice our name?" Tallulah peered through her spectacles at the name on the menu. J. M. Barrie's.

"Oh, how adorable," said Tallulah. She

said to a passing waitress, "Dahling, which Barrie character are you?"

"Wendy Darling."

"Wendy Dahling! How dahling, dahling." To the waiter she said "Hurry, dahling, I'm famished," grateful she hadn't looked at the corpse.

Singer said, "I should wring your neck."

"Why, dahling, is it damp?"

"Do you realize you could have cost Lewis Drefuss his life?"

Tallulah stared at him as she removed her spectacles, set them aside, and applied a match to a Craven A. When she finally spoke, her voice was low and contrite. "If anything had happened to Lewis, I'd have committed suicide."

"Fat chance."

"Don't be unkind, Jacob. Why can't you be more generous at times?"

"I'm a detective, Tallulah, not a philanthropist."

"You certainly aren't a philanthropist. A philanthropist is a person who heads good give."

The waiter brought their coffees with a pitcher of cream which Tallulah eyed suspiciously.

"Peter Pan, dahling. Is this cream fresh?"

"Miss Bankhead," came the reply with exaggerated patience, "a few hours ago it was grass."

"It's going to be one of those days," grumbled Tallulah as she dumped sugar into her coffee. "All right, Jacob. Let me have it. I'm ready for the firing squad, and no blindfold, thank you."

He aimed and fired. "You could have gotten killed when you went to Oliver Sholom's, and you could have gotten Lewis killed when you sent him to the Walsh woman. I want you to stick *out* from now on. The fun and games are finished."

"This has not been fun and games for me, Jacob, I have been dead serious. And one day you'll be man enough to admit I've accomplished a great deal, albeit in my own fumbling way. What I'd like to know is how the hell the killer knew Nanette was in possession of incriminating evidence! How has he managed to keep one step ahead of the police? Is he a genius or is he just plain lucky?"

"He's a genius and he's just plain lucky. He's also made a few mistakes and they'll surface, they always surface."

Tallulah was staring at the sandwiches Peter Pan was serving. "Don't you have any half-sour pickles?"

"Miss Bankhead, this is not Lindy's," said the waiter.

She said something unkind as he went away, which he did not hear.

"About the mistakes," said Tallulah as she spread mustard on the top slice of rye, "exactly what kind of mistakes are they?"

"If I knew, I'd make a collar and mark the case closed."

"Jacob, don't talk down to me."

"For crying out loud, Tallulah, I'm talking plain English. If I knew, I'd make a collar."

"You're not kidding me one bit. You know," she said, and Jacob looked up from his fatty corned beef on white, "but you haven't a shred of evidence. Not a whit of proof. You know, and Jacob"—she paused dramatically—"I know. Remember that little something tucked away in the back of my mind I couldn't remember?"

"That's pretty crowded territory."

"I remember it now."

"What jogged your memory?"

"Nanette's murder. Jacob"—she spoke his name with an authority that commanded his attention—"I'm going to give a party. This coming Sunday."

"That's pretty short notice."

"Don't be ridiculous, dahling. People never have much of anything to do on Sundays except go to brunches or a movie. My program's been prerecorded so I'm free. I assure you, Jacob, it'll be standing room only."

"And what is the purpose of this party besides helping pass another Sunday?"

"Don't be dense, Jacob."

"Don't be obtuse, Tallulah."

"I'm going to unmask the murderer."

He put down the sandwich, swallowed what was in his mouth with difficulty, took a sip of coffee, and then said, "Didn't we agree from now on you stick out?"

"You agreed, dahling, I didn't. You need me to give this party, Jacob. Without it, you'll never get a shred of proof. You'll never make what do you call it, dahling, oh yes a collar—where these colloquialisms spring from I'll never know—and even if you dare make a collar, you'll be hard put to win a conviction. You'll be hard put to get the killer before judge and jury. Even if you did, it'd be a hung jury with all you've got against him now, which is absolutely nothing. You're mumbling under your breath, which is it?"

"It's this sandwich. It's from never-never land."

"Frankly, I don't understand how you can have an appetite after what you've just seen. Thank God I didn't brave a look at her. Was it awful?"

"She wouldn't win a beauty contest."

Tallulah shoved her sandwich aside and lit a cigarette. "I shall invite all the suspects, and of course they can bring a friend. After all, dahling, we don't want to give the impression I'm arranging one of those climaxes William Powell and Myrna Loy do so well in the *Thin Man* films."

"You also don't have a scenarist writing it for you."

Tallulah smiled. "I think I'll do just fine with this one. Now let me see . . ." The guest list tripped from her lips like the Music Hall Rockettes time-stepping from the wings. Some of the names Singer didn't recognize and Tallulah identified them. "I think it's a good idea to populate the party with a few people who have nothing to do with the case. It'll disarm the killer, don't you agree, dahling?" Jacob signaled for more coffee. "And we need some of your men, too, dahling. Adam Todd of course, because he's on my tail, Christ what a deadly expression, and that nice Oscar Delaney and one or two more in case there's violence."

"I'm not worried about violence, Tallulah. I'm a little worried about an action for slander."

"What action for slander, dahling? Have you been keeping something from me?"

"Tallulah, if you name a killer without evidence to back you up, you could be sued."

"Mr. Singer, Bankhead always gets her man. She frequently regrets it, but she gets him. It's only the violence that has me worried. I don't want anyone hurt—"

"Or killed."

"I've a marvelous idea!"

"Help."

"Yes?" asked Peter Pan who was refilling the coffee cups.

"It's only an expression," said Singer. "Don't be stingy, son, fill them to the top."

Peter Pan wondered what Tallulah Bankhead saw in a lunkhead like this. Well, he'd heard rumors about her kinky indulgences. He was dying to know if it was true she used cocaine, and if she did, how to get the name of her dealer.

"What's the marvelous idea?" Peter Pan was finally out of earshot.

"I want your boys dressed as waiters and bartenders. Now isn't that a good idea?"

"Absolutely great."

"I'll need someone to look after the women. How about a policewoman, someone not too tough looking."

Jacob thought of Annabel Forsythe. He suggested her to Tallulah.

"She sounds wonderful. Will you call her for me, dahling, and have her at my suite Sunday at five? Bless you, Jacob."

"And what if this backfires?'

"It mustn't backfire and it won't. I won't tolerate another flop, Jacob. This one has to work because I'm staging it myself." She looked at her wristwatch. "I've got to get moving." She almost offered to drop him at his precinct, but then thought better of it. She didn't want him questioning her errand on the West Side. She reached across the table and grabbed his wrist. "Promise me I have your full cooperation."

"Tallulah, have I any choice?"

Twenty minutes later, Tallulah was sitting on a hard-backed chair looking at Herbert Sholom seated at his sewing machine. The man seemed to have shrunk and shriveled in the past few days.

"So how can I help you, Miss Bankhead?" he asked, threading the needle. She told him. He said nothing.

"I really need you to do this, Mr. Sholom. I think it's the only way we can trap your nephew's killer."

"My nephew. That bum. You should have known his father, my brother. He was just as bad. When he defected from the party, he really *defected*. That was when Hitler and Stalin signed their pact. Well, I suppose it was a betrayal, and I'm sure you know how I feel about betrayals, like how I felt about my nephew. I see you're looking at my portraits of Stalin and Lenin. I'll tell you what they represent for me, Miss Bankhead. It has nothing to do with politics. I was never a very good communist. It was my wife, may she rest in peace, who was a real *tummler*. You know what that means? That's someone who likes to stir things up. She loved going on strike and she thrived on peace marches and she had a dead aim with a rock. Boy, do I miss her. If she was here this place would be a lot neater. I wouldn't even be working, I think. We'd probably be living in Miami

Beach. I'm not a poor man, though it looks it."

Tallulah crossed her legs and lit a cigarette. She needed him. She let him talk. It was killing her, but she let him talk.

"I own this building and a couple of lots out in Bensonhurst, and believe it or not, despite how I felt about him, Oliver would have gotten it all. So now his other cousin will get it." He scrunched up his face and asked, "You really think I can do this?"

"I really do, Mr. Sholom."

He sighed and offered a glass of tea but Tallulah declined. She was in a hurry. Time was precious; there was so little of it. "Well, Miss Bankhead, there's a first time for everything. All right, I'll do it."

"God bless you, dahling."

"I'll be there when you want me. Don't worry, I won't let you down. Betrayal is one thing, but murder, hoo hah! *That's* really something!"

Back at her suite, Tallulah was a tornado of activity. Estelle Winwood adored parties and threw herself into action with enthusiasm. Patsy, to whom a number of chores had immediately been delegated, began screeching. Tallulah never found it difficult to decode Patsy. "For chrissakes!" is what she had screeched. "Do you expect me to spend the rest of my life as your chief cook and bottle opener?" Tallulah asked the hotel caterer to come to her suite immediately and then phoned Mrs. Parker to tell her the news.

"I haven't been to a party in ages," said Mrs. Parker. "I haven't a thing to wear."

"Just throw on any old thing, dahling."

"I will. I have lots of those. Has Jacob really agreed to this nonsense?"

"It's not nonsense, dahling. I promise you fireworks. Believe me, dahling, I promise you fireworks!"

Patsy had the radio on the bar turned on and they listened to an overheated account of Nanette Walsh's murder. The caterer arrived, bowing and scraping himself into the room, and the conference with Bankhead was short and to the point. After Estelle showed him out, Tallulah changed into a comfortable robe, tied a bandanna around her lush mane of hair, torched a Craven A, and settled down with the telephone.

After an hour, she had contacted about half her guest list and left messages for the others. So far there were no refusals or protestations of conflict of invitation. The doorbell rang and Patsy admitted a bellhop who handed her a florist's box. Although it was for Tallulah, Patsy tore off the ribbon and wrapping and flung aside the cover.

"What is it, dahling?"

"It's a single long-stemmed rose."

Patsy held up the rose and Tallulah thought it lovely. "No card?"

"Yeah," said Patsy, and brought it to her.

Tallulah read aloud. " 'When this you see, remember me.' "

SIXTEEN

IT WAS one of those mornings when the obituaries in *The New York Times* were a bore. Estelle Winwood set the newspaper aside and moved to her dressing table. Her favorite wig rested on its block, having been combed and curled the night before. She had decided she'd wear a flowery print to Tallulah's party with a floppy picture hat and a single strand of pearls, and she'd carry her flowing embroidered lace handkerchief, which the late poet Rupert Brooke had given to her when most people were just a whisper in their mother's ear. She thought of carrying a flower, a single perfect rose like the one Tallulah had received. "When This You See,

Remember Me." No signature. Tallulah's enigmatic smile. Her phone call to Jacob Singer to tell him about the mysterious rose.

Murder was something Estelle recognized but did not understand. She saw no reason for wars, for violence, for weapons, or for the Theater Guild. And the party worried her. This wasn't one of Tallulah's last-minute socials planned on a whim; she was giving it as much concentration and planning as she would bring to an opening night. Or the conquest of a prospective lover. This was a new kind of passionate involvement for Tallulah, a mysterious one that Estelle didn't quite understand, involving policemen dressed as waiters and bartenders carrying concealed weapons. Now Estelle understood there might be danger and, good grief, perhaps gunshots. Would a bulletproof vest go well with the flowery print? Where could she get one on a Sunday? For a brief moment she thought of forgoing the party, claiming a sudden attack of anything, braving Tallulah's fury. But Estelle adored parties, and she would never be too old to enjoy an adventure. She would brew herself a cup of tea, nibble a Cadbury biscuit, read the script she'd promised to discuss with a young theater producer tomorrow. Then she would choose an appropriate scent for the evening. And at the party, she would try to stick close to Tallulah, to protect her. It would be simpler to protect a whirlwind.

Patsy Kelly burnt the toast, the bacon, and the eggs sunny-side up. She ate them with relish accompanied by three cups of bitter coffee, read the comics in the *Daily News*, and ran herself a tub. While soaking with a Bloody Mary to keep her company, she decided to accept an offer to tour summer stock in a revival of the cobwebbed theatrical warhorse *Ladies Night in a Turkish Bath*. What the hell, it was a guaranteed ten weeks at three hundred bucks a throw. It wasn't Hollywood money, but it was money. She couldn't go on living off friends indefinitely, specifically off Tallulah. And after tonight, there might not be a Tallulah to live off. Even when thinking, Patsy dangled prepositions. She'd had enough of parties. Thelma Todd had been one of her best friends; they had co-starred in a series of successful two-reelers for Hal Roach. When Thelma was found dead and there was an investigation of sorts, Patsy kept yapping at her lawyer, "I don't want to be indicted by no grand jury!" She was never indicted, but she was questioned endlessly. There had been mysterious phone calls telling her to keep her trap shut. Keep her trap shut about what? Thelma's love affairs were common gossip. When she was found dead she was living with Roland West in the apartment above the restaurant she was running in Malibu Beach. Running, ha! Fronting was more like it. Fronting for the mob. Thelma was always broke, like Patsy. She must have crossed them and that's why she got it.

But Tallulah was something else. Tallulah fronted for nobody. And whether she knew it or not, she was the target for tonight. I'll stick close to her, Patsy thought; I'll protect her. I never knew a cop who could shoot straight. But a maniac. What the hell's with her? A party for a killer? What would my sainted mother make of *this!*

George Baxt and Lewis Drefuss were brunching at Regent's Row on East Fifty-eighth Street. Baxt thought better about ordering a third Bloody Mary, threw caution to the wind and ordered it, knowing there was a fourth in his future, and then told Lewis to snap out of it.

"I'm having these awful nightmares," explained Lewis.

"I shouldn't wonder, those awful pictures of you in the *Mirror*."

"I keep seeing that crushed skull, the mallet that killed her . . ."

"So why'd you order the tomato surprise?"

"Do you want to go to the party with me?"

"I do, but I can't. I've got four shows to watch tonight. I've got three of my charges on Philco and they're a pain in the ass if I have to admit I didn't watch them. Take somebody else."

"I'll go alone."

"What are you doing this summer?"

"I haven't decided. You?"

"God have mercy, I'm sharing a house with the Halls and Flora Roberts at Ocean Beach. Will you stop drumming on the table? My hangover has a hangover."

"Maybe I won't go to the party."

"Like hell you won't. And I expect a full report with quotes."

"Tallulah's crazy."

"So what else is new?"

"Giving this party. She's so vulnerable. You heard about the death threat she got."

"They've heard about it in Tibet. By the way, is 'The Big Show' positively canceled?"

"Down the drain forever." He raised his old-fashioned. "To Tallulah."

"And why not?" He signaled for his fourth Bloody Mary.

Mitchell Zang strutted about his bedroom in the nude, a plucked peacock. The girl in the bed was bored with his endowment, bored with Mitchell Zang, bored with sex, and bored with the thought of going home to Chillicothe and forgetting about becoming an actress. "Tallulah Bankhead invites me to a party! Can you imagine that?" The girl grunted, a displeased sow. "Me! Mitchell Zang! Bankhead! The Big Time! The fucking cow, all the time I was with Nance Liston she treated me like I was invisible, now all of a sudden she invites me up for cocktails! Me! Mitchell Zang!"

The girl said into the pillow, "Him . . . Mitchell Zang . . . shit on shingles." Her voice was a muffled blur and he heard nothing but himself.

"I'm going to take her for every nickel I can get." He stood in front of a floor-length mirror, the one Nance Liston had used to perfect a movement. He preened. He stood full front, then side view. First the left, then the right. "There'll be some very important people there tonight. Producers. Writers. Rich bitches who know all the answers and all the right people. This is my lucky day, baby!" He sprang across the room, landed on top of her, and she screamed.

"You trying to kill me, you asshole! Get off me! Oh, my back, oh, God, you've broken my back."

"Oh, shut up and get dressed. I'll spring for breakfast."

"Big spender."

Her mind was made up. She was going home to Chillicothe.

Joseph Savage stared at the sheet of paper in his typewriter. Then he looked at his wristwatch. He had hours before Tallulah's party. He stared at the sheet of paper. It was still blank. He went to the refrigerator and had a few sips of milk straight from the carton. It was going sour. He dumped the carton into the garbage pail in the closet under the sink. He returned to the typewriter. He stared at the blank sheet of paper. He went to the window and looked out. It was a nice day. Some kids were playing stoop ball. A couple of congenital dog walkers were comparing leashes, or that's what it looked like. His landlady sat on a chair on the sidewalk reading the Sunday paper. Her husband sat on the sidewalk smoking his awful pipe and chugalugging from a can of beer. Joseph returned to the typewriter. He stared at the sheet of paper. He went to the closet and checked the sports jacket and slacks he planned to wear to the party. They weren't wrinkled. They weren't wrinkled the last six times he checked them. He returned to the typewriter. He stared at the sheet of paper. He went to the dresser and looked in his billfold. The eighteen dollars hadn't matured into a larger sum. It was the same eighteen dollars he'd counted the last time. He scratched his chest. He went back to the window. A man in a window of a building across the street was exercising with barbells. He looked as if he might be a model. Joseph never exercised. Getting out of bed in the morning was a major accomplishment. How come an invitation to a Tallulah party all of a sudden? I'm writing a play for her, but that's no big deal. She'll probably ask me not to use my own name. Oh, balls. Not Bankhead. She'd never stoop to a stunt like that. I wonder if Jacob Singer will be there. He returned to the typewriter. He stared at the horrible sheet of paper. It mocked him. It defied him. He would never outwit it. It brazenly defied him. Angrily, he accepted the challenge. His index finger tapped: *The*. He smiled with satisfaction. Now exhausted, he went to the sink, dampened a cloth with cold water, applied the cloth to his head and stretched out on the couch.

And there are those, he reminded himself, who claim eight hours a day at the typewriter. Liars.

Annabel Forsythe's closet was piled high with hats. Annabel lived for hats. She never threw one away. She had an Empress Eugenie, a tricorne, hats galore inherited from previous employers who had quickly gotten bored with them. She had several John Fredericks and at least three Lilly Daches and God knows how many Florells. She wore hats to church and to the movies and to the park and to the toilet and to unemployment, but not too fancy a one there.

She was selecting the appropriate hat to wear to Tallulah Bankhead's cocktail party. Well, get me, girl! Miss Annabel Forsythe has arrived! She is going to a cocktail party at Miss Tallulah Bankhead and we are both Southern girls! True, Miss Forsythe will be passing around the canapés and attending the ladies in the bedroom and washing glasses, but Miss Bankhead said, "Dahling, you dress like a guest! I want you to feel right at home!"

Bless your heart, Tallulah honey. I'm going to make myself right at home. She was trying on one of the Daches for the tenth time.

"Honey!" she yelled. "What do you think of this one? How do I look?"

Ike said from behind a copy of *Confidential*, "It makes you look too Jewish."

Ted Valudni shouted into the phone, "Beth, you're being unreasonable! What's so terrible about our showing up at Bankhead's together?"

"Guilt by association." Beth was waving her left hand, drying her freshly polished nails.

"Come off it, damn it!"

"Ted, we are no longer a twosome. We are no longer an anything. We are permanently separated, like Peter Ibbetson and his sweetie. We won't even meet in dreams. You go by yourself, and I'll go by myself. We'll say hello and then we'll mingle. You by yourself and me by myself."

"Did you talk to her?"

"Who?"

"Tallulah! What's this party all about, anyway?"

"It's a party. Does everything have to have a theme?"

"You haven't said a word about Nanette Walsh."

"She's dead."

"She's dead!" he mimicked her. "I know she's dead! And so's Sholom and Barry Wren and Lester Miroff. They at least had something in common. They were friendly witnesses. But where does Nanette figure?"

"Maybe the murderer killed her because he was afraid he'd be accused of discrimination."

"That's pretty cold-blooded. That's not you, Beth. That's not the Beth I knew."

"Ted?"

"What?"

"Did you ever know me?"

He exploded. "For God's sake, Beth, let's not go into that routine again! Ah, the hell with it! Go by yourself! I don't need you! I don't need anybody!" He slammed the phone down. He broke a vase. He threw a pillow across the room. He smashed a framed photograph of Beth. He burst into tears.

Oscar Delaney's wife was her mother's favorite child. This was because they both shared one odious trait, suspicion. Mrs. Delaney suspected the landlord, the butcher, the grocer, the neighbors, their children, total strangers, and Oscar. She sometimes suspected he wasn't really a detective. She sometimes suspected he was still a patrolman walking a beat out in Brooklyn and kept his clothes in a locker and changed into them to come home, claiming he was a detective. Yes, there was now more household money, but he could be borrowing that from his father, as Oscar was his father's favorite child. Oscar and his father had one trait in common: hatred. They hated their wives.

"Why can't I go to the party with you?" She was calmly attending to her hair, but at any moment the innocent hairbrush could turn into a dangerous weapon.

"How many times do I have to tell you I'm not a guest, I'm on assignment? I'm going to be tending bar."

"Are you getting overtime?"

"Sure, I'm getting overtime."

"How come you're wearing your best suit to the party if you're tending bar?"

"We're going to try on jackets at the hotel! The hotel is supplying us with white jackets! Miss Bankhead's arranged every-thing!"

"Who's *us?*" He recognized the danger in her voice.

"Me and the other boys. They're posing as waiters!"

"And what about the redhead in Coney Island?"

"There's no redhead in Coney Island!"

"Don't you lie to me!"

"Don't you start in again!"

"It's that Spanish bitch on Delancey Street!"

"There is no Spanish bitch on Delancey Street!"

"I want the truth!" The brush sailed past his head and landed on the floor.

"You want the truth? You want the truth?" he yelled as an uppercut sent her staggering against the wall behind her. "Here's the truth! I'm fucking Eleanor Roosevelt!"

"I knew it," she gasped.

Armbruster Pershing thought his wife Eleanor looked particularly beautiful and told her so.

"Thank you, darling. I'll never outshine Miss Bankhead, but I can certainly give it a try."

He put his arms around her from behind and kissed the nape of her neck.

"Now, Armbruster, don't go giving us an appetite there's no time to fulfill."

"We could arrive fashionably late. It's a showbiz party. Nobody will be on time."

"That's why we will. I want to talk to her and know her and laugh with her and make my bridge ladies rotten with envy."

"I hope you won't be disappointed. I'm told she does all the talking at a blue streak, and getting to know her is as hopeless as a federal project."

"Well, I can't be faulted for giving it my best shot. I've always been fascinated by the woman. She's an original, there'll be no one like her again, and this is one experience I'm really looking forward to. I hope there'll be fireworks."

"Knowing Miss Bankhead, you'll get them. I don't think this is your ordinary every Sunday show-business cocktail party. It's a camouflaged time bomb. There's a murderer on the loose out there somewhere and we know Miss Bankhead is involved in the case. She's up to something and I think it's going to be more fun than watching a Democrat lose an election."

Eleanor picked up a glass of sherry and

sipped it. "Don't tell me this is going to be one of those parties where all the suspects are being gathered in one room and then the killer is to be unmasked!"

"Sounds suspiciously like it is."

"Oh, Armbruster! How exciting! Oh!"

"What's the matter?"

"Supposing it's your dreadful Mr. Valudni!"

"Wouldn't that be wonderful! I'd be rid of him once and for all."

"Darling, if you so dislike him, why don't you discard him the way you did your first three wives?"

"For the simple reason his fees pay their acrimony . . . I mean alimony."

"Whatever you do, sweetheart, don't ever bring him around here socially. While I loathe all commies and all leftists and the rest of that ilk"—she was from an old Boston family—"I detest anyone who betrays a friend to save his own skin." She sipped the sherry. "What's become of the noble gesture? Now stop smirking. There *was* a time when people had a finest hour. You know, like Winston Churchill and Calvin Coolidge. Where has it all gone to? If he survives this, what becomes of a snake like Valudni?"

"Oooohhh, I suppose some thirty or so

years from now, if he lives that long, he'll be given a plush testimonial dinner in aid of some charity where they'll show clips of his films, and many of the actors and actresses who worked with him will say wonderful things about him while his darkest hour and most degenerate gesture will be conveniently overlooked. He might even be declared a national monument."

"If for some perverse reason you're trying to depress me, you're succeeding." She put the glass on the bar and went to her husband. "You're such a lovely person, Armbruster. Do you suppose I'm the only one who knows that? I hope not. I hope your next wife will be as appreciative."

David Carney's sister Audrey said to him over the telephone, "Is your suit all nice and pressed?"

"Yes."

"And there's no ring around the collar of your shirt?"

"No."

"And you're wearing a tie that has no stains on it?"

"Yes."

"And you won't forget to take a clean white handkerchief?"

"Yes."

"Did you remember to polish your shoes?"

"Yes."

"And you're going to be a perfect gentleman and behave yourself?"

"Yes."

"And when will you come home to your apartment?"

"After I murder Miss Bankhead."

Miss Tallulah Bankhead was a vision in an infrequently worn Elsa Schiaparelli cocktail dress. She wore her best jewels and her most elegant shoes. Her makeup was subdued, but her enthusiasm wasn't. She perked like a coffee pot as she examined the bar. It was beautifully set up. Oscar Delaney looked smart in his white jacket with blue trim, the blue matching the color of the bruise on his forehead, which she tactfully refrained from mentioning. Adam Todd and the other two detectives looked equally at home in their white jackets, as though born to the waiter's calling. Annabel Forsythe was an oversized vision in a pink and purple number that Tallulah decided had been designed by a couturier named Haphazard. But oh God, that hat, well, forget it, Tallulah. *Chacun*, et cetera. She'll certainly remove it when the guests start arriving. If she doesn't, I'll have Patsy knock it off her head.

"Estelle, you look positively radiant!"

"Thank you, dear, what are you after?"

"I'm after nothing for crying out loud. Can't I pay you a compliment?"

"You do it so infrequently that when you do, I find it worrying."

Radiant, hell, I should have told her the truth. Estelle darling, you're the victim of a poor job of embalming.

"Patsy, what have you done to your hair?"

"Nothing."

"Oh."

"You like my dress?"

"Love it. It's you, it's very you."

And all it lacks, dahling, is the ashes to go with the sack cloth, but oh, what the hell, no matter how you look, I love you. Her press agent Richard Maney, was having a scotch mist and looked worried. Tallulah asked, "Why the frown?'

"The truth? I'm getting bad vibrations."

"Now don't go mystical on me, Maney. This is not the time for it. There's no turning back now."

"And what if this whole mess backfires?"

"I'll retire to the country for the rewrite."

"Tallulah, if this doesn't work, you may not be around for the rewrite."

"Don't be morbid, dahling. How's Gloria Swanson's show doing in Detroit?" She pronounced it Detwah. "Are they fixing? Has she gotten any new lines?"

"Only around her eyes."

Tallulah diverted her attention to Adam Todd. "Dahling, that bulge under your left shoulder is so obvious. Can't you do anything about it?"

"That's the only place I can wear my holster, Miss Bankhead."

"Let's try it with the jacket unbuttoned. There! Perfect! And you have such a lovely flat stomach. You must come up sometime and share your secret. Oscar! Are you sure we have enough ice?"

"Plenty, Miss Bankhead. If we run out, we can always phone downstairs for more."

"Of course we can, dahling. How clever of you to remember."

Jacob Singer arrived with Dorothy Parker.

"Dottie, oh Dottie, that dress, that absolutely perfectly lovely little dress, you look like a painting by Velasquez."

"Dear, that's what you said the last time you saw it." To Adam Todd she said, "A Jack Rose on the rocks. Haven't we met before? Oh yes! You're the tail. Moonlighting?"

Tallulah took Jacob's hand and led him to the bar. "You're looking incredibly handsome, Mr. Singer. You look rested. Did you have a good night's sleep?"

"Your palm's damp."

"My enthusiasm isn't."

"What if you end up with egg on your face?"

"As opposed to a knife in my ribs?"

"You look real spiffy, Oscar," Singer said to the detective as he noticed the bruise on his forehead. "I see the missus remembered to wave you good-bye."

"Cut it out," grumbled Delaney as he poured Singer a drink.

Singer leaned against the bar and sized up the other detectives. "You boys look like fugitives from a bar mitzvah."

"Lay off, Jacob," said Tallulah. "They look exactly right and you should be proud of thcm."

"Hello there, Annabel," cried Singer as she entered from the bedroom. "That's one hell of a hat."

"Beats hell!" retorted Annabel smartly. "This is genuine John Frederick!"

Mrs. Parker almost choked on her drink.

"I'm in the wrong profession," she commented to no one in particular. "How are you, Patsy? Up to anything special these days?"

"Well, yeah, come to think of it, Dottie. I'm starting work on my memoirs."

"How nice. It shouldn't take long to fill five pages."

Patsy moved away from her as though in fear of contamination. Mrs. Parker called across the room to Tallulah. "Dear, supposing nobody shows up?"

"I'm confident I'm still a draw, Dottie. They'll show up."

Estelle was now at Tallulah's side. "I know what you're up to, Tallulah, and I'm frightened for you."

"Dahling, you of all people should know I've spent most of my life walking a tightrope without a safety net for protection."

"I shall be right next to you the entire evening."

"Why?"

"To protect you, of course."

Tallulah was touched. "Dahling, Tallulah is a survivor." She shouted to Oscar Delaney. "It's time I had a drink! Oscar! Mix me a perfect dry vodka martini and leave out the garbage!" The phone was ringing and guests were being announced. Tallulah laughed and then said in her loudest baritone, "Fasten your seat belts, dahlings! It's going to be a bumpy party!"

SEVENTEEN

GABRIEL DARNOFF decided to take another walk around the block. It was just a few minutes past six, and he didn't want to be one of the first to arrive at Tallulah's party. He had seen Jacob Singer and Dorothy Parker entering the hotel, and he was in no mood for either of them. His producers had folded his play abruptly the previous night, having wisely posted a provisional closing notice the number of days required by union rule prior to the play's official opening night. He chewed on a cigarillo while ambling along Park Avenue, and wondered what Tallulah was up to. She'd never made social overtures before, even when he had two big hits going for him. This sudden invitation, her promise that "Something interesting is going to happen, I hope, dahling," piqued his curiosity. He turned onto Fifty-third Street. There wasn't a soul in sight. It was Sunday in New York on a warm spring evening. He looked at his wristwatch. The hell with it. He quickened his step.

The party was livening up, and Tallulah was pleased. The celebrities she'd invited were beginning to make an appearance and heighten the color of the soirée. Mrs. Parker commented to Jacob Singer as *New Faces* producer Leonard Sillman entered with Gypsy Rose Lee, "Here's arsenic and old face."

Gypsy said to Tallulah after they embraced, "Now I hope you're not going to do your strip act and those embarrassing cartwheels."

"Not tonight, dahling. I reserve my outrageous behavior for more formal events. Leonard, you look unusually pretty tonight, have you found some fresh suckers for your next show?"

Patsy asked Estelle Winwood, "Who's that woman by the window talking to herself?"

"That's Cornelia Otis Skinner. She frequently does a one-woman show."

The great Greek actress Katina Paxinou arrived with her equally celebrated husband, Alexis Minotis. She scolded Tallulah amiably. "You haven't been to see our play!"

"Dahling, I can't even pronounce it!"

Paxinou's magnificent eyes widened with mockery. "And what is so difficult about *Oedipus Tyrannus?*"

"Now what made you decide to appear in a jawbreaker like that, dahlings?"

Minotis said amiably, "You know what happens when Greek meets Greek."

"Yes, dahling, they usually open a coffee shop. There's Mel and Helen! Dahlings, how sweet of you to come. Helen, you're as pale as a ghost. What's wrong?"

"It was the cab ride," said Helen Gahagan Douglas. "I'm terrified in taxicabs. I've got rider's block."

Douglas saw and recognized Ted Valudni and his face turned to stone. "What's that shit doing here?"

Tallulah took his hand and squeezed it. "Melvyn dahling, don't make a wave. I can't explain now, but in a little while you'll understand everything."

Melvyn Douglas continued bristling. "He's one of the reasons I'm out of Hollywood."

"I know, dahling, I know. How's your play doing?"

"Splendidly, for a trifle. It proves that lack of taste can be profitable."

"Don't knock it, sweets," said his wife, "it's paying the bills."

A beautifully liquid, sensuously husky voice interrupted. "Hello, you three."

"Maggie! Maggie dahling!" Tallulah embraced Margaret Sullavan, who looked enchanting in a simple blouse, skirt, jacket with her trademark Peter Pan collar, and a beret coquettishly arranged on her head.

"What's the occasion? Not another birthday, is it?"

"No, dahling, it's something special. And don't you dare run away until after my big number."

Sullavan's face fell. "You're not going to sing."

"No, dahling," said Tallulah with a laugh, "maybe I'll ask *you* to sing." She said to the Douglases, "Did you see Maggie in *Shopworn Angel?* She sang 'Pack Up Your Troubles' so deliciously!"

"Tallulah, that wasn't me. I was dubbed."

"Ridiculous, you're just being modest."

"Modest, my eye. You'll faint when I tell you who actually did my singing. Ready? Mary Martin."

Nobody fainted, but they were agreeably surprised. Tallulah grabbed Adam Todd as he went past her carrying a tray of drinks. "Dahling, take care of these celebrities. Give him your orders, dahlings, his name is Adam

Todd and isn't he adorable look at the gorgeous cleft in his chin so much for Kirk Douglas and Cary Grant and oh my God there's Bea Lillie Bea Bea what an adorable pillbox on your head"—under her breath—"and who's the pill with you?"

"Coo Tallu and coo to you too!" greeted Beatrice Lillie to her four friends. "Kisses kisses kisses," she said, her head working in their direction like a hen foraging for seed.

"Who's your friend, dahling?"

"What friend?" She turned to the willowy young man at her right. "This person? He's an impostor!" The young man's face reddened. She continued dizzily. "He's also an orphan. He's an impostor orphan. He used to have a mother, but she hasn't been seen since she went to Sotheby's to bid on an armoire. The police have her listed as missing in auction. La! What madness." Miss Lillie said to the young man who was looking for a hole to fall into, "Madness, dear, introduce yourself, I've forgotten your name. You do have a name, don't you, dear? You'll need it when the police arrive later to identify the bodies."

Tallulah said nothing about how close the comedienne might be to the truth.

The young man was stammering. Mrs.

Douglas tried to put him at ease by taking his hand and shaking it. He finally said with a thick Southern accent, "Ah'm Fortinbras D'Artagnan Winterbottom the Fourth."

"And don't tell us what happened to the other three," demanded Miss Lillie with hands on hips. "I call him Knuckles for short."

"Why Knuckles, in heaven's name, dahling?"

"Because he has ten! Ha-ha-ha-ha-ha and coo. Knuckles writes cookbooks. Tell them, Knuckles, and forever hold your peace. If it's too heavy, hold mine." She winked at Tallulah. Margaret Sullavan considered offering the young man the Sazerac she was holding, but good samaritan was a role she infrequently attempted.

The young man said, "Well, ah have mah best-sellin' book on Southern cookery, *Puttin On the Grits*, and now ah'm headin' west for a book on regional recipes, *Home on the Range*."

Patsy joined them and interrupted, "Say, Tallu, there's some nut who just got here telling everybody he's come here to kill you."

"Oh, that's got to be that dahling David Carney who tried to assault me in the zoo! Jacob dahling! Look who's here, that dahling

David Carney. Go say hello and frisk him, dahling!"

Singer hurried to Carney and said hello and frisked him. Estelle Winwood was appalled and went to Carney with a sweet smile and asked, "Young man, would you like something to drink?"

"I don't drink," said Carney, "I kill."

Estelle said swiftly, "Oh, there's Basil Rathbone and Ouida, do excuse me." She fled to the other side of the room while Carney went to the kitchen to see where the knives were kept.

Bea Lillie spied the Rathbones and said to her group, "Why, there's dear old Nasal Bathroom. And that looks familiar over there!"

"Where, dahling?"

"Near the bar, the little man with the mustache stalking the waiter."

"Oh dahling, that's Tennessee Williams, I didn't see him come in."

Bea Lillie trilled, " *'I was waltzing, with my darling, to the Tennesseeeee Williams . . . !'* "

Gabriel Darnoff and Joseph Savage stood off to one side discussing the trials and tribulations of blacklisting and playwriting. Lewis Drefuss was deep in conversation with a breathtakingly beautiful young blonde actress who had arrived alone. He had seen her on a Philco Playhouse with another blonde newcomer, Eva Marie Saint, and was impressed by both their performances. She wore little white gloves on her hands and sipped occasionally from a glass of chablis. He couldn't remember her name and prayed someone would rescue him.

The actress told him, "I'm leaving for Africa to do a picture with Clark Gable and Ava Gardner. I just found out it's a remake of one he did ten years ago with Jean Harlow, *Red Dust*. Now, it's called *Mogambo*. John Ford's directing and I've been warned that means there'll be a lot of whiskey consumed."

"Are you co-starring?" He was running the alphabet through his mind searching for a clue to her name.

"I'm third billed, but I don't know if it's above the title. I was below in *High Noon* with Gary."

The name clicked now. Grace Kelly. He said, "Gary Cooper and now Clark Gable. Aren't you lucky!"

"Cooper was a bore," she said, "and Gable has false teeth. What fun."

Margaret Sullavan was with Dorothy Parker. "How are you holding up, Dottie?

Leland and I have seen so little of you lately. What are you doing?"

"I'm on the lam."

Sullavan laughed. "From what?"

"Life."

"Oh God, Dottie, you're not thinking of suicide again!"

"Don't mock me, dear, someday you'll learn."

"I'm not mocking. I sometimes wonder if I'd ever have the courage to do it."

"Now who's being morbid?"

Sullavan sipped her drink. "I'll let you in on a little secret. I'm in trouble."

"Pregnant?"

"Christ no, thank God. Dottie, I'm going deaf."

"Oh, my dear, my dear."

"And what will I do when I can no longer hear cues? I won't be able to do theater anymore."

"Can't something be done? There's been so much progress . . ."

Sullavan shook her head. "I've been examined and poked by every renowned specialist here and abroad. It's hopeless."

Mrs. Parker took her hand and held it. The blacklist suddenly seemed unimportant.

Cornelia Otis Skinner asked Tallulah,

"Sweetie, has Estelle Winwood ever played Shakespeare?"

"When they were youngsters, dahling."

"I'm thinking of reviving *The Merry Wives of Windsor*. Would you and Estelle consider co-starring?"

"Me and Estelle on the same stage with you? Are you mad? By the time the curtain comes down on the first act, the audience will have forgotten your name, dahling, all three of them."

Basil Rathbone said to Gypsy Rose Lee, "I don't suppose you saw my werewolf movie? It was a howling success."

"No, I didn't, dear. Say, is that white-haired old man over there Albert Einstein? If it is, I want to challenge him on his theory of relativity."

Armbruster and Eleanor Pershing were feasting on celebrities. "My God," she said to him, "it looks like a benefit. Oh, there's Maurice Evans!"

"Which one?"

"Over there with Helen Hayes, the one who spits a lot."

"My, isn't she tiny? And here comes Ted Valudni. Be nice."

Through clenched teeth she said, "Ted

Valudni, I'd sooner have a kidney removed. Hello, Ted dear! How are you?"

He shook her extended hand lightly and said to her husband, "I don't know why the hell we're here, do you?"

"We were invited" was the rational reply.

"But why? What's Bankhead up to? Look who's here. There's Joe Savage and Gabe Darnoff and that rotten bastard Singer, and you know what, I think the waiters are all cops. I'm telling you, Armbruster, I've directed enough thrillers and I ought to know one when I see one. This is a setup. Bankhead and the detective are up to something and I don't like it one bit."

Eleanor asked him, "How can you dislike it if you don't know what it is?"

"Tell me, Eleanor," asked Valudni, confusing her with an idiot child, "are you always this practical?"

Jacob Singer said to Tallulah, "When do you go into your act?"

"When Herbert Sholom gets here."

"Supposing he stands you up."

"Then, dahling, I'm up on the creek without a paddle."

"You could try improvising."

"Wipe that sneer out of your voice, Singer."

"It's not a sneer. You can't treat detecting lightly. I take great pride in my work."

"Jacob dahling"—her voice was dripping icicles—"it might help if you learned the difference between pride and arrogance."

Beatrice Lillie said to David Carney, "And tell me dear, how many fatalities have you scored in your favor?"

"I don't like to brag."

"How becoming. Tell me, dear, do you hire out?"

"Why, is there someone you'd like murdered?"

"As a matter of fact, I would. Have you ever heard of Noël Coward?"

"Excuse me, aren't you Beatrice Lillie?"

"Who? Me? Let me see. Where's a looking glass? Ah! Right there!" She took Mitchell Zang by the hand, wondering where he'd gotten that delicious scar on his left cheek, and led him to the mirror. "Ah! Here we are! Aha! It isn't Garbo, it isn't Dietrich," she sang in her delightful falsetto, "or that neat trick . . . !" She dropped his hand. "We must stop meeting like this, people will say we're in love."

"I just had to tell you how much I've admired you all these years." Each word was

extremely well greased and emerged effort-
lessly.

"All what these years?" She held up her
hand. "Don't tell me! I'll tell *you*. You adored
me in *At Home Abroad*. You worshiped me
in *Set to Music*. You suh-wooooooned when
you saw me in *The Show Is On!* And what
did you think of my Ophelia in Tom Mix's
Hamlet? Stop! I never played Ophelia. What
do you think of Lillian Gish? Are you interested in joining my movement to help stamp
out Mickey Rooney? Don't toy with me,
you'll burn your fingers. Well, well, come,
come, out with it, what's your name?"

"Mitchell Zang. I'm an actor."

She yelped. "An actor! I've lost interest!
Don't bother waiting for me under the Astor
clock! I've a previous engagement with my
parole board."

"Please don't go. I don't know anyone
here." Except that fink detective and
Bankhead and a couple of commie bastards.
"Please, have a heart."

"My heart's in the right place. You're not.
My heaaaaart's in the highlands . . ." she
sang. "Oh very well, you seductive creature,
get me a gin on the rocks and the key to the
city."

Mrs. Parker said to Tallulah Bankhead,

who kept looking at her wristwatch and saying "Damn," "You're a bundle of nerves, Tallulah, what's the matter?"

"I'm afraid I'm being stood up."

"Are you demented? The party's packed. It's a smash. And for crying out loud, where'd you dig up Mae Murray?"

"Mae Murray? Is she here?"

"Well, why do you think Irvin's playing 'The Merry Widow Waltz'?"

Irvin Graham, the celebrated composer of *The Whale Who Wanted to Sing at the Met*, was playing the piano Tallulah had brought in for the occasion. The diminutive Mae Murray, erstwhile star of the silent screen, stood next to the piano and swayed to the music, waiting to be recognized. Tallulah came to her rescue and said loudly, "Mae Murray, how marvelous of you to come!"

She said in a small voice, "Nils Asther brought me. You don't mind, do you?"

"Of course I don't mind. I would have invited you if I'd known you were in town."

"I'm staying at the Gorham and—"

Bankhead interrupted. "Where's Nils? I haven't seen him since we both struck out with that carabiniere in Roma God knows how many years ago Nils Nils come kneel at my feet dahling you look positively gorgeous you haven't changed one bit how's Vivian? Divorced? When did that happen oh what the hell were you doing getting married in the first place everyone everyone here's Nils Asther and here's Mae Murray and of course they have voices, dahlings, they did talkies too didn't you, dahlings, Mae stop blowing kisses you're dribbling Nils what are you doing here I mean New York not the party . . ."

"Some nut named Georg Baxt tracked me down and got me a part on a Kraft television theater in *Dodsworth* with Anthony Ross and Irene Manning. I loathe television."

"Yes, dahling, isn't it beneath us all, I wish I could get a series. Excuse me, dahling, dance with Mae while I have a word with Patsy."

Gypsy Rose Lee said to Dorothy Parker, "What was it you said to Connie Bennett? I mean did you see the expression on her face?"

"No, dear, she left early and took her face with her."

"I've been to a mahhhhhvelous party," Bea Lillie sang to Tallulah. "Tell me, dear, who's the stud dogging my trail?"

"A stud. Steer clear. He's bad business."

"Aha! You've traded with him. He's bitten you."

"No and God no. He was Nance Liston's fellow."

"Dear sweet Nance. So he's the one who was punching her around, eh? The brute, the beast, the actor." Her voice became confidential. "Tell me, dear, what's this all about? I have a heavy date with a thin baseball player . . ."

"What about young Winterbottom?"

"Oh, I just carry him around for show. His mother was in *Charlot's Revue* with Gertie and me back in the dark ages before man learned to walk upright. Who's the divine little man at the piano?" Tallulah told her. "And who's that thin little woman standing near him making wisecracks."

"His wife Lillian."

"Remind me not to turn my back on her. Ahaaaa!" Four young men were entering. "Here comes the Harvard Hadassah!"

Tallulah went to the bedroom. In her handbag she found the slip of paper on which she had written Herbert Sholom's number and dialed. After ten rings, she hung up.

"I'm going to kill you."

Tallulah spun around and faced David Carney. "Don't creep up on me like that, you almost scared me shitless. Wouldn't you like to meet a nice young girl?"

"No."

"Boy?"

"No."

Lewis Drcfuss entered the bedroom.

"Ah! Here's Lewis! Saved by the bell! Lewis, have you met David Carney? He's a very clever young playwright and outpatient with homicidal tendencies but I think it's all a cry for attention yes attention you heard me attention must be paid now why didn't I invite Artie Miller if anyone should be here it should be Artie I wonder if I could get *him* to write me a play do you think he'd go for *Death of a Saleswoman* or *All My Daughters* Mister Carney will you stop pulling at my dress!"

"Where is the bathroom, please?"

"Right through that door, dahling, and for heaven's sake don't lock yourself in on the other hand though . . ." She pulled Lewis Drefuss back to the party. "Talk about the best-laid plans of mice and men."

Lewis interrupted her. "Tallulah, you'll have to forgive me. I'm not up to this. I don't feel well."

"Nonsense! Of course you feel well! Patsy will get you an aspirin!"

"I haven't been sleeping and Christ knows

I've had no appetite since finding Nanette's body. I've got to go home."

"Absolutely not. I won't hear of it." She looked solemn. "I need you, Lewis. Something's afoot, but I can't tell you what it is. You must stay. I need you. I really need you."

He was beaten. "Okay. I'll get myself a drink."

"Of course, dahling. Have a straight gin. Mother's milk. It does wonders if you have the curse. Ethel at last! What kept you, dahling?"

"What a shindig, Tallu," shouted Merman, and the windows trembled. "Where'd you dig up all the gorgeous men? Who's the bartender? What's his price! Hey you! Bartender! Pour me a red wine!"

Bea Lillie said to young Winterbottom, "The air raid alert's arrived."

"Isn't she Ethel Merman?"

"Yes, dear, and you must forgive her. She's rather subdued tonight. Ah, there she goes challenging the bartender to a hand-wrestling match. Good old Merm, she choses her musicals brilliantly and her men badly and don't we all, tra-laaaaa!"

Tallulah said to Jacob Singer, "My skin feels so tight around my skull. I'll give Mr.

Sholom five more minutes, and then I go it alone. People are starting to leave, damn it. Dahlings! You can't leave just yet! I've a big surprise prepared! You don't want to miss it! Oh, look! Here comes the press! Earl dahling! Walter, you angel!" She greeted Earl Wilson and Walter Winchell as they entered from the hall. "Don't tell me you came up in the elevator together!"

"Along with my lunch," said Wilson. He found pen and pencil in his inside jacket pocket and began noting down the names of the celebrities present.

"Ed Sullivan's going to try and make it after his show. Earl, where's your beautiful wife?"

"Home with Junior. He's got a cold."

"The poor dahling. There, I said it. Doesn't that prove I don't loathe children? Walter, let me get you a drink. I'm sure you know just about everybody here. Ted Valudni, where do you think you're going?"

"I'm tired. I don't like parties. I'm going home."

"I'll be very displeased if you do. Give me five more minutes."

"For what?"

Winchell said to him, "Valudni, haven't

you learned by now never to cross a goddess?"

Said Valudni, "Well, if a mere mortal may speak—"

"Later, dahling, later," she said, and waved him away.

Jacob Singer said to her, "It's like I've been telling you, Tallulah, leave the detecting to the detectives."

"Jacob dahling, why don't you look at this as two sets of hands playing one piano? I'd hate to find out you're a poor sport."

He was looking past her to the little man who had shyly come into the party. "Tallulah, I think that's who you're waiting for."

Tallulah turned and, with a sob of relief, hurried to Herbert Sholom.

Cornelia Otis Skinner said to Mrs. Parker, "Who's the quaint little man Tallulah's talking to? Doesn't he look Dickensian?"

"Yes, he does," agreed Mrs. Parker, "Oliver Twitch."

Lillian Graham said to her husband, who was doing a medley of his own songs at the piano, "Irvin, you're not getting paid for this. Why don't we get the hell out of here?"

"Not until I play some of my new numbers for Leonard Sillman. He's planning a new revue for Imogene Coca and Tommy Dix."

Lillian folded her arms and emitted a sigh that soon shattered against the ceiling. "And who's doing the choreography? Connee Boswell?"

Tallulah guided Herbert Sholom to the bar for a glass of wine. She talked a blue streak en route and he nodded his head sagely, absorbing every word. Here he was at last, taking part in an important drama, or so Miss Bankhead led him to believe. Her instructions were simple and he knew exactly what he must do. What little dialogue she wanted him to speak he committed to memory without difficulty. She said to Oscar Delaney, "Look after Mr. Sholom and guard him carefully. Without him, I'm a disaster area."

Then she hurried to Irvin Graham at the piano. "Irvin dahling, give me a very loud fanfare."

He did as Beth Valudni arrived and unfortunately found herself standing next to her husband.

"It's about time," he said nastily. "Where the hell have you been? I was beginning to think you weren't going to show up."

"I'm beginning to wish I hadn't. Now shut up. Tallulah's going to speak."

"When doesn't she?"

The fanfare had quietened the room. Tallulah moved to the center of the floor with her arms upraised and smiling, she hoped, beguilingly. 'Dahlings . . .'' she said, her eyes traveling from the Valudnis to Joseph Savage to David Carney, then to Jacob Singer and from him to Lewis Drefuss and then to Garbriel Darnoff, who was standing between Patsy and Estelle. "I'm so glad you all came, and I'm really delighted you did."

"She's repeating herself," whispered Merman to Bea Lillie.

"After all these years, why not?"

"Do you suppose she's announcing her retirement?" Ouida Rathbone asked her husband.

"Tallulah will never retire, dear, she'll disintegrate."

"Tonight, you see me in a totally new role, one I never dreamt I'd ever be playing. Tonight, dahlings, I am not Tallulah Bankhead the actress, I am Tallulah Bankhead the detective." She heard a few titters and saw looks being exchanged and heard someone say, "God, she's pissed again," and her eyes locked for a moment with Herbert

Sholom's and he winked. She would remember that gesture always. He didn't know it then, but the wink succeeded in shoring up her faltering confidence. "And I might add," she said with a disarming little laugh, "I hope I don't make a total fool of myself."

Friendly laughter.

Adam Todd found her sexy.

Jacob Singer's eyes traveled from suspect to suspect. There wasn't a nervous one among them. He truly hoped for her sake, and probably for his own, that the scene she was about to play would be one of the most effective in her entire life.

Tallulah folded her arms and got down to business. "I suppose," she said in her magnificent baritone, "you're wondering why I've asked you all here . . ."

EIGHTEEN

JACOB SINGER wasn't humoring Tallulah Bankhead to promote a romance. They had come to the same conclusion as to the murderer's identity by different routes. Singer had followed his usual slow, methodical, tediously tactical procedure of adding, subtracting, observing, digesting, discarding,

345

re-reviewing until he made center target where the answer awaited him. Tallulah the enthusiastic amateur worked like a broken field runner zigzagging her way through the evidence, picking up ideas en route, procrastinating, taxing her memory until it finally unlocked the prisoner who could clinch for her the identity of the murderer. Unlike Singer, Tallulah was totally at ease freewheeling her way through the available information until all the pieces came together in a satisfying tapestry known as the solution. It was the same way she bid her way to a grand slam at bridge.

Holding center stage at her own party wasn't a new experience for Tallulah. Unmasking a murderer was, and it wasn't long before her skeptical guests were spellbound. This wasn't Tallulah the showoff, this was Tallulah the serious, Tallulah the crusader, who campaigned spiritedly and heatedly for a political candidate she was backing, who brandished her verbal sabers before the advertising agency executives who feared she was about to be branded a subversive by the House Un-American Activities Committee. It was Mrs. Parker who said, "Shipwreck Tallulah on a cannibal island and she'll soon have it unionized."

"Dahlings," continued Tallulah, rubbing her hands together, her face composed and serious, unlike the usual comic mask she wore on these occasions, "this is not one of my usual party pieces, although I might later wish it were." She saw Adam Todd and another detective position themselves at the front door. There was no other way out of the apartment. The window led to either fresh air or death. Jacob Singer leaned against a wall behind Mitchell Zang and the Valudnis. Oscar Delaney moved from the bar and remained in the bedroom doorway, near David Carney and Joseph Savage. Carney caught Beatrice Lillie's eye and ran an index finger across his throat in a threatening gesture. She murmured "Caw blimey" to Lewis Drefuss on her left, who sat on the arm of her chair, head bowed and fingers interlaced looking like a displaced worshiper from St. Patrick's Cathedral. Herbert Sholom was mesmerized by the sight of Margaret Sullavan, the only actress who could lure him to a movie house or legitimate theater.

"We have many of us here in some way been tainted by the misapplied brush of the House Un-American Committee. Yes, dahlings, I too have been threatened, but the only thing I ever did with a Russian that might conceivably be construed as subversive was a tumble in a rumble seat in the Hollywood Hills with Sergei Rachmaninoff, and that was terribly uncomfortable too, dahlings." She got her laugh, and it encouraged her to continue. "Now don't look about you so uneasily, dahlings, this party isn't a fund raiser." She got another laugh and wondered for a second if she should accept that offer to play Las Vegas. "You'll forgive me if I dwell somewhat at length on murder, but murder is what this party is really all about. There have been four murders this past week"—she enumerated them—"and the victims were in one way or another connected with the congressional investigations. The men had one thing in common: they were friendly witnesses, to use the polite term. Nanette Walsh made the mistake of finding a missing photograph. Basil dahling, don't look so bewildered." She laughed. "The poor dahling's played Sherlock Holmes so often, I'm sure he'd love to displace me in the spotlight."

"Not at all, Tallulah," said Rathbone with his urbane suavity which now creaked, "I've been condemned myself by Sherlock Holmes. It's tough to get them to let me play anything else."

"That's showbiz, dahling, we must have lunch soon." She lit a cigarette and thanked Lewis for the use of his lighter. She caught Singer's eye and he nodded encouragement. She could have kissed him right then and there for the show of support. She said to her audience, "I won't bore you with the details of each individual murder, I'm sure you've all read about it in the tabloids. I do have a story to tell, and I want you to promise to be very patient and not wriggle and cough the way those bloody awful benefit audiences do." Another laugh, but I'm on my own here, there's nobody holding the prompt book, Jacob Singer swore he wouldn't interfere, I wish that Carney nut would stop pantomiming stabbing me.

"I promise to try not to talk too fast. There, I'm ready. Curtain up. Act One. On stage we find Abner Walsh and his wife Martha, twenty years ago. They're young, they're married and have a son, Leo, and Abner is fiercely ambitious. I'm introduced to them at a rent party and I meet the boy, Leo. I find him withdrawn and introspective, and with hindsight, I realize something was not quite right with him. A few years pass and Abner is in Hollywood, where his career is beginning to take off. He sends for

Martha and Leo. They travel by train and in Arizona there's a ghastly accident. Martha is lucky, a very rare experience in her life as I'll soon explain. She escapes with minor bruises. Leo is deadly unfortunate. It's bad enough that since a fall during a playground escapade he's had to suffer an ugly scar on his left cheek"—she saw Mitchell Zang finger his and then quickly move his hand away—"now he barely escapes with his life. Almost every bone in his body is broken, his face is disfigured beyond recognition, and if he survives, he is doomed to an unspeakable life of torture."

Mrs. Parker pursed her lips, examined a fingernail, and wondered if it would be de rigueur if she crept around the perimeter of the room to the bar and poured herself a Jack Rose.

"There is a sanitarium in Arizona that accommodates him. He is destined to spend years there. He will grow into young manhood there. But first he must undergo the tortures of physical rehabilitation—his body in a cast from neck to toes, plastic surgery at a time when the procedure wasn't as sophisticated as it is today."

Gypsy Rose Lee wondered if the rumor was true that Tallulah had recently had her breasts and her behind done and who, thank you very much, was the doctor and how much did he soak.

"Martha, being a wonderful mother, stayed in Arizona with the boy. A gallant but costly gesture. She lost Abner to Nanette." Tallulah paced under a cloud of smoke. "The years pass, the boy is finally sent out into the world with scars healed, revealing a new face, bones knitted, everything in place again except one item that was apparently overlooked. His brain. The introspection and withdrawal of his childhood, aggravated by his tragic accident and years of confinement, resulted in manic depression. Jacob Singer, whom I'm sure you've all met tonight and if you haven't that's him over there leaning against the wall and blushing, got the cooperation of the Flagstaff police, who confirmed that Leo Walsh was kept on at the sanitarium for treatment of his mental disorder long after his body was healed. When he was released, Leo came to an agreement with his mother and father. He wanted the past obliterated. He wanted a new chance with a new life. I suppose Martha's agreement was somewhat reluctant; Leo was all she had. There was no new man in her life and she didn't want one. But she agreed, Leo was owed this. Abner

351

agreed with alacrity because he had a new wife who wanted no part of his other family and a fabulously successful career. There hasn't been such an obliterating burial of an individual since Vesuvius erupted over Pompeii. May I have a glass of gin, Lewis?"

She continued, "We know Leo went to Los Angeles. He took a new name, a successful new identity, but didn't hesitate to make use of some of Abner's friends there, never of course revealing that he was Abner's son. Thank you, Lewis." She sipped. Fresh color came to her cheeks and fresh strength shored up her voice. "He tried to become an actor but was unsuccessful. He decided to seek work behind the scenes instead, and that proved fruitful. He returned to New York, and yes, he was in touch with Martha and Abner. And now Abner needed him. He needed a strong right arm. Abner was under siege, his career and his life were being destroyed. Nanette had left him. He was such a ruin, he swallowed his pride and once again sought solace from Martha, which she generously gave because she would always be in love with him."

"Coo," whispered Bea Lillie to anybody as she dabbed at her moist eyes with a tissue,

"I haven't wept like this since *Lassie Come Home*."

"Abner, reunited with Leo, realizes what he has missed all those years. He has missed his son. Sorry if I sound maudlin, dahlings, but I'm working without a script. *How* those Actors Studio creatures *do* those endless improvisations I'll *never* know, and don't want to. So here's Abner and Leo together again, father and son, and Leo wants to help the man he has come to love again. But it's hopeless and Abner commits suicide. And less than twenty-four hours later, Martha follows Abner in suicide and Leo has lost the only two people in his life he has ever loved for a second and sorrowfully permanent time. He snaps!" She snapped her fingers and looked to see who had yelped. It was Patsy. She shot her a look and took a swig of the gin. Estelle sat with a silly grin on her face and Tallulah finally recognized why Estelle had never attempted tragedy on stage. "He will revenge his parents. He will murder Lester Miroff and Oliver Sholom and Barry Wren and perhaps me, yes, some of you know I received a death threat over the telephone from Leo. And he murders these people. And he's brilliant! He's positively brilliant! Dahlings, he absolutely doesn't leave a clue! The police can't find a shred of evidence pointing to the identity of the murderer. And what's more, even if they did, they couldn't prove it. The police have a genius for an adversary. Now Dottie Parker knows from experience, as I have just been learning, that Jacob Singer is one hell of a superb detective, but he's hamstrung!"

Singer was studying the faces of his suspects. Only David Carney betrayed any emotion, with thumb and index finger he was taking imaginary potshots at various guests.

Tallulah handed her empty glass to Lewis and continued vivaciously. "At this point, enter Tallulah. No cracks, please, there were no fanfares, no tributes, no red . . . oops . . . carpet, and Dottie had introduced me to Detective Singer and we're now great great friends, dahlings." She brushed her hair back, took a moment to recompose herself, and then continued. "Before the murders began, on the day Martha Walsh committed suicide, I had unconsciously noticed something important, but as I so frequently do, I committed that piece of information to near oblivion in the back of my mind, and it would remain there until just very recently. You see, Martha wrote a note to me and had it delivered by one of the neighborhood boys.

It was a sweet note, thanking me for my continued friendship, thanking me for trying to rescue Abner. I told my dear Lewis here what the note was about, that Martha was going to kill herself, and Lewis fled from the studio to rush to her rescue, but Lewis, dahling, how did you know where she lived?"

Lewis stared at Tallulah. Bea Lillie stared at Lewis. He was standing as if paralyzed.

"I knew you had a drink once with Abner Walsh to explain why we couldn't use him on the show, but was there any reason for you to have known Martha?" She waited, but Lewis remained immobile, not speaking, standing stiffly like a soldier at attention.

"Another piece of good luck came our way. Oliver Sholom's Uncle Herbert." She explained to her guests, "He has a tailoring establishment on the floor beneath the apartment in which Oliver was murdered. And dahling Herbert Sholom is with us right now"—she sounded like Jack Parr introducing his next guest—"and here he is."

"My God," said Dorothy Parker, "it's Oliver Twitch."

Herbert Sholom went to Tallulah, who put her arm around the little man. "Herbert Sholom saw the murderer come down the stairs from Oliver's apartment. He always leaves his door slightly ajar in this warm weather to try and collect a breeze. Mr. Sholom, who did you see leaving your nephew's apartment? Is that person here?"

"He certainly is," said Herbert Sholom, pointing a finger at Lewis Drefuss, "that's him. That's the man."

Lewis turned beet red and screamed, "That's a lie! That's a fucking lie! Your door was shut! I could hear your sewing machine—"

"Bingo!" shouted Jacob Singer as the police closed in.

"Shit," said Lewis Drefuss as he rubbed a hand across his eyes with confusion.

"Lewis dahling," said Tallulah with compassion, "murdering Nanette was such a stupid mistake. It was obvious you had to be the one to kill her. I mean it was only a matter of some twenty minutes or so from the time she phoned me and I sent you to her to collect the photo of Leo Walsh. Didn't Nanette recognize you?"

"No," said Lewis, "she didn't recognize me. Not right away she didn't. The picture was ten years old. It was me with the nurses; it wasn't all that good a shot of me. I had written on it 'When this you see, remember me,' you know, like the card I enclosed with the rose I sent you."

"That was another mistake. Nanette had read me the inscription over the phone."

"I wanted to be remembered by him. He'd left me and Mom. I hated Nanette. I didn't know her, but I hated her. And there I stood in her studio looking at her and the picture in her hand and the bust of Abner she was doing, and every bit of hatred I felt for her came rising up my throat like vomit, and I picked up that mallet and hit her and hit her until . . . until . . . and I tore up the photo and flushed it down the toilet . . . and I went into the kitchen for a glass of water until I could calm down and put together a story for the police. I mean . . . there were still others who had betrayed Abner who had to be killed . . . like him"—he pointed at Ted Valudni, who shrank back against Melvyn Douglas, who moved away from him with a look of revulsion—"and then I was going to go to Hollywood and get rid of . . . well . . . you know who, Tallulah . . ."

Lewis's hands were cuffed behind the back. Oscar Delaney held his right arm and Adam Todd his left. Jacob Singer had phoned for a patrol car while Mrs. Parker finally made it to the bar for her Jack Rose.

Tallulah had a hand on Lewis cheek. "I still adore you, dahling, and I always will. I don't condone what you did because much as I have wanted to commit murder in the past, I have no stomach for it, but I understand why you did it. Dahling, I'm paying for your defense. I swore I would and Bankhead never reneges on a promise. Tell me, dahling, now tell me what I can do for you before they lock you up in the pokey."

He kissed her lightly on the cheek and then said with surprising vigor, "You can get me the late Clarence Darrow."

EPILOGUE

THE FOLLOWING September when Tallulah Bankhead's autobiography, as ghosted by Richard Maney, was published, it soared to the top of the best-seller lists almost immediately. She succumbed to television's seductively beckoning finger and starred in a series of musical extravaganzas called *The All-Star Revue*. The December 20th program featured Patsy Kelly, who was a smash hit, and it looked as though her career was reborn. Estelle Winwood drifted airily from flop play to flop play before deciding to head west and attempt to conquer Hollywood, which she eventually did. Dorothy Parker's collaboration with Arnaud D'Ussaud, *Ladies of the Corridor*, did make it to Broadway and the critics declared open season on it. Its demise was mourned by very few, though several decades later it would resurface in an excellent television production, sadly long after Mrs. Parker's death.

As Armbruster Pershing predicted, Ted Valudni's star reascended, and shortly before his death, as a very old man, he was given a testimonial dinner before a packed house and not one of the testimonials had the bad taste to remind those present of Valudni's deplorable cooperation with HUAC.

Joseph Savage was finally cleared of the blacklist but chose not to return to professional writing. Tallulah didn't do the play he wrote for her because nobody would back it, and Joseph eventually wrote a book about his experience, which didn't sell well.

David Carney was returned to an insane asylum after he murdered his bothersome sister and her husband, who should have paid attention when he asked on the phone, "Can I come to dinner tonight and would you make my favorite pot roast and potato pancakes and then after the dessert and coffee I'm going to kill both of you."

Mitchell Zang extorted a large sum of money from an ignorant opera star (are there any other kind?), had plastic surgery to correct the scar on his left cheek, and went to Hollywood, where he became the star of a long-running television series thanks to having the good sense to switch from wooing actresses to wooing producers. He died last year of AIDS.

Gabriel Darnoff never had another success on Broadway but was astonished at the hundreds of thousands of dollars he inherited when his mother died. Why, that foxy grandma! She had invested and salted away just about every nickel she had managed to wheedle out of him and his father. Darnoff emigrated to France, where he married a pretty Russian refugee who had had some success in her homeland as a Gogol dancer. Darnoff's eldest son, Dimitri, recently won the Nobel Peace Prize for his brilliant book about his grandfather, Michael Darnoff.

George Baxt went to England in 1957 for five years. In 1966 he published *A Queer Kind of Death*, which left him a mental wreck.

Armbruster Pershing died of a stroke while playing tennis with his eighth wife, Natalie, who had affectionately dubbed him "Blue-beard." To Natalie's distress and chagrin, Armbruster left very little money, most of his fortune having been eaten up by divorce settlements and what he called acrimony payments.

Oscar Delaney shot his wife, was acquitted, and won a police citation.

Adam Todd left the force and became a private eye. His adventures are under option to a television network as a possible series for David Bowie.

Annabel Forsythe opened a smart boutique in a better part of the Bronx, lost eighty pounds, and took a young lover; they are now two of the most successful crack dealers on the East Coast.

Several years before her death, on the day Jacob Singer was honorably retired from the police force, Tallulah invited him to dinner at a very expensive restaurant on the East Side. They hadn't seen each other in ages. Old age wasn't kind to Tallulah, and she could have swatted Singer for looking exactly the way he had looked the day they nabbed Lewis Drefuss.

Singer gallantly said to Tallulah, "Tallulah, you look sensational."

"Dahling, I'm not blind. I saw myself in

the mirror several times today and I look like an abandoned mackerel. What the hell, Jacob, I knew eventually my sins would catch up with me. Why, only last Friday, when I was a bit younger, the grandson of one of my British beaux asked if he could come visit me, and shortly after he arrived, the little monster—although he was a divine six foot three and perhaps nineteen or twenty years old at most—said to me, 'Gee, Miss Bankhead, I'd never have recognized you from the pictures Grandpapa had of you starring in the West End.' Ye gods! The West End! The era of the dinosaur. Waiter! Another dry vodka martini for me and another of whatever the gentleman is drinking and I'm sure if you don't hurry your blood will clot and where was I Jacob of course you read that my poor dahling Lewis hung himself in that awful place he was condemned to for the rest of his life his defense cost me a fortune but it was well worth it I adore him and I had him cremated and his ashes strewn across the floor at Sardi's so everyone in the business could continue walking all over him and oh God I'm rattling away like a batch of tin cans tied to the rear of a car containing a bridal couple and Jacob I was good wasn't I. I was a good detective and for crying out loud do you know what we ought to be doing we ought to be harmonizing a couple of choruses of 'I Remember It Well' oh let's do and to hell with the other diners dahling and here's the waiter dahling Mr. Waiter do you think you could rustle us up a pitch pipe well do your best dahling oh Jacob it's so good seeing you again dahling!"

AFTERWORD

THE MURDERER and his victims are fictitious, as is Tallulah Bankhead's involvement with the blacklist. But the tribulations she encountered in trying to use the unfortunates on her program are true. I was there; I was an actors' agent from 1951 to 1957, the worst years of the blacklist, and many of the events written about here are drawn from my own experiences. I have known the theory that Blanche Yurka murdered Smith Reynolds for about six years, since I heard it from an elderly gentleman who was once a celebrated Hollywood costume designer. I have checked and rechecked the facts and I am thoroughly convinced that Yurka (who, I might add, was a friend of mine) did it. And amusingly enough, Blanche was originally to star in my play, *Laughter of Ladies*, but so depressed the producers and director in rehearsal that she was replaced by Winwood.

The facts of the blacklist and the real names I do use are all true and available to the public in Washington, D.C. Besides my own memories, I read Stefan Kanfer's superb *A Journal of the Plague Years;* Gordon

Kahn's *Hollywood on Trial;* Alvah Bessie's *Inquisition in Eden;* Merle Miller's *The Judges and the Judged; Only Victims,* by Robert Vaughan (yes the actor!); William Wright's biography of Lillian Hellman (which has one astonishing error: he reports Hellman as being friendly with a woman named Hannah Dorner and then later in the book tells us Hellman became friendly with a woman named Hannah Weinstein. Dorner and Weinstein are the same person, Dorner being her maiden name. It was Mrs. Weinstein who brought me to England in 1957 and launched my film writing career there). I was also privileged to read the manuscript of Jean Muir's unpublished autobiography (ghosted by Hollis Alpert) and to jog the memories of some others to whom I am eternally grateful. All film and theatrical information was culled from my own recollections.

George Baxt

A note on the text
Large print edition designed by
Kipling West.
Composed in 18 pt Plantin
on a Xyvision 300/Linotron 202N
by Stephen Traiger
of G.K. Hall & Co.